≈ PRAISE FOR *The Guardian Herd* SERIES ≈

"From page one, Jennifer Lynn Alvarez weaves an epic tale of a doomed black pegasus foal named Star, whose race against time will lift the reader on the wings of danger and destiny, magic and hope. It's a world I did not want to leave, and neither will you."
—PETER LERANGIS, *New York Times* bestselling author in the 39 Clues series and of the Seven Wonders series

"Perfect for fans of *Charlotte's Web* and the Guardians of Ga'Hoole series." —ALA *Booklist*

"Richly developed. . . . Compelling." —*Kirkus Reviews*

"Chock-full of adventure and twists, making it difficult to put down. Readers will be clamoring for the next book."
—*School Library Journal*

"Alvarez's world is lush with description and atmosphere."
—*Publishers Weekly*

"Will prove popular with both animal-lovers and fantasy fans. A good choice for reluctant readers. The clever resolution will get kids psyched for more tales from the Guardian Herd."
—ALA *Booklist*

"Filled with fantastical action, and rich with description. A well-paced and engrossing story. Alvarez has created a series that will be beloved by readers." —*VOYA*

THE GUARDIAN HERD

WINDBORN

BY

JENNIFER LYNN ALVAREZ

HARPER
An Imprint of HarperCollinsPublishers

The Guardian Herd: Windborn

Text copyright © 2016 by Jennifer Lynn Alvarez

Interior art © 2016 by David McClellan

ISBN 978-0-06-228616-1

17 18 19 20 21   OPM   10 9 8 7 6 5 4 3 2 1

❖

First paperback edition, 2017

FOR MY GUARDIAN HERD, THANK YOU FOR BELIEVING IN ME

TABLE OF CONTENTS

He was not bone and feather but a perfect idea of freedom and flight, limited by nothing at all.

—*Richard Bach*, Jonathan Livingston Seagull

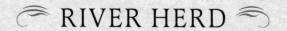 RIVER HERD

The black foal:

STAR—solid-black yearling colt with black feathers, white star on forehead

Under-stallions:

THUNDERSKY—dark-bay stallion with vibrant crimson feathers, black mane and tail, wide white blaze, two hind white socks. Previously Thunderwing, over-stallion of Sun Herd. Deceased

HAZELWIND—buckskin stallion with jade feathers, black mane and tail, big white blaze, two white hind socks

SUMMERWIND—handsome palomino pinto stallion with violet feathers. Deceased

ICERIVER—older dark-silver stallion with powder-blue feathers, white mane, white ringlet tail, blue eyes, white star on forehead. Sire of Lightfeather. Previous over-stallion of Snow Herd. Deceased

GRASSWING—crippled palomino stallion with pale-green feathers, flaxen mane and tail, white blaze, one white front sock. Deceased

CLAWFIRE—white stallion with blue-gray feathers, jagged scar on face, gold eyes. Born to Snow Herd, joined River Herd

Medicine Mare:

SWEETROOT—council-mare. Old chestnut pinto with dark-pink feathers, chestnut mane and tail, white star on forehead

Mares:

SILVERLAKE—council-mare. Light-gray mare with silver feathers, white mane and tail, four white socks. Previously Silvercloud, lead mare of Sun Herd

CRYSTALFEATHER—small chestnut mare with bright-blue feathers, two front white socks, white strip on face

DAWNFIR—spotted bay mare with dark-blue and white feathers, black mane and tail. Deceased

ROWANWOOD—blue roan mare with dark-yellow and blue feathers, white mane and tail, two hind white socks

DEWBERRY—battle mare. Bay pinto with emerald feathers, black mane and tail, thin blaze on forehead, two white hind anklets

LIGHTFEATHER—small white mare with white feathers, white ringlet tail, white mane. Star's dam. Born to Snow Herd, adopted by Sun Herd. Deceased

MOSSBERRY—elderly light-bay mare with dark-magenta feathers, black mane and tail, crescent moon on forehead and white snip on nose, two white hind anklets. Deceased

Yearlings:

MORNINGLEAF—elegant chestnut filly with bright-aqua feathers, flaxen mane and tail, four white socks, amber eyes, wide blaze

BUMBLEWIND—friendly bay pinto colt with gold feathers tipped in brown, black mane and tail, thin blaze on face

ECHOFROST—sleek silver filly with a mix of dark- and light-purple feathers, white mane and tail, one white sock

BRACKENTAIL—big brown colt with orange feathers, brown mane and tail, two hind white socks, golden eyes

FLAMESKY—red roan filly with dark-emerald and gold feathers

STRIPESTORM—liver chestnut colt with bright-yellow feathers, red mane and tail, thin white blaze

SHADEPEBBLE—heavily spotted exotic silver filly with pale-pink feathers, black mane and tail, thin blaze, three white socks. Born a dud and a runt to Mountain Herd, joined River Herd

⟨ MOUNTAIN HERD ⟩

ROCKWING—over-stallion. Magnificent spotted silver stallion with dark-blue and gray feathers, black mane and tail highlighted with white, one white front anklet. Deceased

HEDGEWIND—flight instructor. Bay stallion with gray feathers, black mane and tail, thin white blaze

FROSTFIRE—captain. White stallion with violet-tipped light-blue feathers, dark-gray mane and tail, one blue eye. Born to Snow Herd, adopted by Mountain Herd

LARKSONG—sky herder. Buckskin mare with dark-blue feathers, white snip on nose, black mane and tail

BIRCHCLOUD—lead mare. Light bay mare with green feathers, two white front socks

DARKLEAF—sky herder. Dun mare with black dorsal stripe, purple feathers, black mane and tail, white snip on nose, golden eyes

STARFROST—white colt, pale-yellow feathers edged in white, light-green eyes, curly tail

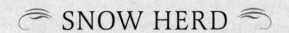

SNOW HERD

TWISTWING—over-stallion. Red dun stallion with olive-green feathers, black mane and tail. Deceased

PETALCLOUD—lead mare. Power-seeking gray mare with violet feathers, silver mane and tail, one white sock, wide blaze on face

STORMTAIL—Ice Warrior. Gigantic gray dappled stallion, purple feathers, black mane and tail, black eyes

GRAYSTONE—Ice Warrior. White stallion, silver mane and tail, pale-yellow feathers each with a silver center, blue eyes

RIVERSUN—black piebald filly, black-tipped violet feathers, wide blaze, green eyes

DESERT HERD

SANDWING—over-stallion. Proud palomino stallion with dark-yellow feathers, wide white blaze, one white sock. Deceased

REDFIRE—captain. Tall copper chestnut stallion with dark-gold feathers, dark-red mane and tail, white star on forehead

SUNRAY—spy and sky herder. Golden buckskin mare with light-purple feathers, black mane and tail, white star and snip on face

RAINCLOUD—legendary mare. Fine-boned palomino. Deceased

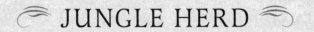

JUNGLE HERD

The black foal:

NIGHTWING—ancient stallion, solid-black with black feathers. Born to Jungle Herd. Known as the Destroyer. Immortal.

SMOKEWING—over-stallion. Speckled bay stallion with brown-and-white spotted feathers, black mane and tail, white snip on nose. Deceased

ASHRAIN—battle mare. Wiry dark-bay mare with yellow and green feathers, one white sock, snip on nose

SPRINGTAIL—battle aide. Light-bay piebald mare with dark-blue feathers, brown-and-white tail

SPIDERWING—legendary over-stallion. Deceased

HOLLYBLAZE—legendary sister of Spiderwing. Spotted bay weanling filly with brilliant gold-tipped emerald feathers, two white front socks, light-brown eyes, black mane and tail, wide blaze on face. Deceased

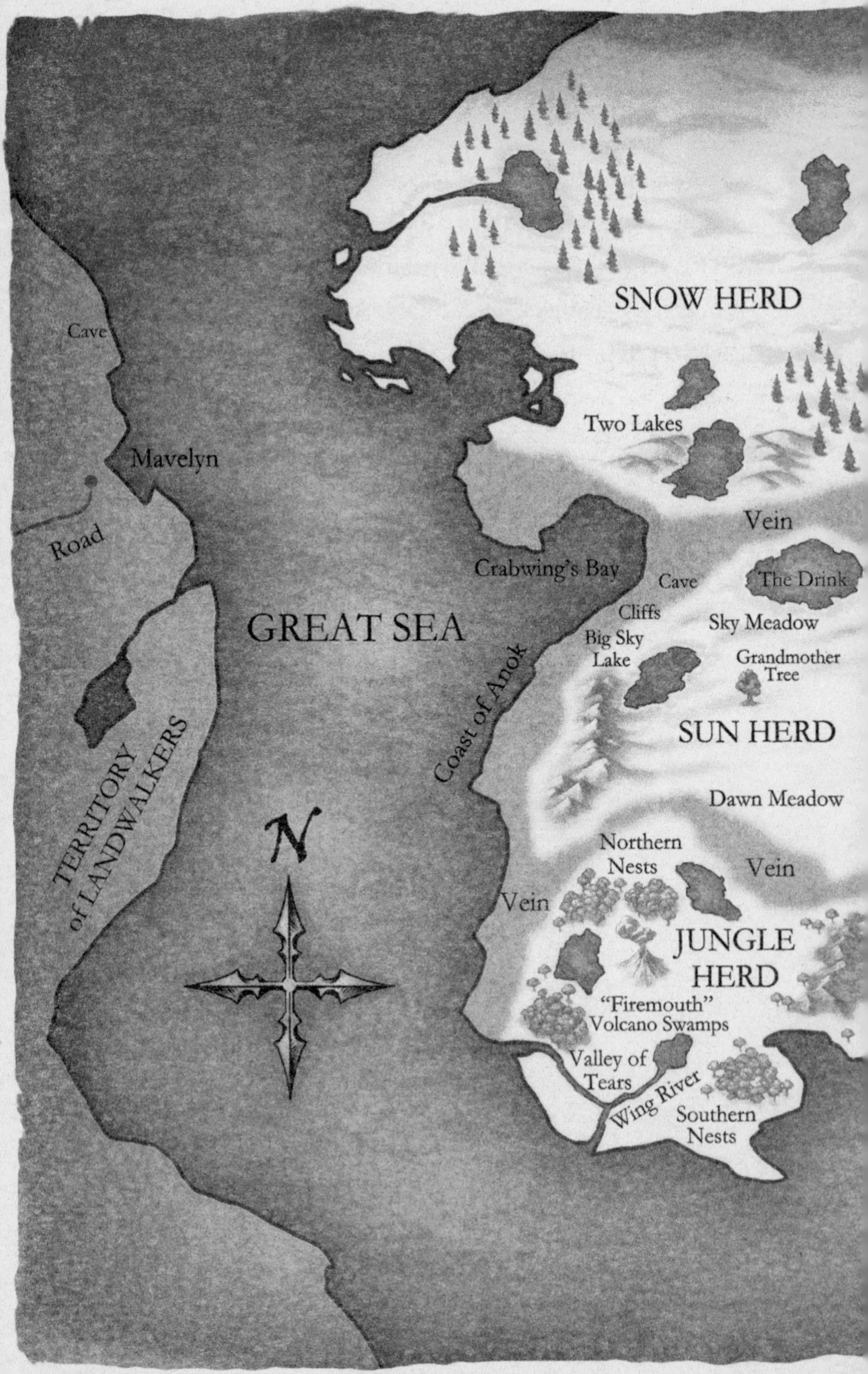
SNOW HERD
Cave
Two Lakes
Mavelyn
Road
Vein
Crabwing's Bay
Cave
The Drink
Cliffs
Sky Meadow
GREAT SEA
Big Sky
Lake
Grandmother
Tree
Coast of Anok
SUN HERD
TERRITORY
of LANDWALKERS
Dawn Meadow
N
Northern
Nests
Vein
Vein
JUNGLE
HERD
"Firemouth"
Volcano Swamps
Valley of
Tears
Wing River
Southern
Nests

Ice Lands

Hoofbeat Mountains

Ice Caves

The Trap

WESTERN ANOK

Blue Mountains

Black Lake

Wastelands

Canyon Meadow

Interior of Anok

MOUNTAIN HERD

Vein

Canyons

Vein

Lower Grasslands

Tail River

Valley Field

Feather Lake

DESERT HERD

Cloud Forest

Turtle Beach

Red Rock Mountains

SEA of RAIN

Vein

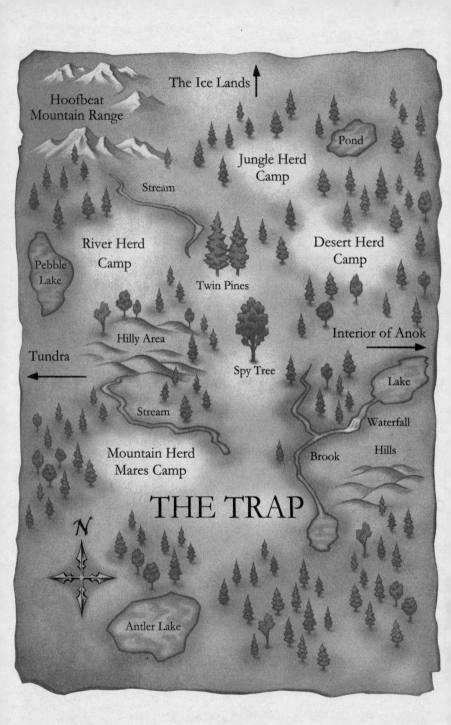

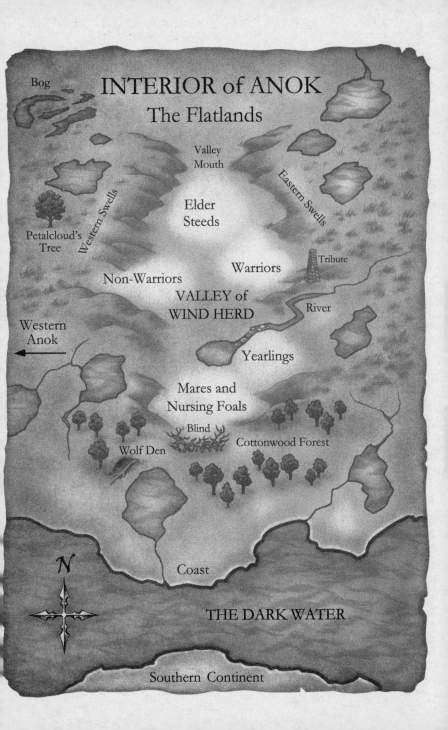

1

TEARS

HEAVY CLOUDS MASKED THE NIGHT SKY, AND cold drizzle collected on Star's feathers as he flapped through the mist, soaring straight up toward the moon. He was searching for the end of the massive cloud layer that blocked his view of northern Anok. Where was his herd? They had just been celebrating the defeat of Frostfire's Black Army at their camp in the Trap. Star was content. He'd used his starfire to heal his friends and his enemies, and the herds that had been hiding from Nightwing the Destroyer were finally united and working together. Star's ultimate goal of bringing peace to Anok had seemed imminent.

But then the cries of an injured pegasus had lured

Star deep into the woods. He'd found Frostfire's mate, Larksong, lying alone beneath a tree, groaning and bleeding. This mare was Nightwing's ally, but Star took pity on her, using his starfire to heal her and her unborn foal. And then guilt had driven Larksong to confess an awful trick: "Run back to your herd before it's too late," she'd whinnied. "Petalcloud did this to me. She beat me and left me here, to lure you away from your friends."

Petalcloud was the leader of the Ice Warriors, an army she'd formed to kill Star and win the favor of Nightwing. Petalcloud had abused Larksong in the hopes that Star would do exactly what he had done: abandon his friends.

Right after Larksong's confession, a flash of silver light appeared from the way Star had come. Then he heard a loud explosion, like lightning striking a thousand trees at once. He'd galloped back to the scene of the celebration only to find ashes covering the ground, a giant hole blasted through the ceiling of branches that sheltered the Trap, and emptiness where his herd had been reveling. Star knew instantly that Nightwing had been there. Perhaps since Frostfire's Black Army and Petalcloud's Ice Warriors had failed to capture Star, Nightwing had changed tactics and decided to capture Star's friends instead.

But where had the ancient stallion taken all of them?

Star burst into the clear sky above the clouds. Bitter cold slowed his blood, and screaming winds pierced his sensitive ears. He flew in a circle beneath the glittering stars, sucking at the sharp air and driving it into his burning lungs, but there were no pegasi here.

Frustrated, he pinned his wings and nose-dived toward land, hurtling through the wet clouds, which felt warm after the heights, and rocketing toward the Trap. He pulled up just before hitting the trees and then roared across them, his hooves skimming the branches, his eyes hunting for any sign of Nightwing or his friends.

Star landed back in the forest, and the pine needles swirled around his hooves. He held perfectly still and listened, his ears swiveling madly, trying to capture any sounds of wingbeats or hoofbeats, or the bleating of the newborns. But there was nothing, just forlorn silence and the wet smell of fog. If his herd was not in the sky and not in the Trap, then where could they be? Star galloped back to the place where Nightwing had blasted the huge hole through the thick canopy of branches.

The area was burned black. The shock of it had not left Star. He felt sick and dizzy, baffled and scared. Many steeds had died; the ashes told the story, but not all—Star held on to that hope: *not all*!

And where was Petalcloud's army? Where were the Ice Warriors? He cantered toward the battleground where he'd last seen them. Petalcloud's huge stallion, Stormtail, had almost killed Star there, but Star had sprang a shimmering golden shield around himself at the last moment. That memory was the only one that was good. Star had learned how to use a new power: a shield. It wouldn't help him defeat the Destroyer, but it would help him defend himself. Star kicked at the bloody soil. Petalcloud's army wasn't here. Even his enemies had abandoned him.

"No," he neighed. "I will find them, all of them." He arched his neck and galloped forward. The hoofprints of Petalcloud's army led straight to the River Herd camp, where his friends had been attacked. Star slid to a halt, certain now that Petalcloud and Nightwing were working together.

Nearby, Star spotted a single black flower. It looked exactly like the magical flowers that grew out of the soil when he cried, except for the color. Star gasped, realizing what it meant. *The Destroyer had shed a tear.* Someone had upset Nightwing, and Star took another sharp breath because he knew that pegasus had to be Morningleaf. Only she was fearless enough, or careless enough, to do it. Star closed his eyes. Nightwing would have blasted her for that—for making him cry.

Star staggered upright and bleated into the darkness, trotting in circles with his head down, sniffing for his friends Morningleaf, Silverlake, or Hazelwind, but all scents had been burned away.

He reared and leaped off the ground, through the gaping hole in the leaves. Nightwing could have taken his friends anywhere, in any direction. Star flapped hard, sending himself straight up, toward the jet streams in the heights. He would have to ride them if he was going to search the entire continent. Star's heart raced as the horizon bowed and the land shrank. The air thinned, and he took deep, slow breaths. He flew in a spiral, unsure which way to go first—perhaps south, to Jungle Herd's territory, which was Nightwing's birthland, or west to the Snow Herd lands, where Petalcloud had trained her Ice Warriors.

Star suddenly halted, shocked. Below him a pegasus rocketed out of the mist, heading straight toward him with his ears flat and his legs tucked. It was a white stallion with pale-blue feathers edged in violet.

A survivor!

Star hovered, watching the stranger.

The stallion glared at him, and as he came closer,

Star saw that one eye was brown and the other blue. He recoiled, stunned.

It was Frostfire—the malicious captain who'd formed the Black Army. He was Star's worst enemy, next to Nightwing, and he was flying straight at him!

2

ENEMIES

"BACK OFF!" STAR NEIGHED AS FROSTFIRE HUR-
tled toward him.

"Where is she?" Frostfire tore past Star, wheezing for
air. He'd flown too high, and his muscles seized, starved
for oxygen. His momentum carried him past Star, but then
his body twirled and he fell toward land, passing Star on
the way down.

Star tucked his wings and dived after Frostfire.
"Where is who?"

With teeth bared, the white stallion dropped upside
down toward the forest. "My mate, Larksong!" he whinnied.

Frostfire was going to smash into the trees. The

impact would break his bones, or kill him.

"Fly!" neighed Star.

Frostfire spread his wings and tumbled sideways over the tops of the branches. His feathers shook loose and coasted behind him like butterflies. Star clenched his jaw and caught up to him.

Frostfire's expression was savage. "Larksong is gone. I left her in the woods, and when I returned she'd vanished, but not her scent—or yours." Frostfire flared his nostrils in disgust. "What did you do to her? Did you kill her? Is this your revenge because I kidnapped Morningleaf and hid her in the lava tubes moons ago?" Frostfire shook his head and then rammed Star in his ribs. "If you hurt Larksong, I'll yank out your feathers, tear off your head, and feed your body to the wolves."

Star's laughter ripped through his body, unexpected and bitter. He flew a circle around Frostfire. Besides the fact that Star had sharpened his hooves and battle-trained with four different herds, he also had his starfire shield. Frostfire couldn't hurt him.

Frostfire's pupils contracted as he roared at Star. "Just tell me what you did!" He'd regained control of his wings, and he glided smoothly next to his enemy.

Star absorbed Frostfire's wrath, understanding that

the stallion loved Larksong and that it was concern for her that was driving his anger. "I healed her," Star said simply. "I don't know where she went after that."

"Healed her?" Frostfire swished his tail. "She was fine when I left her."

"Well, I found her bleeding, dying, in the forest—but her injury was a trick to lure me away. When I returned, my herd was gone. Every steed." Star peered into Frostfire's one blue eye, and their history flamed between them like a raging fire; their words popped like sparks. "What do you know about that?"

"Nothing," he said.

"Are you sure? It was your dam, Petalcloud, who attacked her. Larksong admitted it."

"My mother?" Frostfire's shock was convincing.

"Yes. Larksong would have died if I hadn't healed her."

Frostfire reeled, and Star noticed that their wingbeats had synchronized, creating one steady hum. "Larksong and I are against my mother," said the white stallion. "Petalcloud must have ambushed her and used her as bait, but she did it under Nightwing's orders, not mine. Where is she now?"

"Petalcloud?"

Frostfire's voice rose in pitch. "No. Larksong?"

"I don't know. I healed her, and then she told me to run back to my herd before it was too late." Star coasted on the breeze, feeling heavy with regret. "So we're both looking for our friends?"

"I guess we are." Frostfire slowed and hovered several winglengths above the trees, his flapping feathers created wind that rustled the branches.

Star didn't trust Frostfire, but he doubted a seasoned warrior like him could fake grief or confusion so well. Perhaps together they could unravel the clues and find the missing pegasi.

Frostfire narrowed his watering eyes and sank toward land, looking suddenly exhausted. "And what about my warriors, the Black Army? They never returned to me after your army defeated them. Did Nightwing . . . get them too?" Frostfire touched down on the open tundra and stood with his wings sagging.

Star settled next to him. "Your Black Army follows me now, so yes, they were taken when my herd was taken."

"You stole my army?" Frostfire asked, his jaw agape.

"I didn't *steal* them. They wanted to join me. Most of them."

Frostfire lowered his neck like an angry wolf. "You poisoned their minds."

"I didn't."

The stallion backed away. "You're as dangerous as Nightwing. Did Larksong join you too?" He spat the words.

Star folded his wings. "No, she didn't."

Frostfire peered into Star's eyes, his defiance smoldering but his expression hopeless. "If you're going to kill me, or turn me into one of your slaves—just do it now. Please."

Angry thoughts tumbled through Star's mind. This white stallion had kidnapped Morningleaf, murdered her protectors in front of her eyes, and then taken her to the dark lava tubes in Jungle Herd's territory, where she'd lived in terror until she escaped. If Star released his rage about this, he could be as dangerous as Nightwing. The dark emotions tumbling through his mind horrified him.

But then Star noticed Frostfire's swishing tail, which was curly like his own, and he remembered that this white stallion was his uncle. He and Star's mother, Lightfeather, shared the same sire, Iceriver. And Star's mother had once instructed him to follow his love, not his fear. He had to remember who *he* was, even now when he was alone with his enemy. And he was not a destroyer. Star crammed the silver fire down into a tiny, cold seed.

Frostfire snorted. "I'm right about you, aren't I? You *are* here to conquer us." He looked terrified, but also smug.

"No, that's not true."

"Than *why* are you here? What do you want with the herds of Anok?"

Star arched his long neck. "I don't want to hurt you, or anyone."

"But you *do* hurt us. You don't see how you've ripped the herds apart? You don't see the trail of blood behind you—that every over-stallion is dead, that the steeds of Anok are enslaved, and that Nightwing has returned?"

"I didn't do all that. I united the herds."

"But it all started with you, when you were born."

Star tossed his damp forelock out of his eyes. "No. It started four hundred years ago, when Nightwing was born."

Frostfire shrugged his pale wings. "What's the difference? You both hurt us; you both bring destruction."

"Can we stop arguing? Our friends are missing." Star gazed across the tundra toward the Great Sea, thinking and wondering. "Why did you leave Larksong alone in her condition?"

Frostfire's ears sprang to attention. "What condition?"

Star blinked, only now remembering what Larksong had told him, and that Frostfire didn't know. "Your mare is with foal."

Frostfire staggered as though Star had kicked him. "My Larksong?"

"Yes. It's a colt."

"How do you know?"

"I healed them both."

Frostfire paced in a circle, shedding feathers, excitement building in him like a storm. "I'm going to be a sire?" He pricked his ears forward, his voice rising. "Larksong was supposed to meet me by the little waterfall at midnight. She said she had something to tell me, but she never showed. I think Nightwing took her when he took your herd. We need to save them!"

Star's gut tightened. "Together?"

"Why not?"

Star gaped at him. *Because you formed an army to kill me*, he thought.

Frostfire seemed to read his mind. "Right, I know we're not herdmates, but we have the same purpose, do we not?"

"But I don't need you," said Star. "I can look for them on my own."

Frostfire closed his eyes for a moment, seemed to make a decision, and then peered intently at Star with his odd pair of eyes. "You can, but it will take you many seasons to search all of Anok. I know where Nightwing is taking the pegasi."

Star's heart lurched. "How do you know that?"

"Nightwing told me when I formed the Black Army, before he chose to side only with Petalcloud. But—"

Frostfire stalled, eyeing Star's longer, more powerful wingspan. "If I tell you, you'll leave me behind."

Star hesitated. There was some truth to that. Frostfire could never keep up with him because of Star's powers. Star didn't need to eat or sleep often, so he could fly for many days without stopping. Frostfire would need rest and food.

"I'm not wrong, am I? You'd leave me?" asked the white stallion.

Star shrugged. "Why do you *want* to travel with me anyway? Why should *I* trust *you*?" Star gazed at Frostfire, remembering all the treacheries of their past: the time he yanked Star from Feather Lake and flew him to Mountain Herd's territory to meet the over-stallion, Rockwing; the time he promised to protect Morningleaf and then kidnapped her instead; and the two times he'd beaten Star's friend Brackentail to near death.

Frostfire met his gaze. "I need you, Star."

"Why?"

Frostfire tensed. "Look, I failed to deliver your head to Nightwing, and after you defeated my army, the Destroyer vowed to kill me. It's why Larksong and I were hiding. We were going to meet at midnight and fly away, probably across the sea. But you have starfire. You can keep me safe from Nightwing, right?"

Hysteria bubbled from deep within Star. His worst enemy was pleading for his *protection*.

"Please," said Frostfire. "He'll kill me on sight, and now he has Larksong. I can't rescue her on my own. If you promise to help me free her, I'll help you find your friends."

Star stared at Frostfire's curly tail. His mother would want Star to help him. Through a tight jaw, Star reluctantly agreed. "All right, I'll help you rescue Larksong, and I won't leave you behind. Now tell me, where is Nightwing taking my friends?"

"I won't tell you, but I'll take you there."

Star suppressed a wave of anger. "You trust me to protect you from Nightwing, but you don't trust me to keep my promise? I won't abandon you, Frostfire."

His companion stared at him, saying nothing. Star exhaled, realizing that a lying stallion like Frostfire couldn't trust anyone. "Fine. Let's go."

"It's not that simple," said Frostfire. "Nightwing will visit the territories first, to collect the stray pegasi. He wants all of us, every last pegasus. So if we find him here in Western Anok, maybe you can stop him before he settles the herd. If we can't find him quickly, then I'll take you to the lands where he plans to live."

Star pinned his ears. "Where to first?"

"I don't know exactly. Maybe Mountain Herd's territory," said Frostfire. Then he narrowed his eyes. "This doesn't mean I believe in you, Star—that you're the healer. You can destroy too, just like Nightwing. You're no different."

Star balked, and fresh anger surged through him, but he decided to let Frostfire have his feelings without rebuke. "I hear you," said Star. And the two stallions flew side by side into the sunrise.

3

CAPTURED

MORNINGLEAF'S TEARS SOAKED HER CHESTNUT face and dripped off her cheeks, falling hundreds of winglengths to the ground below. She dangled between her mother, Silverlake, and her friend, Redfire. The two steeds did their best to carry her through the clouds without hurting her worse. Her brother, Hazelwind, and two of her best friends, Echofrost and Shadepebble, flew ahead, creating a wake for the steeds, to ease their burden. Echofrost's brother, Bumblewind, flew behind with Brackentail and Dewberry, whispering about escape.

Leading their herd was Nightwing the Destroyer. The pegasi didn't want to follow him, but Nightwing had shot silver starfire at the ones who'd resisted, killing them instantly. The herd had two choices—follow Nightwing or die—and the pegasi of Anok chose to follow, because they had hope. "Star will rescue us," Morningleaf had insisted, and the news traveled secretly from pegasus to pegasus, lending the herd strength.

Echofrost dropped out of formation and soared closer to Morningleaf. "I have news," she whispered as loudly as she could without Nightwing's warriors overhearing.

Morningleaf's friends crowded together, their wingtips touching as they flew. Echofrost continued. "When we landed earlier to drink, I overheard two Ice Warriors talking. Nightwing is taking us to the Flatlands in the interior of Anok."

"The Flatlands!" sputtered Hazelwind.

Morningleaf watched the guards who patrolled the outskirts of the massive flying herd. "Shh," she warned her brother.

Hazelwind lowered his voice. "Look at the newborns; they'll never make it that far. And what about the winds, and the wolves? Star rejected the interior as a safe home for pegasi moons ago when we were searching for a new territory for River Herd."

Dewberry interrupted. "Legend says that the Lake Herd pegasi blew away in a storm."

"I heard that giant wolves swallowed them whole," said Bumblewind.

Dewberry pinned her ears. "No wolf is that big, or that hungry."

Redfire, who hailed from the desert, spoke. "Our legends say that the Lake Herd pegasi fled Anok when Nightwing became the Destroyer four hundred years ago. That they escaped."

Morningleaf twisted her neck, studying the handsome chestnut stallion they'd befriended in the Trap, remembering that Redfire liked to retell old stories. "If they escaped, then why didn't they ever come back?"

Redfire and her friends were silent a moment, wondering about the fate of the ancient Lake Herd pegasi. Had they been swallowed by a storm, by wolves, or by fear? It seemed important, considering they would soon be living in the same dangerous lands.

"There's a lot of food in the interior," said Bumblewind, causing Dewberry to snort. "Best grazing lands in Anok."

"It doesn't matter," grumbled Hazelwind. "We have a long journey ahead of us, but it also gives us time." He glanced at Morningleaf, his eyes full of grief for what had happened to her in the Trap. "We must plan an escape."

Morningleaf glanced down at the land passing far

below her hooves. They'd been traveling for fifteen days, visiting the five abandoned territories and searching for stray pegasi to join their herd. Many were elders, and when they refused to follow Nightwing, he'd set them all on fire. Each time Morningleaf closed her eyes, she saw the flames and heard the screams.

But the view when her eyes were wide open was just as awful. Her beautiful aqua feathers were destroyed, charred and useless, burned to black shreds by Nightwing. She was a dud now, a walker, a grounded pegasus—she might as well be a horse. Her agony about this seared her mind in waves of sadness followed by overwhelming fury.

"Star will destroy Nightwing," Morningleaf said in a choked breath. Nightwing had also murdered her sire, Thundersky, and trapped him in the Beyond—a realm between life and the golden meadow, a place where souls killed by Nightwing were stuck.

"Of course," said Hazelwind, his voice grim. "But we can't wait, and Star doesn't know where we are or where we're going. Anok is . . . huge. I'm making a plan." With that, Hazelwind flew off to resume his position, taking the headwind to ease their flight, and everyone followed suit, leaving Morningleaf dangling between her mother and Redfire.

Silverlake had been silent during their discussion, but now she spoke. "You look tired," she said, fretting.

But Morningleaf thought it was her mother who looked exhausted. Silverlake had witnessed the murder of her mate, Thundersky, in the Sun Herd lands, and then she'd watched Nightwing maim her filly in the Trap. Grief and rage thundered inside the old mare, threatening to rip her apart.

"I'm okay, Mama," said Morningleaf. "Please don't worry about me."

"I *am* worried, but it's more than that." Silverlake lowered her voice and Redfire turned his head away, giving them privacy to speak. "Your brother is wrong," Silverlake whispered. "He plans to free you so you can rest and heal, but I have a very bad feeling about it." She glanced at Nightwing, who flew at the head of the captured herd. Starfire sparked off his tail, reminding all of them of his power. Silverlake switched her gaze back to Morningleaf, her expression determined. "I . . . I just don't think it will end well. Please be patient. Star will rescue us. And he'll heal your wings."

Silverlake faced away, hiding her rage from Morningleaf. The old mare had vowed to see Nightwing destroyed, but she had no way to accomplish this. Morningleaf knew her mother felt helpless, because she felt the same way.

"I understand, Mama," said Morningleaf, but she couldn't promise to obey. Nightwing was unpredictable, and he knew she was special to Star. It was why he'd hurt her in the first place. Perhaps her mother and friends could wait things out, but could she?

As Morningleaf was carried through the sky, she remembered the horrors of their first day with Nightwing. River Herd had been celebrating the defeat of Frostfire's Black Army in the Trap when Star had done an amazing thing. He'd healed all of Frostfire's wounded warriors, and after doing so, Star told them they were free to go. But instead of leaving, most had joined River Herd and become followers of Star. Morningleaf had felt so proud and joyful, so full of hope.

But one steed had not been healed, and Star heard the pegasus mare groaning far away in the woods. Star left River Herd to find her, promising to come right back, and that's when Nightwing and Petalcloud had landed in their camp. Terror had ripped through the pegasi, and a battle mare named Ashrain had reacted, attacking Petalcloud. The Destroyer stepped between them and killed Ashrain in a huff of silver fire. The warriors charged him, and Nightwing destroyed them too. It was as easy for him as breathing, and Morningleaf would never forget it—hundreds of warriors turned to dust while still upright and poised for battle.

Silverlake had thrown up her wings. "Stop," she'd cried. Morningleaf wasn't sure if she was speaking to Nightwing or River Herd, but everyone had halted, prancing in place, and the only noise was the panicked bleating of the newborns.

Nightwing opened his mouth, and hundreds more terrified pegasi bolted into the woods. He hurled his power after them, and silver beams of light twisted through the trees like snakes, hunting the pegasi who galloped away, and then it curled around their necks and choked them.

Nightwing's power overwhelmed River Herd, and soon all steeds had dropped their heads in submission. A few trotted slowly away, choosing death over capture, and as they melted into the shadows, Nightwing's silver fire caught them and evaporated them.

Silverlake had approached Nightwing, looking desperate. "What do you want?" she'd asked.

The Destroyer folded his wings, gazing at River Herd like a proud sire. "The pegasi of Anok belong to one herd now, my herd. I'm your over-stallion."

Morningleaf had reared, her anger rising like steam.

"Don't do it," Silverlake had whinnied, and Morning-leaf could still hear that warning reverberating through her head. If only she'd obeyed her mother, but at that second she hadn't cared what happened to her, or at least she thought she hadn't. She'd galloped toward Nightwing and halted, facing him.

"You're Star's friend," he'd said, blinking at her. "I remember you from Sky Meadow moons ago, when I stabbed your precious black foal through the heart."

Morningleaf had trembled, remembering when Night-wing had pierced Star's chest with a thin stream of starfire, almost killing him. But an army of weanlings, the ghosts of deceased young pegasi, had come down from the sky. The leader of that Weanling Army was Hollyblaze, Night-wing's past best friend who he'd killed or gotten killed and who now haunted him. When she'd landed with her spirit army, Hollyblaze had called Nightwing a coward, and that had upset him terribly. Then she'd shot bright lights into his eyes and drove him away from Star, allowing Star's friends time to whisk his body to safety.

Morningleaf had taken a breath and then invoked the dead filly's name, hoping to frighten Nightwing with it. "Hollyblaze called you a coward in Sky Meadow. Why?"

Nightwing's eyes had popped wide, and he reared,

shedding feathers. He'd glanced upward, as if the act of saying Hollyblaze's name would bring the filly's spirit down from the golden meadow. When nothing happened, he trained his eyes on Morningleaf. "What did you say to me?"

She'd whipped her tail from side to side. "Hollyblaze called you a coward. I heard her say it. Is it because you murdered her and all those helpless weanlings?"

Nightwing's mouth had opened and shut, but no words or starfire came forth.

Morningleaf had taken a cautious step toward him, sensing his unease. "Tell me," she'd whispered. "Did you murder your best friend?"

Nightwing had gasped, and a single tear dropped from his eye and landed on the soil. Morningleaf watched as a black flower sprouted between his hooves. She smelled something terrible, like rotting trees, and realized it was coming from him. Nightwing twisted his neck, and his eyes drifted off, seeming blank, but she imagined he was reliving his past.

Morningleaf had stepped closer, thinking to drive him off. The River Herd steeds softly rattled their feathers.

"Please no," Silverlake whispered to her filly.

Nightwing had taken a deep, shuddering breath and

then focused on Morningleaf, lowering his head toward her. "I won't kill you," he'd said.

Morningleaf let out her breath in a gasp of hope.

"Not as long as Star lives," he'd added. "You're special to him, and as long as I have you, I won't have to hunt him down. He'll come to me, and I imagine he'll do anything—*anything*—to protect you." Nightwing leaned closer to her, baring his yellowed teeth. "But I'm going to make sure you never get away."

She'd squeezed her eyes shut then, and he'd attacked her. The memory of the pain shot across her mind in colors, brilliant and blinding. Nightwing had doused her wings, only her wings, in silver fire that circulated like water, seeping into her bones and into her feather's roots, killing them so they would never grow back but preserving them so they wouldn't fall out, leaving her wings blackened and ugly, and unable to carry her weight into the sky.

She shuddered, feeling sick even now, fifteen days later.

Her mother had squealed, galloping to her side, and Morningleaf had collapsed. Then Nightwing had lifted his head and roared starfire at the leafy overhang that created a natural ceiling in the Trap, blasting a huge hole in it. "We're migrating," he neighed to River Herd. "Pick up this filly and move out!"

And just like that, River Herd had a new over-stallion—and they left the Trap, and Star, and had flown to the territories to gather any remaining stray pegasi.

Now Morningleaf swept her eyes across the thousands of migrating steeds flying in formation east, to the interior of Anok, but Anok was a massive continent, and the interior was so far away. She guessed it would take until the middle of summer to get there. How *would* Star ever find them?

She chewed her lip, considering what would happen if he did find them. Nightwing would use her to control Star—he'd promised as much, and it was something Star had always feared would happen. It was why he'd once sent her away with Frostfire, so that the white stallion would hide her from Nightwing. She glanced at her brother, Hazelwind, noticing how much his eyes and muzzle resembled their proud sire, Thundersky. Next she peered at her mother, who flew with such steadfast precision that no one would guess the devastating emotions that tumbled within her heart.

When Star comes, I can't be here. The thought assailed her like the wind, tousling her mixed-up feelings and sending them all in one direction—toward escape. But her mother was right; it was too dangerous. Her brother and her friends, they would be killed. No, she couldn't let them help her. She'd have to do it on her own. But how?

Morningleaf closed her eyes and saw nothing but flames and death. Her eyelids flew back open. Now was not a time to feel afraid. Now was the time to think. She sealed off her fears and plotted, letting her imagination fly.

4

TEAMWORK

SEVERAL DAYS HAD PASSED SINCE STAR HAD DIS-
covered his herd missing. He and Frostfire had searched
Snow Herd's territory without stopping, cruising just
below the cloud layer so they could scan the terrain for
signs of pegasi. But the north was empty, abandoned.

The sun was setting when Frostfire begged for a rest.
"I need water," he rasped. There was a river shimmering
in the distance. Star banked and headed toward it.

Star was larger than Frostfire and should have been
taking the headwind to speed their flight, but the white
stallion refused to draft on Star's wake. And it was silly
for Star to draft off Frostfire's, so they flew in each other's
competing currents, slowing each other down, and Star

became frustrated. They landed at the water's edge, and Frostfire plunged his nose into the current. Star spoke. "We're not working as a team."

"So," said Frostfire, water dripping down his chin.

"So we should," said Star. "If you let me lead, we'll travel faster."

"I won't draft off you," said Frostfire, ruffling his violet-edged feathers. "You can draft off me."

Yearlings like Star didn't normally lead a formation, and he understood that Frostfire was once a captain, a leader, and the idea of riding the wake of a younger steed was repulsive to him, but Star had no patience for Frostfire's feelings. "I'm bigger and faster," he said, pointing out the obvious.

"Do you want to split up?" asked Frostfire. "Is that what you're getting at?"

It was tempting. Frostfire struggled to breathe in the heights, and his burly muscles tired easily; he was built to sprint, not to fly for hours on end. He was also moody, and the long silences between them were thick with static that set Star's nerves on edge.

But joy had bloomed in Frostfire's heart at the news of his unborn colt, and it was transforming him. He day-dreamed and fretted, and Star sometimes caught him sighing with pleasure or pacing with worry. In those moments Frostfire's eyes were soft, and when he looked at Star, it wasn't with hatred. In those moments Star found the white stallion tolerable. But none of that changed the fact that Frostfire slowed him down.

"I'm not saying I want to split up," said Star. "I need you to take me to my friends." Star lowered his head and drank from the river, enjoying the cool liquid on his tongue, and he studied the white steed who had streaks of silver in his tail.

He wasn't just using Frostfire to find River Herd; the stallion was also Star's only living family. He didn't believe Frostfire was aware of it or, if he was, that he cared about their blood relation, but Star cared. He'd lost his chance to know his grandsire, Iceriver, and while befriending Frostfire was probably out of the question, the stallion's unborn colt was also Star's relation, and he wanted to know him. "I'm thinking of ways to speed up this search," said Star, hoping to soothe the stallion's suspicious mind.

Frostfire was thinking too, and his eyes brightened with an idea. "You're right that we need to travel faster. Why don't we ride the jet streams? If I fail the exit, you can heal me, right?"

Star pricked his ears, shocked at his proposal. "Heal

you? I'd probably have to bring you back from the dead, but yes, I could do it."

The jet streams were currents of air that whipped across the planet at hurricane speeds. Riding them was difficult, but exiting them safely was near impossible. The skinny, small-boned Desert Herd steeds trained all their lives to ride the jet streams, and they drifted in and out of them with ease, but Frostfire's body was dense and heavy. He would plummet toward land at the mercy of his own momentum. "Do you trust me enough to bring you back from death?" asked Star.

Frostfire paused. "Well, not when you put it like that."

"I don't mean I wouldn't do it. I'm just surprised you'd . . . I don't know . . . trust me with your life."

Frostfire huffed. "Forget it. You're talking me out of it."

But Star didn't forget it. "It would be better if I could prevent your injury in the first place."

"I'll agree with that."

Star pranced, becoming excited. "Maybe I can project my shield around us both."

"Your what?"

"My shield, it's like a . . . like a bubble, but it protects me."

Frostfire flattened his ears and studied Star's body. "So you're immortal *and* indestructible now?"

Star shrugged his wings. "I don't know. Maybe."

Frostfire grunted. "Nightwing has a similar ability, doesn't he? I'd heard from one of my captains that you shot starfire directly at him, but he blocked it. It bounced off without touching him."

"Yes, he has a shield too," said Star, who didn't remember much from that day in Sky Meadow when Nightwing had nearly killed him.

Frostfire paced, thinking. "Have you considered you might have other powers?"

"Of course."

"Have you tried to use them?"

"I don't know what they are, so no."

Frostfire peered up at the sky. "All right, let's try riding a jet stream in the morning."

The pair kicked off and flew to the forestlands to sleep.

Star felt hopeful. By riding the jet streams, they'd be traveling much faster, and they'd catch up to Morningleaf and his friends quicker. How Star would free them from Nightwing, he wasn't sure, but at least he had the shield. Nightwing couldn't hurt him this time. Star wondered what the Destroyer wanted with the pegasi of Anok. Was it just to rule a herd, or something worse? He stretched his long black wings. He guessed that sooner rather than later he would find out.

Frostfire discussed their plan for the next day. "A southwestern jet stream will carry us across Mountain Herd's and Jungle Herd's territories. From the heights, we can scan the lands all the way to the ocean. If we don't find the pegasi there, then we can head east, over Desert Herd's land." Frostfire exhaled. "We're looking for a herd of—I don't know—twelve thousand steeds. We're sure to see signs of them if they're still in Western Anok."

Star glanced at the moon, which was rising. "I'll keep watch tonight."

Frostfire grimaced. "I'll watch out for myself." But soon the captain was fast asleep.

Star stayed awake all night, keeping a wary eye out for predators. Next to him, Frostfire dozed, curled up like a young foal, and Star stared at him, feeling curious.

He knew Frostfire had been abandoned by his mother, Petalcloud, and treated cruelly by his grandsire, Rockwing. Was that why Frostfire thought Star would use his power for evil, because Rockwing had ruled Mountain Herd with such viciousness, forcing steeds to submit to him or die? Or was it because his mother had joined forces with Nightwing and had not included him, her son? Star couldn't blame Frostfire for being suspicious of him when his own family had betrayed him, and he doubted he could ever really trust Frostfire, but maybe during their travels Frostfire would see that he could trust Star?

Turning his gaze from the sleeping stallion, Star scented the wind for predators and wondered where Nightwing could be hiding twelve thousand pegasi. His heart beat faster, thinking about it. His fierce and independent friends—who'd once threatened to execute him in utter fear that *he* was a destroyer—were now under the control of the Destroyer himself. Star found the weight of it all difficult to bear. He didn't know who was alive or dead. Star stared up through the leaves at the pale moon that glowed as it always had, and he wondered if Morningleaf was looking at the same beautiful sight.

5

EXHAUSTION

NIGHTWING LANDED HIS CAPTURED HERD IN THE
scrubby foothills located northeast of Mountain Herd's
territory. They were inland now, far from the coast, flying over a long, winding river. They'd been traveling for
twenty-two days. Nightwing settled the herd once a day
to drink and eat, and once a night to sleep. The pegasi
were weary and hungry, and Morningleaf was no excep-
tion. Her wings ached from holding her weight.

As soon as the herd touched down on the rocky landscape, she stumbled to a halt and let her blackened limbs
hang to the ground. A glimpse of her shadow showed her
how much she resembled Star when he was born: a dud
with black feathers and drooping wings. The thought

wrenched her heart with memories of him and concern for where he was now.

Brackentail landed gently next to her, keeping one eye on Petalcloud's Ice Warriors, who guarded the herd. "They're flying us too hard for such a long journey," he said, gritting his teeth.

Morningleaf exhaled, taking in the brown colt's concern. He'd tried to kill Star when they were all weanlings, but so much had changed since then. It had taken a long time, but he'd earned back Star's trust; then slowly, he'd earned Morningleaf's trust, and also her respect. She no longer saw the past when she looked at Brackentail, but the future. He was growing taller and stronger each day, as were all the yearlings.

Morningleaf stepped closer to Brackentail and nuzzled him, soaking up his warm scent. Her other yearling friends, Shadepebble, Bumblewind, and Echofrost, joined them along with Morningleaf's older brother, Hazelwind.

"I heard we lost another foal," said Shadepebble.

Echofrost nodded. "The filly's wing muscles cramped a few miles back, and she fell. It happened too fast for anyone to save her."

"How is the filly's mother?" asked Shadepebble.

Echofrost winced. "She's . . . gone. She attacked

Nightwing, and, well, you know."

Morningleaf lashed her tail. Nightwing used Petalcloud's army of devoted Ice Warriors to patrol the herd. The big-boned, furry steeds pranced among the captured steeds, biting and kicking anyone who complained or who lay down to rest. Nightwing also patrolled the herd, and he killed pegasi quickly and randomly, sometimes with no warning. It wore on all their jangled nerves. Morningleaf barely recognized the pegasi of Anok—they were shedding feathers, hollow eyed, and skinny, and some had drifted into hopelessness. But Morningleaf's anger, and her concern for Star, kept her sharp.

Brackentail nodded toward the mares and foals who were drinking at a flat blue watering hole. "I overheard Sweetroot advising the mothers to wean the foals early, maybe tonight. Nursing and migrating don't mix."

"Poor things," said Bumblewind.

Morningleaf gazed west, back the way they had come, and imagined Star searching for them. "He'll find us," she said.

Bumblewind flicked his ears, knowing exactly who she meant. "Of course he will."

"I agree," said Brackentail, "but we can't keep waiting for him. Morningleaf won't make it much farther." He looked straight at her. "I'm sorry, but it's true. We have a lot of flying ahead of us, and your shoulder muscles are giving out. You almost lost your grasp on Hazelwind and fell today, like that filly."

Morningleaf tried to deny it. "I—"

Brackentail interrupted. "I saw it, Morningleaf."

"I did too," said Echofrost.

Morningleaf closed her mouth, because they were right. Her shoulders were exhausted from holding her weight as Redfire and now Hazelwind flew her through the sky. If the tops of her wings weren't burned, her friends could use their teeth to carry her; but they'd tried that, and Morningleaf had almost passed out from the pain. But she couldn't travel this way much farther either. And the winds were increasing as they journeyed inland, buffeting her dangling body and making it more difficult to keep hold.

Brackentail lowered his voice. "Echofrost and Shade-pebble are planning a huge fight that will distract the guards. And Hazelwind is working on the rest, getting you out of here while everyone's confused."

"It won't work," said Morningleaf flatly.

"It will," said Brackentail as he wrapped his wing across her back. "Trust us."

Morningleaf leaned against him. "I trust you, but not Nightwing's starfire. Failing means more than just death."

Brackentail's eyes widened. "What do you mean?"

Morningleaf lowered her voice, and the hot wind flipped her mane over her eyes as she spoke the secret that burdened her. "Promise not to tell anyone what I'm about to say."

"I promise," breathed Brackentail.

"Steeds killed by starfire don't fly to the golden meadow where the Ancestors live. Instead their souls are trapped in a place called the Beyond." Her throat tightened as she heard Brackentail's startled gasp.

"How do you know this?" he asked.

"The Ancestors spoke to Star in the north. They told him and then he told me, but we don't want my mother to know. Her mate, my sire, is there, stuck in the Beyond." Tears stung her eyes. "And that's where you'll go if you help me escape and fail. You see, Nightwing hasn't just captured the living but also the dead. And there's nothing we can do; only Star is capable of killing the Destroyer and freeing them. Don't risk your soul for *me*."

Brackentail's muscles tensed at her words, and his wings flared. "But Nightwing will use you against Star like a hostage, or worse. Star won't be able to think straight if that happens."

Morningleaf softened toward him, and the two stood in the sun, each lost in thought. She understood his feelings, but she knew there was no way to escape Nightwing and the Ice Warriors. She was sure her friends would die trying to free her. She also knew she couldn't stop them. They'd proven their bravery and loyalty over and over again, but saving her—it was too much to ask this time, which was why she had a plan of her own.

An Ice Warrior trotted past Morningleaf and her friends. They dropped their heads and grazed. The warrior was Stormtail, the gigantic dapple-gray stallion with the huge hooves who used to guard Petalcloud but who now spent his time patrolling the herd. His black eyes shifted to Morningleaf and her group.

They pretended not to notice him.

He paused, watching them, and his eyes were like shark eyes, empty but searching, his nostrils quivering. Stormtail took a few steps toward them, then turned and trotted away, attracted by a group of sobbing mares.

"The sooner you're out of here, the better," Brackentail whispered to Morningleaf.

She nodded, and her thoughts turned to escape as she

studied the surrounding terrain. Dusty rocks and shriveled plants covered flat-topped stone mesas that stretched for miles, scorched by the sun. Without the ocean breezes and fog, the air was hot, stale. A wide blue river snaked across the bland landscape, the only spot of color.

And beyond this land lay their destination, the lush grasslands of the interior, which were known for their dangerous high winds. But as Morningleaf considered the vastness of Anok, her captivity made even the huge sky feel small. The Ice Warriors never stopped patrolling, never stopped watching. Her world had shrunk to the space between herself and the guards. The sparkling river caught her eye, and she noticed where it disappeared underground and then returned to the surface. An idea formed in her mind. She inhaled, about to speak.

"What is it?" whispered Echofrost.

Morningleaf glanced at her friends, her plan on the tip of her tongue. Then it vanished from her lips. *I can't tell them*, she thought. "It's nothing. I'm just worrying."

Echofrost lifted her fine-shaped head, dazzling Morningleaf with the proud arch of her neck and the glittering determination in her eyes. All traces of the rage and bitterness she'd carried after her kidnapping by Rockwing had vanished long ago. "Don't worry about getting free," she said. "Let us take care of it."

Morningleaf sighed, knowing that Echofrost and Hazelwind had made up their minds too. "When do you plan to get me out?" she asked, playing along.

"In the morning," answered Echofrost.

Then I must escape tonight, Morningleaf decided. She felt her blood rush to her head, and her heart beat like a scared rabbit's. Her plan would probably fail, but so would theirs, and at least hers only involved herself.

6

JET STREAM

STAR BLINKED INTO THE RISING SUN, LETTING THE pale rays warm his black feathers. Northern butterflies fluttered around his hooves as he shuffled through the moss, and he briefly envied the simplicity of their lives. He turned his gaze toward the blue sky. He and Frostfire would travel south by jet stream today. They were on Nightwing's trail, he was sure of it, but they kept missing him. "Are you ready to go?" he asked Frostfire, who was grazing on lichen.

"Yes, I'm ready," said Frostfire, but Star saw his pulse quicken as he took a deep, steadying breath.

Neither stallion had ridden a jet stream before, but Star had seen Morningleaf fall out of one. She'd plunged toward land faster than he'd thought possible. The force of the fall had snapped her wing bones and shredded her feathers. Star had caught her in a beam of golden starfire and healed her ruined wings, otherwise she would have died. Even the fearless ancient stallion Spiderwing, the founder of the five herds, was known to be afraid of jet streams, so Star understood Frostfire's thrumming heart—it matched his own.

Star stepped next to Frostfire and projected his shield, the gold-tinged orb stretched to fit around them both. They kicked off in tandem and surged toward the clouds. Nothing could penetrate Star's shield, not even the damp white mist of the heights. The two stallions emerged above it with dry hides and feathers. Star looked down and saw the land contract as the sky expanded. A quick flash of fur drew his gaze to the tundra below. "Look, an ice tiger," he neighed.

Frostfire glanced at the cat. "I can't wait to be rid of this place."

Star watched the black-striped tiger glide toward the river; her fat paws leaving deep prints in the moss. She lapped at the water and washed her face. Even from their high altitude, Star saw that her fur was covered in blood from a fresh kill. She sat on her haunches and looked up at them, attracted, Star guessed, by the shine of the bubble and the flapping of their wings. When they reached the jet stream, they would leave the north behind, possibly forever. Star's heart clenched; he'd grown fond of the north, even with all its dangers and horrible weather and massive predators, because it was wildly beautiful too.

Star pushed higher, until the river was a tiny blue vein and the tiger had disappeared. Forceful winds buffeted the shield, but Star and Frostfire flew untouched by the currents. Frostfire breathed easily and marveled at it. "I've never flown so high," he whinnied. The atmosphere inside the sphere was warm and pleasant.

"Look," said Star. "The land is curved, not flat."

They pumped their wings, flying higher, until they reached the altitude of the jet streams.

"How do we find the southern one?" asked Star. The fast-traveling currents were invisible to the eye.

Frostfire gaped at him. "I don't know. I thought you knew."

"How would I know? I've never actually flown in a jet stream."

"Neither have I," whinnied Frostfire.

Star rattled his feathers, furious at himself. His mission to rescue his herd was off to a terrible start. "The shield is blocking me from feeling the direction of the air currents," he whinnied to Frostfire. "I'm going to have to release it until we find the southwestern stream."

"But I can't breathe up here."

"Then hold your breath!" Star withdrew the starfire, and the bubble evaporated. Shrill, freezing winds swarmed around them, and the two stallions tightened their wings to their bodies, struggling to stay parallel to the land. In seconds their muscles were quivering from the cold, but the radiation from the sun pricked their sensitive ears and muzzles. Star braced against the biting rays. He had only minutes to find the jet stream before Frostfire passed out. "Stay close to me!"

Star floundered through the crosscurrents, looking for the powerful wake that indicated a jet stream.

Frostfire flapped hard, his body stiff and his eyes leaking tears. Star felt the seconds burning away. He paddled through the currents like he was swimming through water. Far below his hooves, the clouds drifted in fat puffs, and he could see the entire expanse of the north, all the way to where the land ended at the Great Sea. The higher Star flew, the larger the planet appeared. Somewhere down below were his friends, captives of Nightwing. He glanced east, but a distant mountain range obscured his view of inland Anok. Star shook his head—focus!

He glanced at Frostfire. The white stallion's eyes bulged, and he kicked at the sky, beginning to convulse. Star soared higher, his eyes mere slits against the piercing sun. A strong, fast wake shoved him aside. He'd found a jet stream, but it was flowing north.

Star shook his head at Frostfire, duck-dived under the current, and popped up on the other side. Frostfire followed, but the effort cost him the last of his reserves. His eyes rolled back, and his wings stalled.

Star felt the tug of another powerful current, this one flowing south.

Frostfire lost momentum and began to drop.

Star would lose the current if he saved Frostfire.

The white stallion's mouth fell slack, and his body jerked from lack of oxygen. His eyelids fluttered shut.

Star gave up the jet stream, pinned his wings, and plunged after Frostfire. The stallion fell like a stone through the clouds. Star raced toward him, piercing the crosscurrents, his eyes watering and his lips flapping against his teeth. He caught up to Frostfire, spread his wings, and sprang his shield around them both. Now they were connected, but falling faster. Star turned his nose toward the sun and pumped his massive wings. He slowed their descent and then managed to drag them back to their previous altitude. The orb of starfire had its own atmosphere of fresh-flowing oxygen, and Frostfire's eyes fluttered open. "You saved me," he said, sounding surprised.

Star bit back his frustration. Why were the pegasi shocked when he did *exactly* what he promised to do? He ignored Frostfire's comment. "I found the current, but then I lost it. We're going to have to take our chances on finding it again. It's not safe for you if I retract the shield."

Frostfire snorted agreement.

Star flew on, trying to remember the exact altitude of the southern jet stream. Seconds later, he and Frostfire were sucked into a ripping current. "Ack!" Star cried, and Frostfire screamed. The current hurtled them south and sent their orb spinning in violent circles. Snatches of blue and white and brown colors tumbled past in a blur. Star drew in his wings, having no idea how to stop the rolling.

Frostfire flung out his wingtips and rotated against the direction of their spin; his movements were agile and quick, and he soon gained control of the sphere, which was just large enough to encase them both comfortably, as long as they flew side by side.

"How'd you do that?" Star asked once they were stable.

"I learned how to control spins in flight school," said Frostfire.

The clouds zoomed past them as they rode the rapid current south. "I'll watch the land to the west, and you watch the land to the east for the pegasi."

They reached the Blue Mountains and flew until almost sunset, and then Frostfire whinnied. "I see something!"

Star followed his eyes, and what he saw jolted his heart. At the southern end of Mountain Herd's territory, in a meadow called Valley Field, was a huge expanse of black, charred grass.

"Nightwing's been here," said Frostfire, his voice flat.

Star's pulse quickened. "Let's go see if he still is."

7

VALLEY FIELD

STAR AND FROSTFIRE DROPPED OUT OF THE JET
stream and plummeted toward land. "We have to slow
down," whinnied Star as they sped toward the surface of
Anok.

The two pegasi threw out their wings, and the orb
responded, slowing little by little as the ground rushed
toward them.

"The shield will protect us if we crash, right?" asked
Frostfire.

"We're about to find out!"

The orb screamed toward land, with the two pegasi
braced inside of it. Frostfire squeezed shut his eyes, and
Star cringed as they rushed toward the meadow and then

slammed into it. The sphere bounced across the grass, spinning them in a furious circle. When the orb finally rolled to a halt, Star retracted the shield, and he and Frostfire spilled onto solid ground, dazed and panting.

The stallions stood up and glanced around, struck silent. The grass in Mountain Herd's southern grazing field was burned away, and the leaves had melted off the blackened tree limbs. Star had traveled here once as a foal, but not by choice. Frostfire and his warriors had snatched him from Feather Lake and carried him here to meet their over-stallion, Rockwing. The spotted silver stallion had offered to make a pact with Star, to save him from execution and rule Anok together, but Star had refused.

He remembered his first view of Valley Field. The grass had been dark green, unlike the lighter grass in Dawn Meadow. Butterflies, bees, and flies had glided busily beneath the disruptive hooves of the frolicking Mountain Herd foals. The steeds had been content on that hot spring morning, until they'd glimpsed the black foal of Anok dangling helplessly between two of their stallions. Terror of him had sent them into a stampede, and Star had not understood then why the fierce herd was so afraid of him.

Now he was staring at that same meadow, except

it had been scorched by Nightwing's silver fire in what appeared a massive burst of rage. This was why the pegasi had feared Star, even when he was young—they'd worried he'd turn into a destroyer, like Nightwing, and do exactly this to them.

"What happened here?" Frostfire whispered, his body swaying.

Star's blood raced when he saw all the downy feathers littering the black ash, but by the faded scents of pegasi, he was sure this had happened many, many days earlier. "I think some pegasi stood up to Nightwing here. Why else would he destroy them?" Star said, trying to answer Frostfire's question.

Frostfire groaned, overcome by sorrow. He dropped and rolled in the ashes—absorbing his beloved herd into his white hide, staining it black.

Star stepped away from Frostfire, leaving him to his grief, and he nosed the feathers that had settled on the dust. They were the last connection to those who'd died. Star glanced back at the white stallion, thinking. Only Morningleaf knew that steeds killed by Nightwing's fire were sent to the Beyond, a realm between life and the golden meadow, a place where their souls were trapped. Star turned away. He wouldn't tell Frostfire about that.

Right now, the stallion's only solace was his belief that his dead herdmates were in the golden meadow. The way to free them was to defeat Nightwing, and that would be up to Star, not Frostfire.

"This herd . . . ," said Frostfire in a strained voice, stumbling over his words. "I wasn't born to them, but . . . but they were good to me."

Star jerked his head toward the captain.

"It's true that Rockwing was hard on me," admitted Frostfire. "And I had to fight to earn respect in the army, but the rest of them . . . they didn't deserve this." He lay on his side, pressing the ashes deeper into his white coat. He snaked his dark-gray tail through the dust. "You can't heal this, can you?"

Star exhaled. "I'm sorry, but no."

"Can you . . . leave me for a bit?"

Star bowed his head and then galloped into the sky. He soared over Valley Field, searching for any clues that might indicate survivors, or where Nightwing had gone after quelling this uprising in Mountain Herd's territory. Star swooped low when he reached the alpine forest, peering between the trees. Deer and foxes skittered out of his giant shadow, and birds flocked to their nests, silenced by the sight of his huge wings.

After a while another span of blackened grass caught Star's eye. He dropped to the forest floor and pawed at it—more ashes. He lifted off and continued searching, discovering more spots of singed ground. Nightwing had been thorough, finding hiding pegasi and destroying them.

Star flew back to Frostfire, who was standing now. "There are no survivors here," he said.

"I think you're right," said Frostfire, his eyes round and white rimmed. "What has Nightwing gained by doing this?"

Star's anger ignited, and he arched his neck. "Don't you see? He's killing all rivals and rebels—anyone who won't follow him. He wants to rule Anok, and it was only days ago that you were helping him. Have you forgotten that you formed the Black Army to hunt me down and take my head? Because I haven't." Star's voice sizzled, low and quiet, like hot embers.

Frostfire took a step away from him, blinking rapidly as he stuttered for words. "I—I know what I did . . ." He trailed off.

Star advanced on him, swishing his tail. "And now that he's turned on your friends, *now* you change your mind about him? Well, it's too late." Star swept his wing across Valley Field, and then he trotted away from Frostfire as his anger grew. He didn't like it, this bitter wrath, and just looking at Frostfire's guilty face inflamed him further. The white stallion wanted to stop what had been set in motion, now that he'd lost control of it. It was typical pegasus thinking—to leap without looking, to attack without considering all alternatives, and then to regret it—and it frustrated Star to his core.

Frostfire waited until Star's breathing slowed, and then he spoke softly, his tone humble. "Only you can stop him, Star."

"That's probably true, but *how*? I have a shield, but so does he. I had a guardian herd, but they're gone. I don't know how to beat him." Star turned, facing Frostfire, his sides heaving. "I will find Nightwing, but after that I've no idea what will happen." He dropped his wings, letting them brush against the ashes, feeling better to say this truth out loud, to admit that he was stumped, that he was utterly helpless in the face of Nightwing.

Frostfire's eyes glinted in the sun. "Maybe I can train you to fight," said Frostfire. "I trained many steeds when I was lead captain of Mountain Herd's army."

Star snorted. "My herd already tried that, but no skill of hoof or tooth will defeat Nightwing." A sharp image of Bumblewind's jovial face came to mind. They'd trained together as warriors in the Trap, and fresh misery ripped at his heart. He missed his friends.

"You're right, and I know that," said Frostfire, "but they taught you how to be a warrior, not a *defender*."

Star braced. "What's the difference?"

"When I became a captain in Rockwing's army, I noticed that there are two kinds of pegasi: those who thrive on destruction, and those who thrive on *preventing* destruction. You're the latter."

That sounded true to Star. "But how will that help me against Nightwing? He's stronger, and we both have a shield."

"Have you tried using your starfire on him?"

Star stared at the ashes under his hooves. "Yes, but *nothing* good comes from the silver fire," he said, his throat tight. "I won't use it, not ever again."

Frostfire nodded. "Then what about the gold starfire?"

"It heals," said Star. "It doesn't destroy."

"But maybe you can use it another way?"

"I don't know," said Star, "and neither do you."

"Maybe not," said Frostfire, peering at him. "But I was the highest-ranked captain in Mountain Herd's army because I know how to win battles. And I doubt you'll beat Nightwing if you attack him first. You must draw him into attacking you, to activate your defensive powers, like this new one, the shield."

"That almost makes sense," said Star.

"If you don't try, you'll never know."

"Maybe." Star paused. "But the sun is dropping fast. Now is the time to rest—tomorrow we'll fly faster and longer, to cover more ground."

The two pegasi glided to fresh grass on the outskirts of Valley Field. They grazed beneath the dim half-crescent moon, then Frostfire curled into a thicket and dropped into a deep sleep. Star stood over him, keeping him safe and wondering who, if anyone, was watching out for Morningleaf.

8

ESCAPE

MORNINGLEAF WATCHED THE WASTELANDS drift past her dangling hooves, trying to ignore the tingling pains shooting through her wings as she clutched the necks of Hazelwind and Redfire. Her friends had a plan to free her in the morning, but she would be gone before then.

It was dusk, and they were flying over steep canyons, still following the wide river that sometimes tunneled underground and then reappeared elsewhere. Redfire had called it an *aquifer*. Foliage was sparse in the surrounding limestone canyons, and rattlesnakes were plentiful. If her plan worked, Morningleaf didn't think she'd last long traveling through the desert alone. Steeds like Redfire who hailed from the desert were immune to rattlesnake venom, and they knew how to find water. The river was Morningleaf's only hope of survival if her plan succeeded.

Echofrost flew beside her, and Morningleaf watched the silver filly's powerful wings, layered in shades of purple, flapping in perfect rhythm. She was glossy and proud and strong, nothing like the filly she'd been after her kidnapping moons ago. Mountain Herd yearlings had tortured her and Rockwing had allowed the abuse. They'd ripped out chunks of her mane and tail and made a sport of kicking and teasing her. When Echofrost had finally been returned to Sun Herd, it was like half of her had died. Their medicine mare, Sweetroot, had fed Echofrost mashed-up roots each day to calm her nerves.

Only recently had the silver filly forgiven her captors, and in doing so, she no longer needed the calming plants. But Morningleaf wanted revenge on Nightwing, and she didn't like how this desire blackened her heart. Perhaps Echofrost could help her. "How did you stop hating the ones who hurt you?" she asked her friend.

Echofrost peered at Morningleaf and exhaled slowly. "It's not something you *do*, Morningleaf, it's something you *let go*."

"How?"

"I'm not sure how," she nickered. "One day, it's just easier not to hate."

"I hope so." Morningleaf looked ahead at Nightwing, who led the herd. There were no pegasi left in Anok who were free, except Star, and maybe Frostfire. No one had seen the white captain since Star won the battle against his Black Army; it was possible he was dead. Larksong, the mare he'd traveled with, was captured, flying nearby, but she remained silent, speaking to no one.

Morningleaf glanced at the moon, which was a thin crescent between the dark and drifting clouds. Rain drizzled from the sky, beading on her muzzle and making it sparkle. The evening air was cool enough that Morningleaf's breath trailed behind her in twin wisps of steam. Nightwing would land them soon. Far in the distance was a huge expanse of flat, hard mesa, large enough to fit all of them, and he was angling the herd in that direction. She was almost out of time.

Morningleaf took a breath, wishing it were just a bit darker. Echofrost's plan to cause a distraction while Hazelwind whisked her away was brave, but foolish. Nightwing would spot the ruse, and he would hunt her down. There was only one way to ensure that he didn't. She had to die, or at least appear to die.

A large bank of rain clouds drifted across the thin moon; the river flowed slowly below, looking as black as Star's feathers. *Now*, she thought. Morningleaf inhaled, blinking back her tears. "Good-bye," she whispered, so softly that no one heard her.

She relaxed her wings and fell like a large, heavy stone toward land.

"No!" screamed Hazelwind.

Good, cause a fuss, thought Morningleaf. She needed Nightwing to know she'd fallen to her death. It was his fault she couldn't fly; he could only blame himself. But this was her last coherent thought. The rest of her descent was one big rush of sound—her own screaming—and the whipping of her mane in the wind. She hurtled toward land like she'd fallen out of a jet stream, but this time Star wasn't around to save her.

"Morningleaf!"

Her mother's desperate cry squeezed her heart.

Then her friends whinnied and dived after her, and Nightwing trumpeted to his Ice Warriors to stop them and retrieve her. At the last second, Morningleaf angled her damaged wings to make sure she glided straight into the river.

She hit with a painful splash and sank, her body curling into a ball.

When her hooves touched the bottom, she swam through the dark depths, hunting for the web of underground rivers that Redfire had told her fanned off the deep waterway. Behind her, she heard the plunking of bodies hitting the water—her friends and her enemies. She had to lose them all.

Her wings throbbed, her head was splitting, and her chest stung where it had slammed the water. The river was murky from the sediment she'd disturbed, so she had to sense her way through the currents like she was flying, feeling for the crosscurrent that would indicate water flowing off the main channel. She'd spoken to Redfire at length about the aquifers while he carried her through the sky, and she was hopeful she'd quickly locate one. She would hide in it, and when Nightwing saw that her body never resurfaced, he would presume her dead, or she really would be dead—either way, this was her plan.

She glanced behind her but saw only churned-up mud. Her lungs began to burn. She slowed her swimming and let the water carry her. Ah! Now she felt it, a crosscurrent. It was powerful near her hooves. She dived deeper, and it swept her off and down into a tunnel.

Relax, she thought. *Don't waste air fighting.* She had no strength left anyway.

Suddenly, Morningleaf's plan felt hopeless and stupid. But that was also the beauty of it. If she died, it could still be considered a success for the pegasi of Anok. With her out of the way, Nightwing couldn't use her against her best friend, Star. Yes, she was doing the right thing.

Morningleaf drifted helplessly. In a minute, maybe less, she'd be out of air. She began to list, her body twisting sideways.

Then sharp pain sent a flash of energy through her muscles. She hit a ledge with her hooves. Her head rose out of the water. She took a gasping breath and scrambled onto the ledge, panting and huffing. *I made it!*

Moments later her eyes adjusted. A soft, luminescent glow brightened the tunnel just enough for her to make out that she was in a large cavern, resting on a ledge that traveled into the dark distance. There was plenty of air and space to rest. She didn't like that the cavern reminded her of the lava tubes under the volcano Firemouth, but unlike the lava tubes, she had light to see by, and the space wasn't cramped. Besides all that, she was alone, safe. She could stay here for days.

Then a head popped out of the water. "There you are," he said, and he surged toward her.

Morningleaf leaped to her hooves. It was an Ice Warrior!

9

SURROUNDED

THE ICE WARRIOR CLIMBED OUT OF THE WATER onto the limestone ledge and shook himself, flinging water off his hairy coat. Morningleaf backed away from him, noting his easy breaths. Something an elder mare named Mossberry told her long ago surfaced in her mind: *The northern steeds are the best swimmers in Anok. In the dead of winter they break the ice and dive into the cold blue, feeding on sea plants. They can hold their breath for as long as a full-grown seal.* No wonder this blue roan wasn't panting; the swim had been easy for him. How many more Ice Warriors would follow her here? Her gut lurched.

"You can't escape," he said, prancing and surprisingly light on his hooves for such a massive pegasus.

Morningleaf's flanks rammed the back wall of the cavern. The stallion loomed over her, drawing closer. She glanced down the tunnel.

"If I have to chase you farther, I'll do more than just drag you out of here," he warned, his voice echoing in the dim cavern. "I'll break those ruined wings of yours. So don't run."

Morningleaf snorted. Since she couldn't outswim, outrun, or outfight this thick-pelted pegasus—she'd have to outtalk him. "Why are you helping Nightwing?" she asked.

He took a step closer.

"You can't believe he's good for Anok."

The stallion cocked his head, ever so slightly.

"Let me go," Morningleaf implored him. "Tell Nightwing that I drowned and give Star a chance to defeat him. Can't you do that? Just give Star a chance. He'll free us all, even you."

"I am free," he said.

"Right," she huffed. "You aren't allowed to breathe without permission."

He shook his head, getting angry. "Star—Nightwing— what's the difference between them? A black foal is a black foal." He prowled closer, opening his jaws to seize her.

Morningleaf leaped to the side, and her hooves slid on

loose shale, knocking some into the water with a splash. "Star is good!" she whinnied.

"Star is young," he argued. "He will change." He lunged and snatched her injured wing.

Morningleaf shrieked, and her hooves flew, kicking the blue roan in the chest. He held on to her, unmoved.

Then three winged shapes, cruising below the surface, raced toward her, creating a large wake. Morningleaf's heart sank—more Ice Warriors? She yanked her wing out of the stallion's mouth and bolted. The blue roan whistled, stinging her ears, and he galloped after her, kicking up rocks.

Morningleaf slid across the stone cavern, cantering farther away from the main channel. The phosphorescent glow lit her way, but she was no match for the stallion. He grabbed her tail, lifted her off her hooves, and tossed her into the aquifer. She splashed into the cool water, sputtering. He leaned forward to dive in after her.

"Over here, you hairy whale!" It was Dewberry, with Hazelwind and Brackentail. Fresh energy shot through her legs, and Morningleaf paddled away. Her three friends surrounded the Ice Warrior.

"Go that way," neighed Brackentail, pointing with his wing deeper into the aqueduct. Hazelwind nodded, urging her to go, but her brother's eyes darkened and she knew what was coming next—her friends were going to battle the Ice Warrior to the death.

Morningleaf dived underwater and swam farther down the tunnel. When she popped up again, she heard the quick slam of the deathblow. The outnumbered blue roan was dead.

Then another familiar face popped up next to hers. "Bumblewind!" She swam toward him, and they rubbed their muzzles together.

"Where is everyone?" he asked. "I was following Dewberry and then I lost sight of her, and now here you are, alone."

She nickered. "They're that way, taking care of something."

"The Ice Warrior?" he asked.

She nodded.

"You mean I missed the whole thing? The whole rescue?" He tossed his wet forelock out of his eyes.

She snorted, paddling her hooves. "I guess so, unless more Ice Warriors show up."

"They won't," he said. "I mean, there were six others who followed us, but four were swept downstream and never saw the tunnel. They're searching for you along the banks. One struck his head on a rock when he dived in, and he . . . he broke his neck. The other, well, we took care of him before he could enter this offshoot."

"So no one knows I'm alive in here." She swam to the ledge and used her hooves and wings to climb out of the water.

"No one but us." His eyelids flew open. "Wait. Did you plan this? Or did you fall because you were tired?"

Hazelwind, Dewberry, and Brackentail trotted down the cavern toward them, dripping blood that wasn't theirs. Hazelwind's jaw was tight and his eyes narrow. "Oh, she planned it," he said, furious.

Dewberry's wings lilted to her sides. "We won't . . . we can't go back to the herd, obviously. Your mother will think we've all died."

"I know," she whispered.

Hazelwind whipped his head around. "Hasn't Silverlake gone through enough," he growled. "Our father was murdered before her eyes, and now you, her filly—falling to her death and drowning. That's what she'll think, you know. And she'll think I got killed too. How *could* you?"

Tears erupted and flowed down Morningleaf's cheeks. "I didn't . . . I don't . . ."

"Let me guess; you didn't think," accused her brother.

"Don't be so hard on her," neighed Brackentail.

Hazelwind lashed his tail. "Stay out of this."

"I didn't think you'd follow me this far," sputtered Morningleaf.

"Like I haven't heard you and Redfire talking for days about the aquifers," he snapped. "As soon as you let go of my neck, I knew what you were up to." Hazelwind stared down at his battle-stained chest. "I need to clean up."

"Me too," said Dewberry.

The three pegasi who'd attacked the blue roan slipped into the dark river to rinse their hides. They came out glistening, and also shivering.

"Nightwing will search for you, probably for many days before he gives up," said Hazelwind, his anger subsiding. "We're stuck in here for a while."

Bumblewind glanced at the tall limestone walls, his eyes glowing in the phosphorescence. "How did Redfire know this was here?" he asked Morningleaf.

Hazelwind answered. "Redfire's been filling her head with information about the desert. Rivers like these that cut through soft rock, form underground channels like webs that can't be seen from the air. They branch out and surface far away from the main source, which is the river." He glanced at his sister. "Now I know why you were asking so many questions about them."

"She always asks a lot of questions," said Brackentail.

Hazelwind shrugged. "That's probably why I didn't think too much about it until she let go of me."

"What are we supposed to eat in here?" asked Bumblewind.

Dewberry shoved him. "Hungry already?"

Everyone nickered, and the tension melted out of the cavern and floated away with the long, dark river.

"We'll rest here a few days," said Hazelwind. "Then, if it's safe, we'll track Nightwing's herd to the interior."

"We're going to follow them?" asked Morningleaf, stunned.

He grimaced. "Yes, we'll keep our distance, but we'll set up a watch to spy on Nightwing and the pegasi. When Star comes, he'll need information, and we'll be able to give it to him. At least something good has come from your recklessness."

Morningleaf nodded quietly, because her brother was right; she hadn't thought out her plan, or what came next. She was shocked that she was alive at all.

They traveled deeper into the tunnel, found smooth stone, and settled for the night. Before falling asleep, Hazelwind nuzzled his sister, forgiving her. "The four Ice

Warriors who swam downstream didn't see the aqueduct; they'll report that we drowned, and a search won't reveal our hoofprints or our bodies. It wasn't the worst plan."

Morningleaf sighed. "Our mother will understand, someday."

"Yes, someday," Hazelwind repeated, and then he closed his eyes.

10

CAMOUFLAGE

A STRIPE OF ORANGE SPLIT THE DARKNESS, AND
Star watched Frostfire awaken and gaze at Valley Field,
the charred meadow of his homeland. "I may never come
back to this place."

Star paced, feeling anxious. "All that matters now is
finding our friends and defeating Nightwing."

"Of course," said Frostfire.

The two stallions galloped across the field and then
leaped into the air, flapping their wings in perfect rhythm.
They flew straight up and through the clouds, and then
past them, climbing higher. "Come closer," neighed Star.

Frostfire flew beside him, and Star projected his
golden shield around them both. They ducked into the

southwestern jet stream and hurtled away from the mountains. Frostfire controlled the sphere's rotation with his wings, keeping them upright, and Star watched the land pass by in a blur under their hooves, scanning it for signs of pegasi. Hours later they crossed the Vein and entered Jungle Herd's territory.

They coasted over the volcano Firemouth, and the silence between Star and Frostfire sparkled with energy as they each remembered Frostfire's treachery. After he'd kidnapped Morningleaf, he'd hidden her in the lava tubes beneath that steaming volcano.

"I didn't hurt her." Frostfire said, addressing the tension.

Star exploded. "Do you think that because you didn't kick or bite Morningleaf, what you did wasn't *horrible*?" Star's voice cracked. "You killed her protectors in front of her eyes. You forced her into a bat-infested cave. You chased her into a jet stream." Star swallowed, marveling at the fact that Morningleaf had ridden in one of these screaming currents without the protection of a shield. Star turned his head to Frostfire. "Every single bone in her wings snapped on exit." Tears poured from his eyes. "Do you know how badly that hurt her? She would have died if I hadn't been there to heal her."

Frostfire shook his head, looking numb. "I was following orders from Rockwing." The words dribbled from his mouth like the last drops of a rainstorm, weak and changing nothing.

Star clenched his jaw, fighting the urge to retract his shield and watch Frostfire plummet to his death. "I don't see any pegasi in this territory," he said, ending the conversation.

They glided, heading east for many more hours, not speaking. And then the Sea of Rain appeared, green and flat, ahead of them.

"We should check the Jungle Herd nests for pegasi," suggested Frostfire, his voice soft.

Star lowered his nose and directed the golden sphere down and out of the jet stream. They spread their wings, slowing the bubble, but again they were falling too fast.

A crosscurrent knocked them sideways. Seconds later they crashed into the Sea of Rain and sank toward the bottom near the shore. Star paddled his legs, instinctively swimming, but the water didn't pierce the shield. He and Frostfire floated back up and bobbed on the surface. The two gaped at each other.

"This is incredible." Frostfire knocked on the shell

with his wing. Dolphins zipped past them, seeming curious but keeping their distance.

Star directed them to shore and then retracted the shield when they reached land. Hot, moist air assaulted them, and Star felt like he was choking. Sweat erupted on both stallions.

"I know where the nests are," said Frostfire. He lifted off and flew into the rain forest. Star spread his wings and followed.

Below, he saw tall trees and dense foliage. Monkeys leaped from the branches, brightly colored birds flew from tree to tree, and the animal chatter drowned out all other sounds. "How could a pegasus hear a predator coming?" Star wondered aloud.

"They don't," said Frostfire. "Jungle predators ambush their prey. That's why everything here is camouflaged, so the predators and prey can't see each other. It's why the Jungle Herd pegasi have feathers that look like leaves, so they can hide."

Star narrowed his eyes.

"I'm telling the truth," said Frostfire, gliding low over the trees. "And that gives me an idea. Let's land a moment."

The two touched down, and Frostfire continued. "Your starfire forms a shield, like a tortoise shell, right? It protects you. Maybe your starfire can mimic other animal abilities, like maybe you can camouflage yourself."

"Maybe, but I don't know how I discovered the shield. It just appeared when Stormtail was about to kill me."

"That's what I've been saying, Star. When you're threatened, your starfire helps defend you. Here, I'll attack you, and let's see what happens."

Star didn't like the sound of that.

Frostfire trotted away and then returned with a wingful of fallen pineapples. "I'm going to throw them at you."

"Wha—"

Frostfire swooped up the hard fruit and threw them at Star, one after the other.

Star blocked with his wings, growing angry. "Stop! This isn't working."

"Don't use your voice. Use your power."

Star sprang his shield, and the pineapples bounced off it.

"Not *that* power," neighed Frostfire.

Star clenched his jaw and retracted the shield. Frostfire tossed the spiny pineapples at him tirelessly, and the sharper ones cut Star's hide. "I don't feel threatened," grumbled Star. "I feel stupid."

"Because you're letting me attack you," Frostfire neighed, also growing frustrated. "Defend yourself. Try to disappear, like those lizards that change color."

Star's mind drifted into his body, searching through his powers—not the healing fire, not the hard shield— surely there were more. He closed his eyes, remembering how he'd allowed his shield to project. The power had always been there, just awaiting his permission to spring around him.

A pineapple smashed into his jaw, making it throb. This had to stop.

Star opened his eyes, fanned his golden embers of starfire, and then imagined blending into the forest so well that he couldn't be seen. His starfire crackled and then shut around him, like a thousand flower petals closing.

Frostfire paused in midthrow. "You did it!"

Star glanced at himself, but he looked the same; his hide was still black, not camouflaged green like the plants behind him. "No. Nothing's changed," he said.

Frostfire dropped his wingful of pineapples and

swallowed hard. "Not true." Frostfire stared in Star's direction, his eyes bulging. "You didn't change color, but you . . . vanished."

"What?" Star spread his wings, examining his black feathers. "I didn't vanish; I can see myself."

"But *I* can't see you," said Frostfire. "Try to retract the power."

Star did.

"You're back," nickered Frostfire. "Now I can see you again."

"My starfire is getting easier to control," said Star, astonished. "You were right. These powers have been there all along. I just have to let them work."

The sun turned from bright yellow to soft orange, and Star grew anxious for Morningleaf. "This is good, helpful, but we need to catch up to Nightwing. Let's go."

"All right, but we should at least check the Jungle Herd nesting ground first," said Frostfire. "Survivors may be hiding there."

Star followed Frostfire back to the nesting grounds, where the white stallion banked and swooped over the uppermost leaves, cruising above hundreds of pegasi nests. "They're empty," said Star, feeling anxious.

"Look," whinnied Frostfire as he circled lower. "It's Spiderwing's old nest. I've heard of it, but I've never seen it."

Star looked and saw a nest that was burned black. Everything else around it was green. "How do you know it's his?"

"See there?" said Frostfire, nodding toward a thick rim of charred flowers, feathers, shells, and shiny stones. "For hundreds of years the Jungle Herd pegasi have left gifts here, as a memorial to Spiderwing. It's why the nest is so big—they keep adding on to it."

"So it's like a shrine, a tribute?"

"Exactly." Frostfire glanced around in disbelief. "But it's the only thing that's burned. Nightwing must have done this."

Star tried to remember the legends. "But why? I thought Nightwing liked Spiderwing."

Frostfire snorted. "He did, but he was also jealous. When Nightwing conquered the herds four hundred years ago, he killed all the rival over-stallions except one: Spiderwing, the brother of his best friend, Hollyblaze. The two stallions split Anok in half, and Spiderwing's herd thrived but Nightwing's did not. Spiderwing's steeds worshipped him, and still do, as you can see by his nest. He lived a long life and had thirty-two healthy foals. Night-wing had none. No mare would have him, and his herd despised him."

Star pricked his ears. He hadn't known this about the Destroyer. He tried to imagine an over-stallion who was unable to attract a mate, who lacked respect from his herdmates, and he couldn't. He'd never heard of such a thing. Nightwing must have been humiliated. "But none of that is a reason to come back and hurt *us*," said Star.

"Don't you get it," said Frostfire, snorting. *"We're* Spiderwing's descendants—all of us. Nightwing's herd reproduced no foals. The mares turned barren. All of us come from Spiderwing's line, and Nightwing didn't prom-ise *not* to kill us. Or you." He peered at Star. "You're his new rival, and I doubt he'll make the same mistake twice. He won't let you live."

Star shuddered. All he'd ever wanted was to be a regu-lar colt. He hadn't asked for any of this.

Frostfire and Star hovered closer to the ancient nest. Frostfire spoke. "For Nightwing to see this . . . this mon-ument to his oldest rival—still being tended after four hundred years—I imagine that angered the Destroyer pretty badly."

Star lifted his head, feeling overwhelmed by the depth

of Nightwing's hatred. "We're on his trail, but we keep missing him. Let's go now, *right* now, to Desert Herd's territory. It's the last place to search. If they aren't there, then they've left Western Anok, and they're on their way to their new home."

Frostfire nodded, and the two stallions surged toward Desert Herd's lands, flying all night.

11

WATERING HOLE

FOUR DAYS PASSED FOR MORNINGLEAF AND HER friends in the underground cavern. They'd survived by drinking from the aquifer and grazing on patches of wet moss, but now it was time to go.

"Nightwing may have left warriors behind to patrol the river," said Dewberry.

"And in the sky," said Hazelwind. "We'll have to travel at night." He glanced at the yellowish rock walls that leaked water like tears. "If we're spotted . . . ," he began, but didn't finish his thought. They all knew that if an Ice Warrior spotted them, Hazelwind would have to kill the steed before he or she could inform Nightwing about them.

"We won't let that happen," assured Brackentail.

Morningleaf had felt triumphant the last four days, but not anymore. Exiting the river, tracking Nightwing, and spying on him would be as dangerous and stressful as traveling with him. Besides that, her confrontation with the Ice Warrior in the cavern had reminded her how young and small she was against her enemies. Even fleeing from them would be tough. Morningleaf stared at her ruined feathers, feeling useless.

Brackentail edged closer. As if reading her mind, he said, "We'll protect you. That's what a herd is for."

Morningleaf's crumbling resolve thumped to life at his words. She gazed at him and nudged him gently with her muzzle. "Thank you." He'd said the exact words she needed to hear. Louder, she spoke to the group. "Instead of heading to the main channel, why don't we follow this outlet a little farther. It should eventually lead to the surface, but far from the river."

Dewberry and Hazelwind looked skeptical.

"We have time to try it," said Brackentail. "We know Nightwing is taking the herd to the interior of Anok, and it'll be safer to follow this branch than to return to the main channel, where Ice Warriors might still be looking for us."

"That's true," said Hazelwind, glancing at Morningleaf,

"but I'm worried about getting lost. What if this tunnel takes us deeper underground and we become trapped?"

Her brother's gaze was unwavering, and Morningleaf saw their sire reflected in him—Thundersky's bravery and his commitment to his family. Hazelwind had abandoned Morningleaf and their mother once to form his own herd because he didn't trust Star. She'd been furious with him, but since then Hazelwind had decided to accept Star. Now their broken bond was healing, and like a broken bone, it was healing stronger than before. "Trust me," she said to her older brother. "I was trapped in the lava tubes, and I found my way out."

"All right," Hazelwind said. "Lead the way."

Morningleaf turned and walked deeper into the aqueduct, with her friends following.

Many hours later, the rocky ledge ended abruptly, but the river channel continued, flowing ahead. A smidgeon of light in the distance indicated that the surface might be near. "We'll have to swim the rest of the way," said Morningleaf.

Bumblewind lowered his nose to the dark water. "Are

you sure this leads to the surface?"

Morningleaf had counted on a breeze to indicate open land above their heads, like she had in the lava tubes, but underground the air was still. "Wait here; I'll check it out."

Before they could stop her, Morningleaf slid into the water. Without the sun to warm it, the cool liquid chilled her bones. She paddled forward and relaxed, feeling for a current. Small, luminescent creatures glowed along the sides of the rock tunnel. She had the eerie feeling of being watched. She swam on, kicking gently. Then she felt it, rising water, but the tunnel narrowed ahead, cutting off her air. She'd have to duck under the surface and swim the rest of the way underwater. But would this aqueduct take her to the surface, or trap her under land and drown her? She returned to her friends.

"What did you find?" asked Brackentail.

"A way out, I think. Just a few winglengths that way I can feel the water sifting upward."

"That's good," said Brackentail.

"Not if it's leading to a dead end," said Dewberry.

"Well, if I don't come back, then it's a dead end." Morningleaf nickered as if she were joking, but her friends just blinked at her in silence.

"I'm coming with you," said Brackentail.

Morningleaf peered into his soft golden eyes, opening her mouth to speak.

"You can't change my mind," he said.

She exhaled, nodding. "All right, follow me." He jumped into the water, and she led him back the way she'd come. When they reached the spot where the river filled the entire tunnel, they each took a huge breath and dived under the surface. They paddled on and then upward, toward the dim light above.

Soon, Morningleaf's heart was thudding. She thought they'd hit the surface by now, but they were still swimming, and she'd passed the point where she had enough air to turn back. With her chest burning, she glanced behind her, but it was too dark to see Brackentail. She swiveled her ears, hearing only the quiet swish of her paddling hooves.

Morningleaf swam on. Her lungs swelled. Sharp cramps seized her gut. Desperate now, she bolted, kicking as hard as she could and wondering if Brackentail was doing the same. Was there no end to this tunnel?

Her muscles clenched in a spasm.

Her brain shut down.

Her mouth opened.

Then she burst through to the surface. A second later, Brackentail emerged beside her. They pulled hard on the fresh air, sucking at it like starving newborns. "We made it," she gasped.

They were floating in a small watering hole nestled deep within a rock basin in the Wastelands. Far away a lone coyote slunk into the shadows, disturbed by their sudden presence. Morningleaf stared up at the sky. The moon was a sliver, casting a pale glow, but she didn't see any winged patrols flying in the sky.

Brackentail dragged himself out of the watering hole, sniffed the wind, and flicked his ears. "It's quiet," he said.

Morningleaf also pulled herself out, and she stood, shivering on the shore, dreading the moment of going back into the water. "We'd better return for the others," she said. "Before they decide we've drowned."

Brackentail tossed his mane. "Why don't you keep watch? I'll get them."

"But—"

He lowered his head. "I'd feel safer if you stayed and protected the area. I don't want to come back and find a pack of coyotes here."

Morningleaf peered at him, knowing he wasn't afraid of coyotes, but she understood the reasoning behind his plea: he didn't think she'd survive that swim a second time. She'd barely had enough air the first time, and now her legs were trembling. Brackentail was larger, and he could hold his breath longer, but he also knew that she wouldn't stay behind without a reason, and lame as it was, he had given her one: to keep watch for coyotes. Morningleaf studied him, feeling grateful and curious. For the second time he'd said the exact words she needed to hear. "Okay, I'll keep watch."

He nodded and lifted off. "I'm going to get a flying start." He flew several winglengths in the air, and then he dived like an eagle into the water, splashing down and disappearing into the depths.

It seemed forever that she waited, but then each of her friends surfaced in the watering hole and swam to shore, breathless but safe.

"So far the way is clear," said Morningleaf. "No Nightwing. No Ice Warriors." She nudged Brackentail fondly with her muzzle. "And no coyotes."

Bumblewind climbed out of the water and swept his eyes across the dusty canyon. "The first thing we need to do is find food." Then quickly, before anyone could harass him for saying it, Bumblewind added, "Tell me you aren't starving?"

Morningleaf's belly had shriveled like an old blackberry, but she hadn't noticed that until Bumblewind mentioned it. "He's right," she said. "We need to rebuild our strength."

"We'll eat soon, but not yet," said Hazelwind, glancing behind them. "We need to find better cover. I'll fly a quick patrol, see what I can find." He lifted off, sweeping a radius around them, watching for Ice Warriors, and then he landed. "There's nothing here but desert. We'll have to stick close to the canyon walls and travel until morning. Farther inland there will be trees and plants to eat—the faster we move, the faster we'll find them." He cantered off and soon settled into an efficient lope. They traveled by hoof since Morningleaf couldn't fly and they were all too tired to carry her.

"And what about Nightwing?" asked Morningleaf, following her brother.

"We know he's heading east to the Flatlands. We'll follow, keeping our distance. Once he settles the herd, we'll hide as close as we dare to keep watch on him, and we'll wait for Star to find us. As long as it takes."

Morningleaf nodded, shuddering as a desert breeze blew across her water-soaked hide. Beside her, Brackentail loped and listened for danger. She felt safe between her brother and her friend, and she took the rare opportunity to relax, to let them worry about what happened next. Her thoughts drifted to Star. She'd done everything she could to protect him, and so had his guardian herd, but now the pegasi were captured, and she couldn't fly, and Star was alone. She knew he was looking for them—and the hope of seeing him again kept her moving forward, in spite of the thin voice in her head that told her all was lost.

12

FAMILY

STAR AND FROSTFIRE SWOOPED DOWN FROM THE clouds and hurtled across the hot, flat desert. They'd left Jungle Herd's territory two days earlier, and they'd been searching Western Anok for sixteen days since Nightwing had captured the pegasi. Today they arrived in the Desert Herd lands, and Star marveled at the wide expanse of dusty soil, as unmarked as the ocean, dotted only with scrubby brush and short cacti.

"It's bleak," said Star. The Red Rock Mountains and the steady march of the sun across the sky were his only reference points for navigation. His sharp eyes could see for miles in every direction, and there was no sign of pegasi, let alone twelve thousand of them. The striated mesas of the scarlet mountain range, however, piqued his interest. The plateaus were stepped and angular. Deep canyons created sheer cliff walls that were pocked with thousands of caves. "Look there," said Star. "Are those caves deep enough to hide pegasi?"

Frostfire nodded. "Yes, those caves are the homes of the Desert Herd steeds. Each family has one."

"This is the last territory," Star reminded Frostfire. "If we don't find Nightwing here, then it's time for you to take me to the place where he plans to settle them. All along, we keep missing him."

"I know. He's making good time flying with such a large herd," said Frostfire.

"And they have nursing foals with them," said Star, shaking his mane. "He should be stopping often to rest, making it easy for us to catch him. The mothers will have to wean their foals early to keep his pace, and that's not healthy."

Star swooped toward the desert canyons, feeling the dry air burn his lungs. He and Frostfire hovered along the cliff walls, examining the caves. They darted up and down the steep divide, searching for fresh signs of pegasi. Each cave was about the size of the one Star had lived in on the coast of Anok, just large enough to hold four or five steeds comfortably. "Are the caves connected?" he asked Frostfire.

"Not that I remember," said the stallion. "I was here to fight, not to explore, you know." They landed inside a cave to look around.

Star's hooves clattered as he explored the foreign steeds' home. The rock floor was worn smooth from years of pegasi lying on it. Layers of ferns and feathers softened the area. The rest of the rocky surface was scuffed with hoof marks. Three straight red lines were painted on one wall. "What are these?" Star asked, tracing the lines with his wingtips.

"Desert Herd uses ochre to mark their caves. Three lines mean that three pegasi live in this one. It's how they count their numbers."

"Morningleaf would love to see this," Star said, his spine tingling. "She counts well in her head, but I think she'd be interested in these lines that keep track of pegasi."

Frostfire erased the red ochre with his wing and started walking away. "Well, no one lives here now. Let's move on."

Star flew out of the home, feeling suddenly claustrophobic as the truth slammed him. Western Anok was empty; all the pegasi were gone. He spread his wings and glided through the narrow, hot canyons. The air in front of him rippled, and his sweat dried instantly as the sun scorched his back. "There's no one left," he whinnied to Frostfire.

The white stallion cruised beside him, trying to comfort him. "We'll find them, Star."

Star leaked tears, and a trail of white flowers sprouted up through the dry, solid ground. Frostfire stared at them, almost crashing into Star. "That's incredible."

Star shook his head. "Not really." He could grow flowers and heal wounds, but what use was that against Nightwing?

"Come on," said Frostfire, trying to distract Star. "I think it's time I washed these ashes out of my hide." He veered left, and Star followed, soaring over the flat desert at top speed. Soon they were descending into another, much smaller canyon. Star drifted over the ridge and sucked in his breath at the sight below his hooves. After miles and miles of flat, brown terrain, the river ahead was an oasis of lush, green foliage and clear, rushing water.

The stallions landed on the shore.

"This is the Tail River," said Frostfire. "It travels from the Black Lake through the Wastelands, and then dumps into the Sea of Rain."

"Do crocodiles live here?" Star asked, thinking of the jungle.

Frostfire nickered. "No, this water is safe."

The two plunged into the cool, wide river that ran through the divide. Star heard the distant roar of a waterfall and inhaled the comforting scent of damp soil that drifted from the shore. He ducked under the surface and swam with his eyes open. Large trout flitted past him, unafraid. He dived to the bottom, and then he cruised just over the small pebbles and plants on the river floor, swimming upstream so as not to end up tumbling down the waterfall.

Over his head, Frostfire kicked his hooves, paddling against the current. Star glided underwater, remembering his daily swims in Crabwing's Bay when he was a weanling, and then he popped up next to Frostfire, speaking the thoughts that had been on his mind for days. "What will I do when we find Nightwing? My shield and invisibility might help me *survive* him, but they won't help me *defeat* him."

Frostfire floated on the surface with his wings tucked high on his back, like a swan. Star lifted his wings and folded them in the same fashion. They mirrored each other, he and Frostfire, but they were opposites—one shimmering white and the other shining black.

"Maybe you should focus on who *you* are and not who *he* is," said Frostfire, preening his feathers.

Star jolted at his words.

"What is it?" the stallion asked.

"Silverlake said almost those exact words to me in the north." Tears filled Star's eyes as he thought about Silverlake, wondering if she was alive.

Frostfire looked away, whistling softly. "I'm beginning to understand why your guardian herd isn't afraid of you."

Star pricked his ears. "No one should be afraid of me."

Frostfire slapped Star gently on the shoulder. "Nightwing should."

Star huffed and wiped his eyes. "We're done searching the west. Take me to where you think he's going."

Frostfire nodded, and the two lifted straight out of the water and surged into the sky. "Head east," said Frostfire.

They traveled in a pattern, zigzagging across the sky, covering as much ground as possible and scanning the terrain for signs of the missing herd of pegasi—trampled grass, droppings, or molted feathers. After passing over towering mountain ranges, they came upon a dusty plain that spread for miles and seemed absent of all life except for a long, winding river.

"We've reached the Wastelands," said Frostfire over the wind.

A bright splotch of color caught Star's eye. "Look, feathers!" He dived toward a dirt mesa that was surrounded by shallow canyons. He touched down and cantered across the stony plateau, sniffing for the scents of his friends, but what he smelled was his enemy. "Nightwing's been here," said Star, curling back his lips.

"And Petalcloud," said Frostfire, who'd also landed and was exploring the mesa.

Thousands of hoofprints marked the ground, and Star began to catch familiar scents, but they were so jumbled together, he couldn't separate them into individual steeds.

Star's heart swelled with hope. "Look at all these hoofprints; thousands of pegasi are still alive. This is good." He trotted to the edge of the plateau and gazed east. The sky was clear of clouds and layered in gradient shades of blue. He could see all the way to the far horizon. He squinted, searching for pegasi, but as far as he could see, the sky held only birds. "I think I know where they're going," said Star. "To the interior of Anok, to the ancient lands of Lake Herd."

Frostfire halted, not saying a word.

"The flatland territory is the largest in Anok. It's nothing but grass and water. It's perfect for pegasi," said Star, glancing at his companion.

Frostfire avoided his eyes.

"But it's dangerous," Star added, waiting for a reaction from the white stallion that would indicate if Star's guess was correct. "When I was looking for a territory for River Herd, Morningleaf's sire told me all about the Flatlands. It's infested with gigantic wolves and high winds, and no pegasus has traveled there in hundreds of years. If that's where Nightwing is going, he doesn't know what he'll find. And no one knows why the Lake Herd pegasi disappeared long ago—perhaps they couldn't survive there. It's too risky." Star felt suddenly angry. "And it's thousands of miles away. They won't all make it."

"But Nightwing won't have any trouble feeding them there," said Frostfire.

Star peered at his old enemy. "So I'm correct? Nightwing *is* heading to the Flatlands?"

Frostfire's wings drooped. "Yes, you're correct." He looked at Star with his one blue eye. "Are you going to leave me behind? Now that you don't need me?"

Star spread his wings, feeling the hot breeze blow

through his feathers. He stared at Frostfire, frustrated. "Did you know we're related?"

Frostfire took a deep breath before answering. "Yes. My sire, Iceriver, told me. Your mother is . . . was my sister." His lips curled over the words, and Star saw how distasteful the relationship was to Frostfire.

Star leaned closer, forcing the stallion to meet his gaze. "I won't leave you behind, Frostfire, and I won't let Nightwing attack you."

Frostfire's eyes dropped to his hooves. "Why? Because I'm your uncle?"

"No," said Star. "Because we made a deal and because I'm the only pegasus in Anok who can save you."

"But I don't deserve your protection," said Frostfire honestly.

"Maybe not, but you don't deserve to be killed by Nightwing either."

The two were silent for a long moment, and then Frostfire said, "Come on. It's a long way yet to the interior."

"Then let's not waste time." Star galloped forward, his hooves clopping across the rocks, and he leaped off the edge, free falling a moment before gripping the wind with his wings. He swooped out of his dive and cruised fast over the lower plains. The two stallions glided side by side, but after a while Frostfire dropped back and drafted off Star's dominant wake.

Star was shocked at first when the older stallion took the submissive position behind him, but then he relaxed. And for the first time since Star's herd was captured, he didn't feel alone.

13

THE INTERIOR

ALMOST A FULL MOON PASSED AS STAR AND
Frostfire tracked the pegasi toward the interior of Anok.
They'd slowed their pace when they'd noticed fresh droppings and trampled ground, signs that they were close.
Star didn't plan to confront Nightwing immediately. He
would wait until the Destroyer settled, so he could assess
the condition of the herd and Nightwing's plans for them.
Also, Frostfire needed to rest, so each time they landed
to graze and sleep, Star practiced turning invisible. He'd
sneak up on the white stallion and whisper, "Do you see
me?" Frostfire would practically leap out of his hide and
whinny, "Stop doing that!"

As they traveled deeper inland, the dry, rocky terrain

gave way to green grass and abysmally flat land. It was now midmorning. Star had flown to a higher altitude than Frostfire to examine their surroundings. Ahead was a grassy plain so large it swallowed the land all the way to the horizon. It was dotted with hundreds of blue lakes and ponds and patches of forest. But over this land, the clouds were dark, turning darker, and flashes of lightning glowed deep within. Star dropped down to Frostfire's elevation, and the two stallions hovered in place. "I think those are the ancient lands of Lake Herd," said Star. "But a storm is coming, and fast. We need to get out of the sky."

"There's enough grassland here to feed *ten* herds," said Frostfire. "It's so different from the mountains where I was raised, where grazing time had to be rationed."

"True, but I rejected this place for River Herd. Thundersky told me that besides the gigantic wolves and winds strong enough to toss yearlings, lightning storms are frequent."

"None of that worries me," said Frostfire.

"It should because if Nightwing chooses this territory for his home, your colt will be born here."

Frostfire's eyes snapped to his surroundings, studying them all over again from the perspective of a sire.

Star watched the storm quickly blow toward them.

"Come on, we'll have to wait this out on the ground." Star dipped his nose, and the two plummeted toward land.

Farther above them, in the center of the clouds, lightning flashed. Star sniffed the air, smelling rain. He glanced at the long grass that rippled in the wind as far as he could see. In Sun Herd's territory, and in the north, there had always been tall foothills and huge mountain ranges to shelter the pegasi from the wind. Here there was nothing. He and Frostfire stood taller than anything for miles around, except for a few clusters of trees, and Star felt exposed. "This is not a good place for pegasi."

Frostfire nudged him, staring into the distance. "Look there, it's a herd of buffalo."

Star followed his gaze and saw at least a thousand buffalo trotting across the grassland, disturbed by the storm. The creatures' deep grunts and groans reached Star's ears and then drifted off with the wind. The clouds seemed to rumble, and rain poured from the sky. "Let's head into those trees," said Star.

They galloped into a small grove and stood for hours, covering their backs with their water-repellent feathers. When the center of the storm reached them, the wind blew the rain sideways. Star clamped down his tail and shook the water off his wings, but soon he was drenched. Next to him, Frostfire leaned closer, resting and shivering.

Star stayed awake and watched the rain until he noticed something odd appear in the clouds, like a shadow. "What's that?" he whispered, jolting Frostfire awake. The two peered skyward.

The figure flew circles in the depths of the black clouds as lightning crackled around him. "It's a pegasus."

"Our friends must be close," neighed Frostfire. "But why is this one flying in the storm, alone?"

"Maybe he's scared?"

The pegasus flew loops and rolls, and glided, dodging lightning bolts. "Or maybe he's crazy," exclaimed Frostfire.

Thunder boomed, and the lone figure burst from the clouds followed by a streak of white lightning. Star flinched, expecting the bolt to strike the pegasus, but the steed twirled toward land, avoiding it. Then he leveled off and flew over the buffalo, spooking them. The lightning bolt struck the grass, and Star watched the herd lurch into a gallop. The stallion swooped back up toward the clouds, and his delighted whinny pierced Star's ears, making them ache.

"It's him," gasped Frostfire.

But Star had already figured that out. The dark shadow was Nightwing.

"Don't move," warned Star.

The Destroyer soared high over their heads. Star and Frostfire ducked deeper into the thicket, and the herd of buffalo galloped out of sight.

Star watched the black stallion twist through the raindrops. He hadn't seen the Destroyer since the day he'd landed in Anok and said to Star, *There you are.* Then, he'd been bone thin, with hollow eyes and a ragged mane and tail. Now, flying in the sky, he looked only slightly better. He'd gained some weight around his hips, and he'd shed out much of his ancient coat, but his hair was still dull and dry. Star understood what this meant: Nightwing's healing powers were weak. Maybe Frostfire was correct. Maybe Star was stronger in ways he didn't understand.

Star guessed the cause of Nightwing's haggard appearance was his long hibernation. When Star's injuries had sent him to sleep, he'd woken weak and thin too, but he'd been asleep less than a moon—not hundreds of years. Also, he'd had his guardian herd to care for him. The medicine mare, Sweetroot, had appointed steeds to watch him day and night. They'd bathed him, rubbed him with plant oils to keep him free of flies and gnats, rolled him over twice a day, and massaged his muscles to keep his blood flowing. At the thought of it, his throat constricted with gratitude. It was obvious no pegasus had watched over Nightwing.

The Destroyer cruised in and out of the clouds, teasing out bolts of lightning. When they caught up to him, he sprang his shield, protecting himself.

As the storm stretched over them, the clouds sometimes parted, and the sudden peaks of bright sunlight burned Star's eyes. The heavy winds created waves in the grass, and the tree leaves crashed against each other, making a loud racket.

The storm eventually passed on and so did Nightwing. He flew opposite of it, heading farther east. Star watched the black stallion until he disappeared.

"He plays with lightning," breathed Frostfire.

The awed tone in Frostfire's voice caused the last of Star's confidence to drain out his hooves. "I . . . I can't do that."

"Don't lose courage, Star. Anything he can do, you can do."

Star shook his head. "But we're different. I'm a healer." *How could a healer battle a destroyer?*

"Look at me, Star."

Star met his uncle's gaze, noting the earnest look in the stallion's mismatched eyes. Frostfire lowered his voice. "I'm not wrong about you. You *will* overcome his strength. When the time comes, let Nightwing attack you with *all* his power. Only then will you discover yours."

Frostfire nudged him. "Think about it, Star—how do we sharpen our hooves?" He didn't wait for an answer. "On solid rock, right? Not on moss. His powers will sharpen yours." Frostfire lifted his head, his eyes glittering with excitement, his voice rising. "Battle will bring out the best in you, Star. That's what warriors understand, and it's what defenders learn to appreciate. You'll discover yourself through your opponent. Don't fear him. Embrace him."

Star's heart surged under Frostfire's rallying words. He stood taller, and his starfire coursed through his veins, causing golden sparks across his feathers.

"That's it!" neighed Frostfire. "Believe!"

And suddenly Star saw his mother's beautiful face reflected in Frostfire's. He threw out his wings, touching Frostfire's shoulders. "You're my family," he said, excitement bubbling in his chest. "And here we are, working together. My mother—your sister—would have been pleased."

Frostfire pulled away, looking startled. "No, Star. I never knew my sister. I was already gone when Lightfeather was born to my sire, and then my mother drove her off and Iceriver disowned her. Yes, we're family, but really, what does that mean?"

Star pricked his ears. "It means we share blood. Isn't that important to you?"

Frostfire met Star's gaze. "Larksong and my coming colt are all who matter to me. Look, I'm here, I'm helping you, but I don't feel the same. I don't think of you as family."

Star's wings dropped to his sides. "But—"

Frostfire bristled. "Come on, let's stay focused on our mission, on Nightwing."

Frostfire kicked off and flew fast over the grass, heading east—following Nightwing. Star glided behind him, shaking off his disappointment with Frostfire. Was it so foolish to think the stallion would change, would accept him? Star blinked hard, fighting tears. Yes, it appeared so.

But they'd found Nightwing, and that meant that Star's friends were close. Soon he would see them. He would find out who had lived and . . . who had not. He pricked his ears; his anticipation was hot, like a fever, but his dread was cold, like ice.

Moments later they crested a low hill and Star gasped, curling his wings and slowing. Before him spread a huge valley, and grazing inside it were twelve thousand pegasi.

He'd found them.

14

BROKEN

IT WAS DIFFICULT TO BELIEVE THAT STAR HAD finally found the missing pegasi after searching and traveling for over a moon. They stood grazing before him like a mirage, like the false appearance of water in the desert. He heard Dewberry's voice in his head: *Trust your eyes, Star.* She'd said this to him once when they were living in the Vein, after Star received his power, and it had proved sound advice.

"There they are," he whispered to Frostfire.

The two stallions landed and crouched in the grass, sneaking forward, placing each hoof softly in front of the other. Star sensed danger, a static in the air. He halted. "Something's wrong."

Frostfire pranced, his nostrils flaring. "I feel it too."

Star flattened his ears and peered around him, but saw nothing amiss. His heart raced as if he were galloping. Next to him, Frostfire's tail twitched like a ground squirrel's. They waited, which made them each tenser, but nothing unusual happened. Star crept forward, and Frostfire followed. Ahead was a shallow valley rimmed on the eastern side by rolling swells and framed on the southern end by a forest of cottonwood trees. Star and Frostfire crouched at the western end of the wide valley, watching the herd.

The pegasi walked in large groups, grazing on the tall grasses or staring vacantly at the sky. A light-gray mare trotted past with a silver yearling at her side, and then they split apart to join different groups of pegasi. Star's heart skittered at the sight of them. "It's Silverlake and Echofrost," he whispered. Next he saw the Desert Herd stallion Redfire, then the runt filly Shadepebble. They appeared unharmed.

He searched the herd eagerly for Morningleaf and Bumblewind. Frostfire groaned softly when Larksong cantered across the valley and settled next to Silverlake and Sweetroot. Star noticed that the buckskin mare's belly had rounded with her growing foal, and Frostfire nickered with relief. "They're safe."

But Star saw no sign of Morningleaf, Bumblewind, or Dewberry in the throng of steeds. Hazelwind and Brackentail also appeared absent. His breath hitched, and desperate tears formed in his eyes.

"Look, there's my mother," whispered Frostfire. Star followed his gaze and saw a striking gray mare standing by herself. It was Petalcloud, and she was staring proudly at the sky.

Star followed her gaze. "And there's Nightwing."

A black shadow rocketed through the clouds, his eyes trained on Star.

"Look, he sees me!" Star's blood drained from his ears. The last time he'd faced Nightwing, the ancient stallion had pierced his heart with starfire, almost killing him. But there was no hiding from Nightwing now, so Star put the past behind him and stood taller, spreading his wings and quickly catching the eye of Petalcloud, and then all the captured pegasi.

A hush fell over the valley as thousands of heads swiveled to face him. Hope rose in their expressions as the pegasi realized that the black stallion standing on the ridge was Star the Healer. The steeds of Anok had once wished for his execution, but now they stared at Star with devoted fervor.

Star cantered into the sky and hovered above their heads.

"It's you!" bellowed Nightwing. He dropped out of the clouds like a diving hawk. Star braced for an attack.

"Steady," neighed Frostfire from the grass below. "Let him come to you."

Nightwing pulled out of his dive and flew a large circle around Star, snapping his jaws. "I knew you'd come for them," he said, nodding toward the pegasi in the valley. He drew a breath and then shot starfire across the sky, blasting it toward Star.

Star threw up his shield, and the destructive fire swirled around it and then fizzled away, leaving Star unharmed. Sharp whinnies and startled gasps erupted in the valley.

"Ah." Nightwing tossed his heavy mane, which fell in clumps across his neck. "You've discovered the shield." He sounded disappointed.

Star hovered, his anger steaming. Silver sparks crackled across his hide, and he had to shake them off, to resist the dark fury that threatened to bloom in his heart. Below his hooves, the pegasi galloped into one large group, craning their necks to watch the two stallions. Star heard Petalcloud command her Ice Warriors to guard the herd.

There was still no sign of Morningleaf among them. "Let the pegasi go," Star said to Nightwing.

Nightwing drew closer, his head cocked. "Why don't you try and take them from me?"

Star dropped his shield and shot his golden fire at Nightwing. It hit the ancient stallion square in the chest, and Nightwing halted midair, stunned as his brittle hide turned glossy. Then he mocked Star, braying loud enough for all the pegasi to hear him. "I think the idea is to hurt me, Star, not heal me."

Petalcloud's nickering drifted up from the valley.

Star ignored the ridicule, took a breath, and faced Nightwing. "You're not wanted here," he said evenly. "The pegasi follow *me*, not *you*."

"Is that right?" Nightwing dived toward the herd of steeds, skimming just over their heads. "Whoever wants to follow Star is free to go."

The pegasi stared warily at Nightwing, and Star's heart lurched. The Destroyer was lying, and the pegasi knew it, but three elder mares shot out of the grass toward Star, their eyes locked on his.

"No!" he neighed to them.

But they kept coming, tears streaming down their

cheeks. "We'll die free," whinnied the mare in front, a palomino.

No you won't, thought Star, thinking of the Beyond.

Nightwing spiraled below the mares and exhaled silver light, catching them in its deadly beam. Star watched all three pegasi melt and then combust, disappearing into the wind. Several steeds screamed. The newborn foals, now weanlings, bleated in fear.

"Stop!" Star whinnied to the pegasi and to Nightwing. "No one move. Please."

Nightwing swooped closer, panting like a tiger. "You see? The pegasi are safer with me." He looked triumphant. "This is my herd, Star. I protect them now, not you. Go. Leave this place. Leave Anok."

Star glanced at Frostfire standing on the ground, wondering what to do. He and Nightwing each had a shield. How could they fight each other when they couldn't hurt each other?

Nightwing followed Star's gaze and spotted Frostfire. He blinked, looking surprised. "You're alive?" he said to the white stallion, diving toward him.

Star hurtled toward his uncle. "Leave him alone! He's with me."

Frostfire glanced desperately at his dam, Petalcloud, who stood in the distance. The dark mare's eyes sparkled with curiosity, but she did nothing to help her son.

"Your Black Army failed me," said Nightwing, drawing up his starfire.

Frostfire gulped. Star landed next to his uncle and sprang his shield around them both just as Nightwing blasted the stallion. The silver fire burst without harm against the orb.

Nightwing twisted his ears, his eyes smoldering.

Feeling bold in the shield, Frostfire spoke. "If you won't free them all, then give me Larksong."

"What are you doing?" rasped Star. "We aren't here to bargain."

Nightwing paused, thinking, and then his eyes glinted and he snaked his head toward Star. "I see," he hissed. "You two have come for your mares, is that it?"

Star's heart thudded as he thought about Morningleaf.

"Yes," said Nightwing. "That's it. I see it in your eyes."

Star blinked rapidly and pranced forward, bringing Frostfire with him inside the shield. "Where *is* Morningleaf? I can't find her in the herd."

Nightwing flicked his tail, his eyes bright with pleasure. "You're too late, Star. She's dead."

Star recoiled with a sharp grunt. *Dead?*

"It wasn't me," said the Destroyer, looking regretful. "She drowned herself in the Wastelands. For you, I imagine. So you'd stop doing stupid things like healing your enemies, traveling with traitors, and challenging me for my herd. Things like you're doing right now." He clacked his teeth at Star.

Star dropped his head, wheezing for breath. This couldn't be true; Nightwing was lying.

Petalcloud flew up the low ridge where Star and Frostfire stood. She nuzzled Nightwing, showing off their alliance, and Star noticed that her body was full and glossy while the rest of the pegasi looked thin and dull. Petalcloud lifted her chin and appraised them. "A captain without an army and a black foal without a guardian herd—you're a sorry pair," she said, her voice lilting. "But you heard Nightwing. You're free to go. He won't make that offer twice."

Frostfire arched his neck, holding his mother's gaze, still encased safely inside the shield. "We shouldn't have sided against Star," he said to her. "We were wrong."

Petalcloud pranced closer, her delicate muzzle flaring. "You're just angry because you failed to make a pact with Nightwing and then your army abandoned you."

Frostfire glared at her, swallowing back his emotions.

"I'm lead mare of this herd," Petalcloud announced to both of them while nodding toward the valley. "And so I'll make you my own offer. If you pledge yourselves to Nightwing, you can join our herd as under-stallions. But you'll have to decide right now."

Frostfire's jaw circled helplessly as he choked on words that he wanted to say to her but couldn't.

Tension crackled between the four of them. Star braced, ready for anything, and Frostfire pinned his ears.

Petalcloud glowered, and she reminded Star of the vibrant flowers in the jungle—the ones that lured you close with their beauty and then killed you with their poison.

Nightwing broke the silence, realizing that they had reached an impasse. "You two had your chance; now leave this territory." His voice boomed across the valley. "This land belongs to me."

"Come on, Star," Frostfire whispered. "We need to regroup." Frostfire glanced behind him to where Larksong stood, touching her belly with her wing. "We'll be back," he whispered to her as though she could hear him.

Star and Frostfire, still encased in Star's golden sphere, kicked off and flew over the valley of pegasi.

Echofrost and Silverlake and the rest of the herd watched them leave, and Star saw the hope lift from their eyes. He faltered, almost falling from the sky. Frostfire bolstered him. "This isn't over, Star."

Star nodded as his vision blurred with tears. Morningleaf was dead. As soon as they were past the valley, he moaned aloud, seized by pain that was worse than anything he'd ever experienced.

"You're thinking of your blue-winged friend?" Frostfire guessed.

Star blinked acknowledgment, and his wings stuttered, throwing the golden orb into a spin. Frostfire tried to correct their balance, but Star sank like a dead weight toward land. "Star, help me fly this thing!"

The ground rushed toward them, threatening to break them, but Star didn't care.

He was already broken.

15

GRIEF

STAR OPENED HIS EYES, GROANING, HIS HEAD throbbing. He stood up and stroked his forehead with his wing. He was standing alone in a field of grass. It was morning, still early. Bugs crawled through his mane, and sweat drenched his hide. "Frostfire?" he called.

The white stallion trotted into his line of sight, looking unharmed.

"What happened?"

"We crashed," said Frostfire. "You hit the ground pretty hard. I landed on top of you, so you took the worst of it."

Star tossed his mane at the buzzing flies and quickly regretted it. The painful throbbing increased, pounding his brain like surf against the shore. Star squinted at the bright sunlight. The heavy clouds were gone, and the rain had dried on the grass. A memory tugged at his thoughts, something Nightwing had said—something Star didn't want to remember. "How long was I out?"

"The rest of yesterday and all night."

Star flinched. "What's happened since then?"

"Nothing, really," replied Frostfire. "I've been spying on the herd. The pegasi live in that valley we saw, but they travel out to the Flatlands each morning to graze. Petalcloud's Ice Warriors guard them."

Star's body ached with bruises, and he quickly sent his starfire through to heal his wounds. His tension unwound, but when he was finished, his head still hurt. That was unusual. "I'm going back," he said, spreading his wings. "I'm going to end this now."

"Wait!" Frostfire moved closer. "Remember what I said. Nightwing has to attack you first. He will draw out your strength, but if you rush this, you'll lose."

"But he knows I have the shield, so he's not going to attack me. He said we're free to leave." Bitterness choked Star's words. "How do I fight that?"

Frostfire rubbed his eyes with his wings. "I don't know, let me think about it. But I do know that charging blindly at him isn't tactical, Star. Think about it; we have twelve thousand allies in that valley." Frostfire's mismatched eyes glimmered as he pointed toward the herd of pegasi. "The reason Nightwing didn't attack you is because he doesn't know how to beat you either. This is good. It gives us time to make a plan."

Star lowered his wings.

Frostfire interpreted his gesture as acceptance and continued. "We need to establish contact with the herd, to organize them, and we'll need several spies to watch Nightwing and . . . my mother. Who do you suggest?"

Star's first thought was Hazelwind, but he hadn't seen the buckskin stallion in the valley. "Silverlake for sure," he said. "And the Desert Herd stallion I met in the Trap, Redfire."

"And what about spies?"

"Silverlake and Redfire can choose the spies." But Star knew that Echofrost and Shadepebble would volunteer.

"All right. Let's get out of the open," suggested Frostfire. "The cottonwood forest on the southern end of the valley is a good place to watch the herd without being too obvious."

The two took off and whisked over the grass, skirting the edge of the valley. The wind blasted across the plains, buffeting them. Star squinted against it.

"I already can't stand this wind," grumbled Frostfire. Their loose feathers detached and swirled behind them. He glanced at Star, looking worried. "Are you sure you're okay?"

"I think so," said Star, but his heart twitched. What was he missing? What had he forgotten?

They reached the grassy cottonwood forest and landed. Star's wounded head thumped harder when his hooves touched the ground. He glanced around him, noticing the trees were spread wide. "There's not much cover here."

"The forest thickens that way." Frostfire pointed farther south with his wing.

Star slumped against a tall elm tree, feeling dizzy from the pain in his head. He sent starfire there and waited, but the pain did not cease.

"What's wrong?" asked Frostfire.

"It's my head," said Star. "It hurts, and I can't heal it."

Frostfire halted, peering at him. "You didn't land on your head, Star. You're not injured there."

"Then why does it hurt so bad?"

"My head hurt for a long time after my mother gave me away." He trotted closer. "I think it's grief causing your pain."

"Grief over what?"

Frostfire stiffened. "You don't remember what Nightwing told you? About Morningleaf?"

The image of Morningleaf's bright blaze, warm eyes, and aqua feathers blazed across Star's mind, and in an instant, he remembered. "Oh no," he whispered.

"Nightwing said she drowned herself."

"He's lying. She wouldn't do that." Star held his head in his wings. *Or would she?* Star imagined her amber eyes, shining with devotion, and he remembered when she threw herself in front of the deathblow meant for him, and the time she rode a jet stream to save her brother, knowing she wouldn't survive it, and the time she'd used herself as bait to lure the Black Army and the Ice Warriors away from Star's body when he was injured. Star reared back, shaking his heavy black mane. *Oh, she might! She might drown herself if she thought it would help him.*

Star landed from rearing and stood, trembling from ears to tail. All the confidence he'd earned as a warrior in the Trap was gone. He was a shell of a stallion—a husk of a pegasus. One more blow and he would disintegrate into a thousand tiny pieces and drift away with the rushing winds of the Flatlands.

The excited growl of a wolf broke the silence. Star's

head snapped up, and he pricked his ears forward.

Beside him, Frostfire flared his wings. More growling came from the woods. "It's a pack," he said quietly. "They're hunting something."

Star twisted his ears and caught the low rumble of hoofbeats and the snarling of the wolves. They were chasing something hooved, like deer or horses, or maybe buffalo. Star's heart fired with hot energy. "I'm saving them," he neighed.

"Saving who?" cried Frostfire.

"Whatever creature those wolves are about to kill." Star galloped and lifted off the ground, flying through the trees.

Frostfire followed, angry. "Don't risk a fight with wolves, Star. They're just hunting."

"I don't care." Star pinned his ears, his veins pulsing with blood and starfire, his fury driving him faster.

"I know what you're doing," whinnied Frostfire. "Your friend is dead, so you're going to save some animal since you can't save her. It's a waste of your energy."

Star pinned his ears. "I'm doing it anyway!" But maybe Frostfire was right. Maybe because he couldn't save Morningleaf, he would save a deer or a horse. Maybe he was going crazy, but his need to protect the poor creature consumed him like fire.

Star rocketed into the depths of the forest, neck flat, following the low growls of the wolves and the panicked breaths of the prey. A patch of gray fur flashed between the trees. He was catching up to them.

A sharp snarl and piercing squeals erupted. The wolves had cornered their victim. Star knew he had only seconds to stop the attack. He narrowed his wings and jetted forward, dodging branches. Ahead was a tumble of hooves and fur and gnashing teeth. Four gigantic wolves had their quarry pinned to the ground. Colorful feathers exploded around them, and Star reeled.

These weren't deer or horses.

They were pegasi.

16

DISCOVERY

STAR DROPPED ON THE ATTACKING WOLVES, FOL-lowed quickly by Frostfire, striking them with sharpened hooves, but their thick fur resisted tearing. Star changed tactics and struck at their heads. The wolves were monstrous, the size of yearling pegasi. Star slammed a black one between the eyes, and it reeled off a pinned mare. She cracked it in the ribs, pushing it the rest of the way off. "Take that, you big coyote!" she neighed.

Star's heart fluttered at the familiar voice. "Dewberry!"

She rolled to her hooves as one of the two gray wolves leaped for her, snarling and showing long, white fangs. Star landed in the wolf's charging path and butted it in the chest like a mountain ram. The furry beast somersaulted into a tree and collapsed in a daze.

"Use your starfire!" whinnied Dewberry.

But Star had sworn never to use the silver fire again. He tossed his mane and dived into the fight, relying on his hooves and teeth. The black wolf recovered and leaped toward Frostfire. The white stallion kicked him in the chest, sending him flying across the clearing.

Dewberry lifted off, joining Frostfire in attacking the other wolves. Her lip curled in disgust at the sight of the past Mountain Herd captain. "Is he with you?" she whinnied, but Star was too busy to answer.

Star galloped toward the pinto who was trapped under the giant paws of a white wolf, kicking for his life. Star saw streaks of yellow and brown, and his heart thumped with hope. "Bumblewind?"

The bay pinto lifted his head. *It was Bumblewind!* The second gray wolf, which was darker and bigger than the one that attacked Dewberry, dashed for his friend's throat. Star whirled and let loose both hind hooves, knocking the wolf out cold. Bumblewind flew toward Star just as a giant white she-wolf snatched his tail and hurled him into a tree. Bumblewind's head cracked against the bark, and he slumped onto the dirt.

Star, Dewberry, and Frostfire landed to protect Bumblewind, kicking the circling wolves. The beasts' eyes flit between the four pegasi as though they were thinking, assessing their odds. "These aren't normal wolves," Star said.

"No," rasped Dewberry. "They're dire wolves."

"Those don't exist," said Frostfire, kicking one in the ribs.

"Tell *them* that," said Dewberry.

Bumblewind shook his head and rolled onto his hooves. "Can you fly?" asked Star.

"Yeah. I'm fine," said Bumblewind, but his eyes were still swirling from his impact against the tree.

The white dire wolf, the leader of the attack, growled low and angry, then signaled the others to follow her. They slunk back into the woods, returning to the shadows.

The four pegasi lifted off, hovering between the trees. Bumblewind stared at Star, his eyes full of joy. "I knew you'd find us," he said.

Star looked away. Yes, he'd found them, but he was too late to save Morningleaf.

"Does Nightwing know you and Dewberry are here in the woods?" Frostfire asked Bumblewind.

"No. We slipped away from Nightwing in the

Wastelands and followed the herd here, and we've been hiding and watching them ever since, waiting for Star to arrive." Bumblewind peered at Star again. "I can't believe you're really here."

Star battled back fresh tears. They'd grown up together, and Star would never be able to look at Bumblewind or Echofrost again without also seeing Morningleaf.

Dewberry huffed, jerking her head toward Frostfire. "So what's with him? How'd you two end up together?" she asked Star.

Frostfire bristled, but they were all out of breath, and Star merely said, "Long story."

The pinto mare looked doubtful.

"We need to get out of here before the Ice Warriors come," said Bumblewind. He turned to Star and explained, "They fly patrols through here sometimes." Bumblewind lifted off, and then his eyes fluttered and rolled back in his head. He fell toward land.

Star and Dewberry dived after him and snatched Bumblewind's wings, preventing him from crashing onto the soil. The retreating wolves yipped and snaked back through the trees, coming closer as they sensed Bumblewind's weakness.

"He's hurt," said Dewberry through a mouthful of

Bumblewind's feathers. She glared at Frostfire. "Take this wing from me. I'm going to look for herbs before his bites become infected."

Frostfire did as she asked and took the wing from her.

Dewberry turned to Star. "See that deer trail?"

A thin path wove through the trees, barely visible unless someone was looking for it. He nodded.

"Follow it until you reach the tallest elm tree. Turn left and then land and walk the rest of the way. When you reach the old fallen cottonwood, stamp the soil three times and then wait." Dewberry darted off in search of healing plants.

"Wait for what?" nickered Star, but Dewberry was gone.

"She's enchanting," grumbled Frostfire. "Let's go."

Star and Frostfire flew slowly above the deer path while Bumblewind slipped in and out of consciousness. "He might have injuries inside, where we can't see them," said Frostfire.

Bumblewind's bite wounds had already clotted, and Star saw no sign of swelling around the pinto's belly or ribs. "No. I think this is all from hitting his head against that tree."

Star traced the path, looking for the tallest elm.

Several trees gave him pause, but they just weren't large or distinctive enough to be landmarks. He kept flying.

"I think that's it," said Frostfire.

The elm ahead towered over the rest, and Star felt sure it was the one Dewberry had described. They reached it, landed as Dewberry had instructed, and turned left. They walked as straight as possible until Star spotted a cottonwood that had been struck by lightning and toppled over years ago, as evidenced by the plants growing around it and over it. The tree lay alongside a rounded berm of land. They stopped and released Bumblewind gently on the ground. Birds chirped, ignoring them and gathering seeds.

Star inspected the area and saw nothing special about it, but he trusted Dewberry and so he stamped his hoof three times.

Their ears pricked forward as Star and Frostfire heard sounds below their hooves. Something was moving underground. Seconds later a branch, heavy with leaves, slid across the soil. A black hole appeared behind the fallen cottonwood tree, and a head popped out—it was Hazelwind.

"Star!" he nickered. He climbed out of a steep passageway and then tensed when he saw Frostfire.

Star waved his wings. "It's okay. He's with me."

Hazelwind glared at the white captain. "How so?"

"I'll explain," Star promised. "But later; Bumblewind is hurt."

Hazelwind glanced at Bumblewind, who was lying unconscious on the ground. "What happened to him? And where's Dewberry?"

Star explained about the dire wolves, the injury to Bumblewind, and Dewberry taking off to search for herbs.

Hazelwind nodded. "Let's get him inside."

"What is this place?" Star asked. "You live underground?"

"There's nowhere else to hide," said Hazelwind. "We escaped from Nightwing after he captured us by hiding in underground aqueduct caves. Then we followed the pegasi here, and when they settled in the valley, we dug day and night into this wolf den to make it big enough for all of us."

"Wolf den?"

Hazelwind grimaced. "Yeah, we stole it from the dire wolves, and they aren't too happy about it."

Bumblewind groaned.

"Come on, let's hurry." Hazelwind glared at Frostfire, leaning forward with teeth bared. "But you stay out here."

Star sighed, weary and heartbroken. "Hazelwind, please trust me. Frostfire won't hurt us."

Hazelwind lowered his voice. "It's not that. I'm worried about Morningleaf."

Star froze. "What?"

"After all he's done to her . . . and what she's been through . . . I don't know if she can bear to see him."

"You mean . . . she's alive?" Star's broken heart shuddered.

"Yes," said Hazelwind, looking confused, and then understanding dawned. "Ah, you must have been to the valley. You heard she was gone."

Star nodded; he was breathless. *Morningleaf hadn't drowned?*

"She's inside, Star," nickered Hazelwind, gesturing into the den. "Go see her, but leave him out here." He glared at Frostfire.

Star's heart soared, but now the full repercussions of his alliance with Frostfire hit him. It was one thing to trust the captain when they were alone; it was another to trust him with the lives of his friends—and to bring him to Morningleaf. But he'd also promised not to abandon the captain. "But what if someone spots him, Hazelwind? Or the wolves return? I think he should hide with us."

"Are you *certain* he's on our side?" asked Hazelwind, his voice gruff.

Star remembered what his uncle had said about not considering Star family, but they'd also relied on each during their journey here, and Frostfire had softened toward Star. Still, the captain had lied to him before. Star realized he didn't know what to believe. "Maybe I'm not certain," he admitted, avoiding Frostfire's sharp glance. "But his mate's been captured, and she's with foal. By helping us, he's helping himself too."

Hazelwind locked eyes with Frostfire. "All right, I'll let you inside, but you're not welcome. Do you understand?"

Frostfire nodded.

Star's heart thrummed with sudden worry. "So Morningleaf is alive, but is she okay? Why does Nightwing think she drowned?"

Hazelwind sighed, and Star noticed how weary the stallion looked. "Just go to her."

Star groaned. "Then she *is* hurt?"

"I think you should see for yourself."

Star's heart pounded. Soon he would be with Morningleaf. He ducked into the dark passageway, with Hazelwind and Frostfire following.

17

THE DEN

STAR LOWERED HIS HEAD AND SQUEEZED INTO the wolf den. The soil was moist and cool, and smelled of dirt worms. His head scraped the ceiling, and loose mud chipped off and dropped onto him, sifting through his feathers and falling to the packed dirt floor. Hazelwind wrapped his wings around Bumblewind's front legs and dragged him as gently as he could into the hole.

They entered a chamber shaped like a hoof. It was rounded on all sides except one, which was straight. Hazelwind slid Bumblewind's sleeping body to a sidewall and positioned him so that his wings weren't smashed under his body. Star stood, looking around, but the ceiling was too low for him to lift his head much higher than his shoulders. Otherwise, the four of them fit comfortably in the chamber, and several more pegasi would also fit.

"This is the main den," explained Hazelwind. "Farther in there are two more lairs, which are connected by tunnels."

Star squinted, adjusting to the dim light that illuminated the dust floating in the air, and he saw the tunnel that led out of the first chamber and to the next. "The dire wolves let you take their home?"

"Not exactly," said Hazelwind, and Star squinted, noticing scratches and bite marks on the buckskin's hide. "But there's another benefit to living here. The stench of wolf masks our scent from Nightwing and his Ice Warriors."

"You look tired," said Star. Hazelwind had sagging wings and bleary eyes. It must have been difficult for him to steal and defend the den from those wolves, and then to dig it out. Star wished to restore him, and heal Bumblewind too, but he was positive that if he used his starfire here in the den, it would lead Nightwing directly to his friends' lair.

Dewberry returned and entered the den with her wings full of herbs. Star remembered that her dam had been a medicine mare. She'd worked with Sweetroot in the Sun Herd lands before she'd died of illness herself, and Star guessed Dewberry must have picked up some healing knowledge. The pinto mare dropped the herbs and rushed to Bumblewind's side. "You can't let him sleep," she scolded Hazelwind. "Not after a smack to the head." She shook Bumblewind awake.

"Where am I?" the pinto asked.

"You're safe in the den," said Dewberry. She packed his wounds with a poultice she made from chewed-up yarrow plants.

"Is he going to be all right?" asked Hazelwind.

"Why wouldn't he be?" she snapped.

Star sensed the fear lurking behind her outburst. "Let her work," he said, drawing Hazelwind's attention. "Where's Morningleaf?"

"This way."

Star followed Hazelwind into another tunnel, keeping his head low so as not to scrape it against the dirt above him. It was a short journey to the next chamber, which was empty. "She's in the last chamber," Hazelwind whispered, pointing to the final tunnel. Then he moved aside so Star could enter. "Brackentail is with her. They're sleeping."

Star tensed. He hadn't thought much about Brackentail

since Nightwing had stolen the pegasi in the Trap. He'd assumed the brown yearling was in the valley with the rest of the captured steeds, not here with Morningleaf. His heart sped a notch.

Star proceeded forward. The tunnels were dark, but each chamber had a ceiling hole that reached the air and light above, casting a stream of pale light. He walked through the short tunnel that opened into the last chamber. He stepped into it and halted, his feathers flexing and his heart racing. There was Morningleaf—curled in sleep against Brackentail, who had laid his head across her back and his orange wing over her ribs. Star's stallion blood flared, causing his feathers to rattle, and the grip of icy shock froze his heart.

"Easy," warned Hazelwind, who had followed behind him.

Star shook his head, trying to rid himself of the terrible feelings cycling from his head to his sharpened hooves. Brackentail had become Morningleaf's trusted friend—he knew that. He'd accepted it. He just hated *seeing* it. He swallowed and spoke to her. "Morningleaf, I'm here."

Morningleaf stretched and opened her eyes, sniffing the air. "Star!" She leaped to her hooves and slammed into him, thrusting her muzzle into his mane. "I knew you'd find us."

He wrapped his wings around her, gripping her as tight as he could. Brackentail stirred and woke, and Star watched the big colt's face brighten when he saw him. Star relaxed. Brackentail was his friend too, and he'd asked the colt to watch out for Morningleaf when they lived in the north. His jealousy was unfair.

"I'm sorry," Star whispered into her mane. "I returned to the celebration in the Trap, and all of you were gone."

Morningleaf stepped back from his embrace, and Star noticed the haunted look in her eyes. "I'm glad you weren't there when Nightwing came," she said, and she folded her wings across her back.

"Your feathers!" Star whinnied.

Morningleaf flinched. "Please don't look at them."

Star gaped at her, horrified and unable to stop staring. Her eyes welled with tears, and so did Star's. "Nightwing did that to you?" he asked, but he knew it was Nightwing.

She squeezed her eyelids shut, and Brackentail rushed to her side. "It doesn't hurt her . . . anymore," he said.

The few sunrays that permeated the hole in the den's ceiling spotlighted the damage to Morningleaf's feathers. They were black and dry, and had curled into themselves, and her flight feathers were gone, burned to their roots. Only small patches of aqua color remained.

"She stood up to Nightwing," explained Brackentail. "Rather than kill her, he . . . grounded her."

Star had guessed it was Morningleaf who had made the Destroyer cry. He'd known it when he encountered the single black flower that had grown out of the ash-covered tundra in the north.

He stared at her ruined feathers, and fury boiled up from his belly and shot through his muscles. Nightwing had turned her into a dud. He'd punished her in the worst way, and for what? Star's breathing quickened, and static charges fired across his black hide in small explosions of light.

"Please, Star. Calm down. This is our hiding place."

Star slowed his breathing, lowered his wings, and let his eyes readjust to the dark. "Nightwing won't get away with this," he said, staring at her feathers.

"Let's not talk about it, all right?" Morningleaf exhaled and leaned into Star's chest, taking deep breaths of him. "I've missed you."

Star felt an avalanche of tears threaten to break loose, but he held them back, thinking. Was it her devotion to him or his to her that was more dangerous? Nightwing only hurt Morningleaf because he knew that Star cared about her. She would never be safe as long as he was near her. Star gazed into her amber eyes, knowing she'd do anything for him, and that it would one day get her killed for real, but he also saw that she had no regrets.

Sadness washed over him as he realized that he'd have to stay away from her, to let her go, to let *all* his friends go if he hoped to fulfill his destiny and defeat Nightwing. He briefly closed his eyes. To accept his destiny meant trading away his own dreams. He would never be a regular pegasus, never grow old, and never die a mortal death. But if he freed the pegasi of Anok from the Destroyer, it would all be worth it.

"How did you find us?" Morningleaf asked, drawing him from his thoughts.

Hazelwind and Star exchanged a glance, and Star dreaded telling her that his uncle was here, but she would find out soon enough. "I had help," he said. "From Frostfire."

She jerked away, looking sick. "Frostfire?"

"He's on our side."

She snapped her blazing eyes to his. "Since when? How could you trust him after what he's done?"

Star glanced at her ruined feathers and thought of all she'd suffered—struck by a deathblow, captured by Frostfire, broken in a jet stream, attacked by crocodiles, and now grounded by Nightwing—all of it because she was friends with him.

"I'm sorry," he said to her. "I didn't bring Frostfire here to hurt you, or remind you, but he did help me find you."

Morningleaf met Star's eyes and he held her gaze, willing her to trust him and not to be angry. After a long while she said, "I trust you, but I don't trust him. I'm sorry. He lied to you once before, when he told you he'd protect me. Bringing him here—I think it's a mistake."

Star saw that it distressed Morningleaf to question his judgment openly, but he understood, and she was right. Frostfire had betrayed him in the north. "Don't be sorry," he said. "You're right, but it's too late. He's here."

Morningleaf set her jaw. "Keep your eye on him, Star."

"I will," he promised. "And there's something else you need to know. Bumblewind is hurt."

"How?"

"Frostfire and I found him and the others being attacked by those huge wolves. We helped drive them off, but Bumblewind hit his head pretty hard. We carried him back here."

"These dire wolves are more aggressive than our wolves in the west," said Morningleaf. "Let's go see him."

Star led her and Brackentail out of the sleeping

chamber, and they followed Hazelwind to the large first chamber. There, Bumblewind's reclining body took up a lot of space, so they all slouched against the dirt walls, watching him. Morningleaf and Frostfire avoided each other's gaze. Dewberry spoke. "The dire wolves' fangs just grazed him. It's his head that's the problem." She snorted. "But that's nothing new."

No one reacted to her weak attempt at humor, and Dewberry's expression quickly sobered as she continued. "We can't let him fall asleep; that's crucial. He's confused, and he can't remember the attack well. If his head clears tomorrow, I think he'll be fine."

"What attack?" asked Bumblewind, his eyes dull and swirling.

"See?" said Dewberry.

"This isn't good," said Star.

"I'm watching him closely." Dewberry stood over Bumblewind, guarding him like a sentry, and Star saw the depth of her concern. She teased Bumblewind relentlessly, but if Star thought about it, the two were always together.

The pegasi slouched in the chamber, waiting for nightfall. Star's eyes flicked continually to Morningleaf's blackened feathers, and he had to drag away his stare. The den grew stuffy. "So what is Nightwing's plan?" he asked his friends. "Is it to rule the herd he's collected, or to harm them?"

"It's both from what we can tell," Hazelwind answered. "He's separated out the weanlings. He and Petalcloud are training them to be Nightwing's warriors."

Star balked. "He took them from their mothers?"

Hazelwind nodded. "Since they eat grass now, they don't need their dams for milk."

"But—"

"It makes sense," interrupted Morningleaf. "He's getting them young and raising them to adore him. He gives them special privileges and keeps them from the elders, and from the stories of our past. They don't know anything except what he wants them to know."

"Is it working?" asked Star.

"It's starting to," said Brackentail. "The weanlings are the only ones allowed to fly. They love it. They aren't afraid of Nightwing or Petalcloud."

The pegasi in the den stood in silence for a long moment. Finally Star spoke. "And what about the rest of the pegasi, what are his plans for them?"

"We're still figuring that out," said Hazelwind.

Dewberry gestured toward Bumblewind. "Can you heal him, Star?"

"I can, but it could attract Nightwing to the den. If he's not better by tomorrow, we can move him somewhere else and I'll do it there."

"I can hear you guys talking about me," said Bumblewind. "I'm fine, just tired."

Hazelwind flicked his tail, thinking. "If Nightwing can track you, can you track him? So we know where *he* is?"

Star's ears drooped. "Sometimes I see Nightwing in visions, but I can't control them."

Hazelwind looked disappointed.

Star changed the subject. "We have several hours until dark. Please tell me what happened in the Trap."

Hazelwind opened his mouth to speak, but then Morningleaf interrupted. "I'll tell the story." She began with Nightwing landing in the Trap, just after Star had left them to heal Larksong, and then continued with what had happened next.

Star listened intently, feeling guiltier for not being there the longer she spoke. But could he have stopped Nightwing? Probably not.

"So when did you arrive here?" he asked.

Brackentail answered. "Only four days ago. How about you?"

"Frostfire and I searched the territories first, and the

coast, then we flew east. We found the herd yesterday."

"You made good time," commented Hazelwind.

"We rode the jet streams when we could."

"Him too?" Morningleaf asked, pointing at Frostfire.

"Yes. I sheltered him in my shield."

"Not a bad idea," said Hazelwind.

"So what do we do now?" Star asked.

Hazelwind flared his wings, excited. "We have a plan, Star. The soil here is soft and loose, easy to dig through with our hooves and carry with our wings. We have an idea to construct a tunnel from this forest to the valley where Nightwing keeps the pegasi at night. We've already started working on it. Once it's finished, we can smuggle steeds out of the herd in small numbers. We'll free as many as we can before Nightwing notices."

Star felt discouraged. "But where will the freed pegasi live? Nightwing will find them wherever they go."

Hazelwind shifted. "They'll leave Anok and cross the Dark Water. They'll find a new home on the southern continent."

"But what about the Landwalkers," exclaimed Star. "They infest the neighboring lands."

"True, but they can't fly. They aren't as dangerous as Nightwing."

Star had heard stories about the Landwalkers from the elders. They controlled the soil, caused food to grow where they willed, made slaves of wolves and horses, and cut down forests. Besides that, they were skilled hunters. It was said they fed on bears, moose, sharks, and other large creatures. Star thought they were at *least* as dangerous as Nightwing. "And what about the steeds who don't escape?"

Hazelwind locked eyes with him. "The point is to rescue as many as we can, so that the pegasi will live on, if not in Anok, then somewhere. This way you can fight Nightwing, and it will be . . . less devastating if you lose. We just need you to wait. Don't attack him . . . or let him attack you, until we have enough pegasi gone from Anok to start a new herd."

Star sighed. "No pegasus will truly be safe as long as Nightwing is alive. The fear of him will poison the herds no matter where they live—like it has for four hundred years. It's time to be rid of him for good."

Morningleaf moved across the chamber and pressed against him, laying her cheek on his neck. "This is your destiny, Star."

He nuzzled her. "Then I cannot fail." He felt her heart pulse against his chest. Star believed her destiny was to lead a new herd, a free herd, and the feeling washed over him like ocean waves, in cold, rolling bursts. And for the first time he feared that his destiny and Morningleaf's destiny might be different, that their futures might be lived not together, but apart.

18

WIND HERD

AFTER THE SUN SET, STAR, HAZELWIND, AND
Morningleaf slipped out of the den to visit the tunnel that
the hiding pegasi had already begun to dig. Brackentail
and Dewberry stayed behind to watch Bumblewind and
keep him awake. The evening air was moist and cloying,
reminding Star of the jungle. Crickets and frogs chirped
in an incessant rhythm, and Star had never seen so many
flying bugs. He tossed his mane and lashed his tail, but
the insects became entangled in his hair and harassed
him worse. "How do you stand it?" he whispered, brushing
a throng of mosquitoes away from Morningleaf.

She nickered. "Dewberry has plant oil that she rubs
down our backs. It doesn't keep them entirely away, but

it stops them from landing on us. I'll make sure you get some when we return."

Frostfire trotted up behind them. "Where are you going?"

Morningleaf halted and whirled around, flaring her charred wings. "*You* can't come," she said.

Frostfire pinned his ears, and the two stared at each other, their history raging between them.

Star intervened. "Why don't you guard the entrance to the den, Frostfire? If the wolves come back, Dewberry will need your help."

Frostfire tore his eyes from Morningleaf and nodded curtly at Star, accepting his post as sentry.

The group trotted away, and as they left, Star noticed that Morningleaf carried her wings at an awkward angle, as though they were painful to her. He wanted to heal her, and his golden starfire flamed, ready to obey.

Guessing at his intentions, Morningleaf said, "Not here, Star. We're too close to the den, and please stop staring at my feathers."

"I'm sorry. I—"

Star turned his eyes away, remembering their time in the Trap when they were hiding from Nightwing with the foreign herds. Then, Star had noticed many young stallions staring at Morningleaf, especially at her bright-aqua feathers and her fluffy flaxen tail. Whenever she caught them staring, she'd face them, and her challenging gaze had melted their brazenness, but when she trotted off—they returned to staring. One time Star had said to her, "They're still watching you, you know."

"I know," she'd said with a playful snort. "I can feel their eyes."

But now Star's glances upset her because her feathers were ruined. Hatred for Nightwing blazed, but Star squashed his bad feelings, knowing they were dangerous.

Hazelwind pranced ahead. "We're almost at the tunnel," he whispered. "We take a different route each night so we don't wear down a trail. Echofrost or Shadepebble will meet us there; they're our spies."

A few stars dotted the black sky, and the moon was a crescent, shedding a pale glow. Star smelled rain and the distant scent of buffalo. Cottonwood, ash, and elm trees stretched above him, and the singing of insects filled his ears. The interior of Anok had a beauty of its own, despite the wolves and bugs.

Suddenly Hazelwind disappeared. Star halted, and Morningleaf bumped into him. "Where did he go?" Star asked.

She nickered softly. "Follow me." She skirted around him, and then she too disappeared.

Perplexed, Star advanced slowly, his nostrils flared. He traced Morningleaf's scent to a blind of leaves and branches, woven like a nest but creating three walls and a ceiling that hid them from view. Star understood right away. His friends had found a way to create camouflage.

"Come inside," said Hazelwind.

Star entered the shelter.

"We've begun digging the tunnel here," said Hazelwind, indicating a large hole in the ground that was partially covered by a woven band of tree branches. "And from this wall here, we can see the valley." Hazelwind pointed to the north wall. "Take a look."

Hazelwind moved aside, and Star placed his eye against the back wall, peering through a gap in the branches. The huge valley was spread before him, filled with pegasi. He balked, whispering, "I didn't realize we were so close."

"We're as close as we dare get," said Hazelwind. "Nightwing doesn't allow the pegasi into the forest. He keeps them in the open, where he and the Ice Warriors can see if anyone tries to escape. When his patrols fly overhead, they can't spot us through the tree branches Morningleaf wove."

Star examined the interlocking branches. When they'd lived in the Trap, the Mountain Herd mares had woven baskets to keep their birds' eggs safe and warm for eating. Morningleaf had asked to learn the technique, but the mares had said no. "Didn't the Mountain Herd mares refuse to teach you this?" he asked.

Morningleaf lifted her head. "They did, but I took one of their baskets and unraveled it. I studied the patterns they used, and I copied them. It took a few days, but I figured it out. It's not hard once you understand it."

Star whistled softly. "I doubt I could have made sense of it," he said.

Hazelwind nodded. "I still can't figure it out."

"You two just don't have any patience," she nickered, but Star knew that wasn't it. He didn't see patterns like she did. He couldn't count as high or as quickly either.

Star returned to watching Nightwing's herd in the valley. The light was dim, but it didn't take long for him to realize that the steeds were sectioned into groups that didn't look natural. He pricked his ears, trying to sort it out.

Morningleaf sensed his confusion. "Nightwing's

sorted the pegasi. The northern end is for the elders. The northeast side is for warriors; the southeast is for yearlings; the west is for nonwarriors; and the southern end, closest to us, is for the mares and foals. Each section is further divided by gender. See? All the mares and stallions are apart and are not permitted to speak to each other."

Star gasped. "Not permitted?"

Morningleaf nodded. "They can't do anything without permission, not even drink from the lake. Petalcloud's Ice Warriors guard the groups. By keeping the pegasi separate, it's easier for Nightwing to control them. Only on the open plain, during the day, are they allowed to be together."

Star examined the valley, seeing that all she said was true. The proud pegasi of Anok stood where they were told, with their heads hanging low. Some grazed, others stared vacantly as though dead. Thick-bodied white and gray Ice Warriors patrolled them, prancing with arched necks, looking for trouble. Their long hair flashed in the moonlight as they moved. He saw Stormtail, the granite-colored stallion who'd delivered the deathblow to him, only to have it blocked when Star sprang his shield for the first time.

And there was Petalcloud, trotting in her flowing gait toward the weanlings. The youngsters huddled together, watching her, and she took her time, greeting each one with soft nickers. She preened their bright feathers, mothering each foal, and one by one they relaxed. Star felt sick to his stomach watching it.

"She's winning them over," he said, his throat tight with anger.

"Don't lose heart. We have a plan, Star," Morningleaf reminded him. "This tunnel is the answer." She slid the branches away from the hole. "We take turns digging out the soil with our hooves, and then scooping the dirt in our wings and carrying it to our dump sites. It's going to take a long time to reach the valley, but through this tunnel, we'll be able to move a group of pegasi away from Nightwing and out of Anok."

A sudden shadow crossed the moon, darkening the blind. "Don't move," rasped Hazelwind. Star looked up through the leaves and saw an Ice Warrior soaring overhead, patrolling.

When he was gone, Star let out his breath. "He didn't see us."

"That was Graystone," said Hazelwind. "He's one of the few Ice Warriors who's on our side. When it's his turn to patrol the forest, he lets our spies out to visit us, which means one of them is on her way here now."

Star listened closely and caught the sound of gentle hoofbeats. His heart raced with excitement at the thought of reuniting with another friend. Soon the pegasus ducked into the blind of leaves.

Star nickered with pleasure—it was Echofrost.

"Star! You're here," she said in a fast breath, like she didn't believe it.

He greeted her, nuzzling her white mane. Then he glanced at the sky. "How do you know you can trust this Graystone?"

"Not all the Ice Warriors are under Petalcloud's spell," she explained. "Some hate what's happening as much as we do, but they can't speak up, or stop it. If they do, they'll be killed, but they help us when they can. Graystone doesn't know exactly what we're doing here, and he doesn't ask, but he knows there are rebels hiding in the woods."

Rebels, thought Star. It seemed a strong word for a tiny group of pegasi who were just trying to . . . what? Save the herds from an ancient destroyer? He swished his tail. Yes, maybe *rebels* was the right term.

"Have any other pegasi escaped?" Star asked. "Besides your group?"

Echofrost sagged. "Oh, many have left, but none made it far. They're all dead, killed by Nightwing or the Ice Warriors. No one has tried to escape recently."

Hazelwind fluffed his feathers, changing the subject. "Give us your report."

Echofrost groaned, and Star saw how much she regretted the news she was about to give. "It's about the walkers," she said.

Star pricked his ears. "How are there walkers in the valley if Nightwing made you all fly here?"

"Most were carried by their families, and some were injured along the way and can no longer fly," said Echofrost. "Anyway, Nightwing plans to execute them at sunrise."

Star choked on his tongue. "He—he can't."

"He can, and he is. He says he doesn't have enough Ice Warriors to protect them, and since they can't get off the ground when the dire wolves are hunting, it's for their own good." Echofrost grimaced, her voice bitter. "Everything Nightwing does is for our own good: separating us, controlling us, rationing us. Aren't we fortunate."

Star's thoughts reeled. "How will he do it?"

"He'll line them up and burn them. That's what he does to any pegasi he catches misbehaving."

"But they aren't misbehaving," cried Star. "They're just . . . different."

Echofrost gave him a helpless stare. "He killed an elder because she stepped on a rock and damaged her hoof. He called her injury a 'burden.'"

The pegasi stood in silence, each drained by the conversation. Finally Hazelwind spoke. "And Petalcloud is okay with this? As lead mare, she's in charge of the foals and elders, and most of the walkers are elders."

Echofrost snorted. "She doesn't care, and most of the Ice Warriors don't care. They seem to get nastier each day."

Hazelwind nudged Echofrost with his muzzle. "If there's no other news, you should get back. We'll work on the tunnel."

"There's one more thing," she said. "Nightwing has given us a name. We're Wind Herd."

Hazelwind nodded. "That's a good sign. It means he's making a permanent home here. It gives us time to dig. Thank you, Echofrost."

The silver yearling nodded and slipped out of the blind.

Star's head spun with all he'd heard. He'd been a walker once—dragging his huge, malformed wings around for most of his first year of life. He'd migrated by hoof with the Sun Herd walkers, who were lead by Grasswing. He was a mighty warrior who'd treated Star like his own colt. Anger stormed his heart. He couldn't let Nightwing execute the innocent.

"I know what you're thinking," whispered Morningleaf.

Star avoided her eyes. "No you don't."

"Star, we have a plan. Don't veer from it."

Star stomped the dirt. "But the tunnel isn't ready, and the walkers will be killed at sunrise."

"What's going on?" asked Hazelwind, coming closer and peering at Star and Morningleaf.

"He's going to try and stop the execution tomorrow." Morningleaf lifted her chin, daring Star to deny it.

"There are *hundreds* of walkers and duds in that herd." Star paused, letting the heft of the number settle on his friends. "I know you need time to dig the tunnel, and I won't ruin your plan, but murdering innocent walkers? I can't let it happen. Not while I breathe air." Star's muscles twitched as he wrangled his feelings.

Hazelwind interrupted. "The night is slipping away. We need to start digging. Don't ruin this, Star. Please." Hazelwind walked into the tunnel and began scraping dirt with his front hooves.

Star's attention diverted to their task. "Digging this tunnel all the way to the valley will take many moons," he said. "What if Nightwing moves the herd?"

Morningleaf lashed her tail. "We have to try, Star, and I don't think he'll move them. He's claimed this territory and named the herd, and over-stallions hate wandering. It's why everyone thought you'd claim the Sun Herd lands when you grew up. It's odd for a herd to *wander*, but it's not odd for one this size to stay put."

"I guess so," said Star.

Morningleaf nickered. "Will you help us?"

"Of course."

Morningleaf kept watch while the stallions took turns digging. Then she helped them remove the piles of fresh dirt and spread it to hide it. They each took short breaks to drink from a clear creek that was nearby and swarming with small, brown fish. The work was hard, but it kept Star busy while his mind raced with ideas. How could he save the walkers without ruining Morningleaf's plans?

Just before dawn they returned to the den. Bumblewind was awake and doing well, but he still couldn't remember the dire wolves or hitting his head. Hazelwind and Morningleaf retreated to the third lair to sleep. Frost-fire stayed outside.

"Is that you, Star?" Bumblewind asked when Star entered his chamber.

"Yes. I'm here." Star dropped his head and nuzzled his friend.

Bumblewind's powerful muscles relaxed. "I knew you'd come." He gazed at Star with his warm brown eyes. "Warriors don't give up on each other."

"Not ever," Star agreed. He glanced outside the den at the brightening morning sky. "I have something I have to do, but I'll come back soon." Star turned to leave.

"Watch out for the wolves," warned Bumblewind. "Dewberry said they attacked me."

Star glanced at Bumblewind's bite marks. "I see that." Star nodded to Dewberry and whispered, "Are you sure he's going to be all right?"

Dewberry tugged gently on Bumblewind's tail, her eyes glittering. "He's fine; he made it through the night. It'll take more than a few gigantic wolves to get rid of this yearling."

Star saw Bumblewind was in good care. "I'll watch out for wolves," he promised Bumblewind, and then he stepped outside.

Brackentail followed him. "It's almost dawn. Where are you going?"

Star turned and faced him. "I'm going to save the walkers," he whispered. The horizon took on a hazy glow.

Frostfire, who was still guarding the entrance to the den, heard them talking and trotted closer. "Take me with you," he said. "No one wants me here."

Brackentail pinned his ears at the white stallion who'd once broken his orange wing at the root, but he looked at Star. "Take me too."

Star tossed his long, black forelock out of his eyes, staring at his two friends who'd each once been his enemies. "If this doesn't end well for me, it won't end well for you two either."

Frostfire snorted. "If this doesn't end well for you, it won't end well for *any* of us." He turned to the brown yearling. "But you should stay behind, Brackentail. Nightwing already knows I'm here—he saw me with Star—but he doesn't know about you. You're supposed to be dead like Morningleaf—you can't risk being spotted."

"That's true," agreed Brackentail, looking dejected.

Star noticed Brackentail's tight muscles and pinned ears. Frostfire was causing his friends nothing but distress. "I'll take you with me, Frostfire."

"Saving the walkers is a dangerous idea," warned Brackentail, looking from one to the other. "If we lose you, Star . . ."

Brackentail didn't finish the sentence, and Star faced him. "Just focus on that tunnel, no matter what happens to me." Star lowered his neck and pressed his forehead against Brackentail's. His breath hitched as he spoke. "And take care of Morningleaf . . . if I don't come back."

"I will," Brackentail promised.

Star turned and flew toward the valley, followed by Frostfire. He had to save the walkers. It would tear his soul to shreds if he didn't. As he flew away, he realized something awful: he hadn't yet healed Morningleaf's aqua feathers. "I'll come back," he whispered over his shoulder. "I promise."

19

TEN THOUSAND STONES

STAR AND FROSTFIRE GLIDED TOWARD THE VALley on the wave of a fast current. The sun was beginning to rise, swathing the green grass in pale streams of yellow light. The Ice Warriors had already marched Wind Herd onto the Flatlands to graze, and the harsh winds whipped their tails against their flanks.

Star thought it was not the worst place to settle a herd of pegasi, and it was probably the best place to settle a herd this large. He scanned the terrain, viewing it as an overstallion might. The interior of Anok provided enormous grazing space and hundreds of shimmering freshwater lakes. Rounded, leafy trees dotted the plain, shading the pegasi as they walked with heads down, their teeth ripping at the grass. But the high winds, giant wolves, and violent storms made this home less than ideal for the pegasus foals.

Star circled the valley once, purposefully showing himself to the five herds that were now one—united, but conquered. He had not abandoned them, and he hoped that the sight of him would bolster their mood. Frostfire landed, waiting as Star swept over the herd. Thousands of heads rose and eyes blinked, mistaking Star's shadow at first for Nightwing, but when they recognized the shining white star that marked his forehead, they nickered delighted greetings.

Silverlake was there. Star spotted her shining feathers quickly, but her gray coat was dull and her eyes barren. She didn't know that her filly, Morningleaf, and her adult colt, Hazelwind, were safe, and so close to her. But it was her genuine grief that made Morningleaf's "death" all the more convincing. Star wished he could land and whisper the good news into her ears, but Silverlake's relief would change her attitude, and any sudden joy would alert her guards that something was amiss. Star flew away from her, noticing that many of the pegasi were in similar shape: dull coated and slouching, empty of their former fire. In this land of plenty, they were not thriving.

Nightwing thundered across the grass, whipping his tail and looking stunned. "You're back," he brayed.

Star landed in front of him, and the two stared at each other. The starfire rumbled in Star's belly, and he prepared to project his shield should Nightwing attack him. He advanced on the ancient stallion, biting back his rage. "What are you doing with those walkers?" he asked.

Petalcloud and her Ice Warriors had forced six hundred walkers, mostly elderly pegasi but also dozens of disabled warriors and several dud foals, into a straight line. The dark stallion watched Star, his head cocked, his eyes curious. "I think you know or you wouldn't be here," said Nightwing. The nearest Wind Herd steeds had stopped grazing to watch the two black stallions meet on the plain.

Standing before the ancient Destroyer, Star felt young and inexperienced, and his long legs threatened to crumble beneath him. But he arched his neck like an over-stallion and pricked his ears, feigning confidence. "If you don't want them, set them free," he said.

Nightwing slit his eyes. "I won't do that."

"Then return them to the herd."

"They're duds, Star," hissed Nightwing. "You remember what that's like, don't you—being stuck on the ground like a horse. I can't protect them." He flattened his neck and panted, fanning his starfire.

"Then give them to me," said Star. "I'll protect them."

Nightwing pricked his ears, realizing Star was serious. "Why? They're useless." The walkers lowered their heads, seeming embarrassed by all the attention.

"Stand tall," Star whinnied to them. "It was Grasswing who ended the battle in Sky Meadow. He's a legend now, and he was also a walker. You're not useless, you're needed." Star turned back to Nightwing. "I want them and you don't. Does it matter why?"

Nightwing paused, his eyes narrowing. "Suppose I let them go, what do I get in return?" He glanced at Star's chest where he'd once pierced it with his silver fire, almost killing Star.

Star winced, remembering the pain of that attack, but he would not offer the Destroyer his life in exchange for the walking herd. "What do you want?" he asked, and then cringed. The Destroyer could ask for *anything*.

Nightwing's silver starfire crackled across his back and down through his hooves, sparking against the moist grass. He pranced, and Star saw the hatred glowing in his dark eyes, the telltale heaving of his sides.

Star threw up his shield.

Nightwing roared starfire at him.

The pegasi in the Flatlands spooked and bolted. The Ice Warriors tore after them, and Petalcloud whinnied commands.

Star braced, but the massive blast of silver light streamed around his golden orb. He spoke from inside his shield. "You can't kill me."

Nightwing threw back his head and poured starfire into the sky.

Star pricked his ears, waiting for the Destroyer to finish.

Then Nightwing turned on the walkers and took a huge breath.

"No!" Star leaped in front of Nightwing and kneeled, lowering his head like an under-stallion. "Tell me what you want!"

Nightwing pranced around him. The Wind Herd pegasi regrouped and stared, their wings limp. Star knew how it looked, like he was submitting to Nightwing, and he was, but not in his heart. Star hoped they could strike a bargain.

Nightwing's eyes snapped to Star's, and his expression changed from frustrated to triumphant. "I'll tell you what I want—a tribute! One that is greater than Spiderwing's nest in the Jungle Herd lands. One that will reach the clouds. One that cannot be destroyed by fire and that will stand for ages." He arched his neck around the idea, savoring it. "And I want *you* to build it for me."

Star rose from his knees. "I don't understand. How would I do this?"

"Build it on the top of that swell," said Nightwing, pointing to the eastern side of the valley at the highest ground. "There's a riverbed on the other side. It's full of large, flat stones. Pull out ten thousand and stack them as high as they'll go. I want my tribute visible from the ocean in the west to the ocean in the east."

Star's eyes rounded. "Ten thousand stones?"

Nightwing peered at the walkers who were gaping at Star. "Do it and I'll let them live."

Star squinted toward the riverbed. Spiderwing was the Destroyer's rival four hundred years ago, and the Jungle Herd pegasi had turned his nest into a monument to honor him. Now Nightwing wanted to be honored too, and since no one would do it, he would force Star, his *current* rival, to build it. Constructing a tribute to Nightwing would also serve to humiliate Star in front of the Wind Herd steeds, but it would save the walkers' lives. Then he glanced at the hill where the tribute would be built.

It would take many moons to complete. *But so would the tunnel.* Building the tribute would give his friends time to finish their project and begin smuggling pegasi to safety.

Finally Star spoke. "All right. I'll build it."

Nightwing folded his black wings and drew in his starfire. "I'm setting three conditions," he said. "No steed can help you, you cannot use your starfire for *any* reason, and you must live alone, in banishment."

The closest pegasi who were listening gasped. To them, banishment was a punishment worse than death.

Nightwing continued. "Every time you violate a condition, I'll kill a walker. If you fail to finish the tribute, I'll kill them all. When you're done, I'll let the walkers go, but until then they'll live with Wind Herd."

Inside Star, his resolve melted. Moving ten thousand stones, by himself? It was near impossible. But when Star turned his head and looked at the walkers, he saw their relief. "And what about him?" Star asked, nodding toward Frostfire.

Petalcloud interrupted with a huff. "Keep him or kill him. He's banished too."

Star heard Frostfire's short gasp of shock, and he felt sorry for the white stallion. Perhaps it was better to have no mother than an evil one.

Nightwing glanced at the hill. "Well, what are you waiting for? Get started."

The six hundred walkers dipped their heads gratefully to Star and then trotted back onto the grassland, guided by seven Ice Warriors. Star flew to the riverbed, dropped his wings into the water, and lifted out the first stone. Frostfire stayed close, still too shocked to speak.

Nightwing trumpeted his victory into the sky and then joined his massive herd on the Flatlands. Star noticed that he wouldn't let the pegasi fly higher than the trees—like they were all newborns. The herd returned to grazing, looking dejected. Star was building a tribute to Nightwing—and he understood how it appeared, like he was doing the opposite of fighting for them. Like he was giving up. But what the pegasi didn't know was that Hazelwind was near, and that he was a digging a tunnel to save them.

Star turned to the work ahead of him. The sun rose higher, and the heat awakened the bugs. He knew Echofrost would tell Morningleaf what he had done, and the reality of it was settling on him, more cloying than the heat.

He would be busy building this tribute for many

moons, and Nightwing would be watching him. When would he visit Morningleaf? He hadn't said good-bye to her or healed her wings. With his heart heavy and his wings already tiring, Star set down the first stone.

20

LETTING GO

MORNINGLEAF WOKE IN THE COOL DEPTHS OF the den. Brackentail had slipped into the chamber and fallen asleep next to her. His warm breath blew against her singed feathers, making them rise and fall. His ears twitched and his eyelids fluttered—he was dreaming.

She stretched, being careful not to wake him. The bright splotch of sunshine that streamed from the hole above her head indicated that it was near the middle of the day. They normally slept until dusk. What had awakened her? And where was Star?

The sound of whispering sifted gently through the silence, and she recognized the soft voices of Bumblewind and Dewberry. Morningleaf slipped out of the lair and crept through the center chamber where Hazelwind was sleeping. She followed the tunnel to the den's first chamber and entered, yawning.

Bumblewind glanced at her with startled eyes. "Why are you awake?"

"That's an odd question. I can be awake if I want." She peered at her two friends, who looked guilty. "Why? What's going on?"

They looked at each other, arguing with their eyes as they often did. Morningleaf realized Star was missing, and her belly twisted. "Where's Star and Frostfire?" Before they could answer, she knew where they'd gone. "They went to save the walkers, didn't they?"

"We couldn't stop them," said Dewberry.

Morningleaf's eyes burned, and her throat tightened. She stood for a moment, her wings trembling, and then she charged out of the den and galloped toward the blind that overlooked the valley.

"Morningleaf!" Dewberry grunted, and sped after her.

Morningleaf flattened her neck and galloped faster.

But Dewberry was older and stronger. She caught up to Morningleaf and snatched her tail in her teeth, tugging hard to stop her.

"Let go!" Morningleaf squealed, kicking Dewberry

in the chest. The mare released her, and Morningleaf resumed her gallop toward the blind.

Dewberry lifted off, flying just over her head. "Get back to the den," she snapped. "Now."

"No," whinnied Morningleaf. "I have to know what happened to Star."

"But it's daylight! It's not safe."

"I don't care."

Morningleaf reached the hiding place, out of breath, and skidded inside.

Dewberry followed and bit Morningleaf's mane, yanking out some hair.

Morningleaf whirled on her. "Why did you do that?"

Dewberry nipped Morningleaf again, hard, like an angry dam.

Morningleaf snapped her jaws, but Dewberry's dark eyes hardened to stone. "Don't try it, filly."

Morningleaf closed her mouth and rubbed the top of her neck with her wing, which throbbed from the bite. "What's your problem?"

"*You*," huffed Dewberry, pointing behind them. "You tore out of the den without scenting for wolves, without checking the sky, and without telling us where you were going. Are you trying to get us *all* killed, or just yourself?"

"But Star—"

Dewberry stamped her hoof. "Star left the den without telling you for a reason, Morningleaf. Did you consider that? He didn't want you to stop him or follow him."

"Why?" asked Morningleaf, trying to catch her breath.

"Because of stuff like this," said Dewberry. "When it comes to Star, you don't think about anyone else, or yourself." Dewberry folded her ruffled wings. "You take too many chances."

Morningleaf tossed back her flaxen mane. "What are you talking about?"

"I'm talking about *everything* you've done," rasped Dewberry. "Baiting armies, flying in jet streams, galloping through a wolf-infested forest by yourself. Do you expect Star to drop everything and save you?"

"Of course not," said Morningleaf, tears forming in her eyes.

Dewberry continued. "Did you ever stop to think that you're putting Star in danger too? He can't focus on Nightwing if he's got to run after you and save your life. It's why he left you behind. He's not the dud foal you grew up with,

Morningleaf. He can take care of himself."

Morningleaf exhaled as if the mare had kicked her.

Dewberry leaned toward her. "Let Star go so he can become who he is meant to be."

The two friends faced each other, panting, their eyes shining. Dewberry had said too much, pushed Morningleaf too far, but the fierce mare did not back down. Morningleaf's thoughts swirled madly, leaving her confused and sad. *Was she holding Star back?*

Dewberry softened. "You don't see him the way we do, but I wish you would. His love for you will destroy him one day, if you don't release him of it." She stroked Morningleaf's mane. "He'll throw us all away for you. Running off and putting yourself in danger will only distract him from his purpose, and it will probably get you killed. Let him go."

Morningleaf staggered toward the nearest tree and leaned against it. Her throat closed, and she couldn't breathe. She dropped her head and sucked at the hot air, drinking in bugs and dust and coughing terribly. Dewberry stood near, watching. Morningleaf's knees gave way, and she sank into the soil. She knew Dewberry was right, but her heart was breaking. "How?" she wheezed. "How could I do something like that?"

Dewberry sank down next to her. "I don't know how, but I know you must."

The two mares pressed their foreheads together. Morningleaf sobbed, feeling lost.

"Echofrost's dam told me your story when we were living in the Trap," said Dewberry. "That Silverlake forced your birth early so she'd have milk for Star, and that you tried to protect him from the mean foals like Brackentail. And I saw you take the deathblow that was meant for Star, and I watched him bring you back to life. You've lived *for* him and *through* him since your first breath of life, but you have to understand that maybe you have your own destiny."

Morningleaf squinted. "I take care of Star; that's what I've always done."

Dewberry shook her head. "And you've done it well, but he doesn't need you anymore."

Morningleaf took a deep, shuddering breath, and her wretched tears subsided. The two lay quietly in the shade for a long time.

Dewberry eventually stood. "Since we're here now, you might as well peek at the valley and see what happened to him."

Morningleaf sighed. "No. You look."

Dewberry peered out of the blind and then turned back to Morningleaf. "He's alive, and so is Frostfire."

"What about the walkers? Did Nightwing execute them?"

"Nope. They're fine. It appears Star and Nightwing have made an arrangement."

Morningleaf grit her teeth. "How so?"

"The walkers have been let go, and Star is . . . well, he's stacking rocks on a hill."

"That makes no sense."

Dewberry shrugged. "Nothing Star does makes sense to me. If I had that starfire . . ." Dewberry trailed off, her eyes bright with her imagined conquests. She blinked. "Anyway, Echofrost or Shadepebble will explain it to us later. Let's get back to the den before Hazelwind comes after us."

Before leaving the blind, they sniffed for wolves and checked the sky. When they were sure the way was clear, they returned to the den—but they returned to madness. Brackentail and Hazelwind were prancing in the first chamber, wild eyed and pawing the soil, their bodies shaking and their lungs wheezing.

"What happened?" asked Morningleaf.

Hazelwind trembled; his eyes were swollen with tears. "It's Bumblewind."

"What?" cried Dewberry.

"He's dead."

21

HONOR

MORNINGLEAF DID NOT BELIEVE HER EARS. SHE rushed to Bumblewind's side and pressed his body with her wings. "Bumblewind? Wake up!"

His large eyes were closed, and his jaws were parted. Morningleaf nuzzled him, trying to exchange breath, but his lips were cold. She rubbed his chest and pulled on his stiff legs. "Get up, Bumblewind. Please get up."

Dewberry reared, hitting her head on the den's ceiling. "It's my fault," she whinnied, her eyes rolling. "My fault." She kicked the walls, causing dirt to fall on their heads.

Hazelwind tackled her and tried to subdue her before she collapsed the den.

Morningleaf threw up her head and moaned.

Brackentail wrapped his wing gently over her mouth. "Shh," he said. "You'll draw the wolves." Morningleaf fell onto her side next to Bumblewind and pressed her nose into his stiff neck, crying silently.

Dewberry knelt by Bumblewind's head and whispered into his ear, "I left you. I'm sorry. I let you fall asleep." Her tears rolled down her cheeks and splattered the dirt floor.

Hazelwind soothed her. "This isn't your fault."

Dewberry tossed her mane, her agony causing her to twitch as though infested with bugs. She buried her head in her wings.

"No, it's my fault," cried Morningleaf. "I took Dewberry away from him."

"No, you're both wrong," said Hazelwind, his voice raw. "I heard you both leave, and I came to see what was going on, and Bumblewind was awake. I stood with him and we talked for a while, and then I noticed he'd closed his eyes. I immediately pressed on him and shook him; I even bit his ear as hard as I could. He just . . . slipped away. It couldn't be stopped."

The lair blurred, and Morningleaf wiped her eyes. "Let's take him to Star."

Dewberry shook her head sadly. "We can't. Nightwing is watching him."

Hazelwind rubbed his face in his wings and then looked at each of them. "She's right. Now listen, and please hear me. Bumblewind died in his sleep, without pain. He's safe in the golden meadow with the Ancestors. This is over for him." Hazelwind gazed at Bumblewind, who looked peaceful.

Fresh sobs wracked Morningleaf, Dewberry, and even Brackentail. Hazelwind curled to his knees, and the four of them soaked Bumblewind's coat in salty tears. After a long while they began whispering their favorite memories of him into his motionless ears.

Hours passed, and finally the talk subsided and the steeds rested with Bumblewind until the temperature cooled and they knew it was dark outside. The four friends stirred. It was time to bury Bumblewind.

Just then hoofbeats sounded outside the den. Shade-pebble, the Mountain Herd filly who spied for them along with Echofrost, poked her head into the crowded chamber. "The wolves are near," she whispered. The group squeezed aside to let her in. She saw Bumblewind's stiff body and froze. "Oh no."

Hazelwind grimaced. "Yes, he's gone. We need to return him to the soil, but we can't let Nightwing see the burial stones."

"We could put his body in the last chamber of our den and then collapse it," suggested Brackentail.

Shadepebble shuddered. "No. The wolves will dig him up."

Morningleaf gasped.

"I'm sorry," said Shadepebble, hugging her friend.

Hazelwind pawed the den floor. "We have to do something with him, and soon." He shed a few jade feathers, showing his stress.

"I have an idea," said Shadepebble. "Star is building a stone tribute for Nightwing."

"A tribute?" whinnied Hazelwind.

"Just listen," said the filly. "In exchange for the lives of the walkers, Nightwing is forcing Star to build a monument to him of ten thousand stones on the tallest hill."

"That will take many moons," cried Brackentail.

"Yes," she said. "But Star saved the walkers, for now anyway, and bought you time to complete your tunnel."

"But why would Nightwing want Star to build his tribute?" asked Brackentail. "He's Nightwing's rival."

Hazelwind knew the answer. "It's to make Star look weak in front of Wind Herd and to embarrass him." Hazelwind exhaled, looking tired. "It's not unprecedented. Rockwing once forced an enemy over-stallion to bury his own dead captains after Rockwing beat him in a battle. It was long ago. . . . He was a Snow Herd steed, I believe. After the over-stallion finished, Rockwing broke his wings. Then his warriors flew him up to the clouds and dropped him."

Morningleaf shuddered, imagining Star with broken wings.

"So what's your idea, Shadepebble?" asked Dewberry.

"If you want to give Bumblewind a stone burial and honor him—have Star bury him in the tribute."

Hazelwind sucked in his breath. "How are we honoring Bumblewind if we put him in Nightwing's tribute?"

"No, she's right," said Morningleaf, catching on to the idea. "It will make the tribute special to *us*, and it will encourage Star. He'll be building it for his friend, not for the Destroyer. It'll be our secret."

"And something Nightwing can't take from us," added Brackentail.

The five pegasi agreed, and Morningleaf's broken heart stumbled back to life. Bumblewind's death would mean something.

"Now comes the hard part," said Shadepebble. "Getting Bumblewind to Star."

"Brackentail and I will carry him," said Hazelwind.

"Shadepebble, you'll need to give the news to his twin since you're in the same group. But wait until tomorrow and tell Echofrost on the open plain. The crashing winds will dry her tears and deafen her cries. Nightwing can't know anything is amiss. Understand?"

Shadepebble nodded and slipped out of the den, rising into the sky, flying through the trees and heading back toward the valley. She would land at a rendezvous point where Graystone, the sympathetic Ice Warrior, would meet her and walk her back to her group. The risks of her friends' comings and goings terrified Morningleaf, but she was glad Shadepebble had brought them news of Star.

Hazelwind turned to Morningleaf and Dewberry. "All right, we'll be back as fast as we can."

Morningleaf and Dewberry whispered their good-byes to Bumblewind, while Hazelwind and Brackentail tugged on the pinto's wings and slid him out of the den. They were careful, brushing away the dirt that lodged in his feathers. Once out, they lifted him by the roots of his wings and carried him away.

When he was gone, Dewberry dissolved, her body quaking with sobs. She'd teased Bumblewind without mercy when he was alive, but the two were almost always together, and suddenly Dewberry seemed half a pegasus without him. Morningleaf's throat tightened. Bumblewind's twin sister, Echofrost, would also be a half without him.

Dewberry kneeled and rolled on the spot where Bumblewind had died. "You were the best of us," she said, her voice cracking. She sniffed the soil and the loose feathers that remained, and then closed her eyes.

Morningleaf rested near her, saying nothing, and they waited for the stallions to return.

22

THE SECRET GRAVE

THE DAY PASSED SLOWLY AS STAR WORKED AT building the tribute. Clouds covered the moon, darkening the riverbed, and Star could no longer distinguish one stone from another. He'd moved nineteen huge rocks to the monument today, his first day. *Nineteen of ten thousand.* Star felt defeated and silly for agreeing to build it. Frostfire kept him company, but the strong stallion wasn't allowed to help.

It was early evening now, and Frostfire glanced at the large stones Star had carried. "You should rest."

Star wasn't tired, but his wing and back muscles throbbed. It was difficult to locate the flattest stones underwater and then to pull them out of the river. They were often half buried under heavier rocks and mud, and the riverbank was slippery. He sometimes fell and then watched in frustration as his stone tumbled back into the water.

Once he was soundly on the shore, Star cradled the stones in his wings and carried them up the hill. It took time also to place the rocks correctly. Nightwing's tribute would topple if not well built, but Frostfire had buried enough warriors in stones to give Star tips on how to construct the base. It would have to be substantial to support the expected height of the monument. Frostfire advised using the red clay in the river to help stick the rocks together, and so Star slathered it between the stones with his wingtips. But this extra step, while important, also slowed him down.

Star followed Frostfire down the side of the hill, and they grazed on oat grass as the sun dropped in the west.

"Your feathers are frayed," said the white stallion.

"I know." Star folded his wings across his back. He'd noticed the damage, but he couldn't use his power to heal himself. If he tried, Nightwing would execute a walker.

Frostfire glanced at the sky, and Star followed his gaze. The Ice Warriors patrolled Wind Herd, flying in lazy circles. Star heard splashing and looked toward the pond.

"There are the weanlings," he said. Nightwing, Petalcloud, and the young pegasus steeds swam in the pond nestled at the southern end of the valley, splashing each other and then floating like ducks.

The weanlings' mothers stood in the distance, guarded by Ice Warriors and forbidden to be with their foals. The mares twitched anxiously, molting feathers all over the trampled valley terrain. When one mother bleated to her youngster, an Ice Warrior kicked her hard in the flank. Petalcloud ignored the plight of the mares, but it was clear she adored the weanlings. "A good lead mare doesn't separate foals from their dams," said Star.

Frostfire watched his mother play with the weanlings, his entire body tense. "I can't let that happen to Larksong. If Petalcloud takes away our foal, I'll kill her."

Star jerked his head toward Frostfire, studying the white steed, whose mismatched eyes were rooted on his mother. The stallion's expression was twisted with confusion. Star knew the story; that Petalcloud had lied to Frostfire when he was a weanling and then sent him to live with her sire, Rockwing, trading him for her freedom. Rockwing had sired eighteen dead colts and two live fillies. He wanted a breathing colt so intensely that he was willing to take his daughter's. But when he got Frostfire, he bullied him into the army, pushing and training him to the limits of his endurance. And now Frostfire faced the possibility that his mother might take his coming foal and keep the newborn for herself.

Petalcloud and Nightwing walked out of the pond, followed by the youngsters. They shook, tossing water droplets off their hides, and then lifted off on a short flight to dry their wings. The foals bleated happily, gliding across a pink sunset sky. Their mothers watched in helpless fear. When they'd all landed back on the grass, Petalcloud wrapped her wings around her belly and nuzzled Nightwing. Frostfire gasped and staggered into Star.

"What is it?" Star asked.

"Petalcloud is pregnant," he said. "With Nightwing's foal, I think."

Star's heart thudded at Frostfire's words, and he thought back, remembering how plump Petalcloud had appeared when he first saw her in the valley. Nightwing pranced next to Petalcloud, and the ancient stallion glowed with pride. Understanding clunked into place, quick and simple. "This is what he wants," whispered Star. "What he's always wanted."

"What?" asked Frostfire.

"A family." Star turned away as sudden tears sprang

to his eyes. He blinked rapidly, controlling himself but feeling desolate.

"How do you know?"

"I just do," said Star. But he was certain, because he recognized Nightwing's need in himself. Star wanted it too: a family of his own. He'd lost everything when his mother died. And now he was immortal, different from everyone else, but he just wanted to be a regular pegasus stallion. Maybe so did Nightwing.

The difference between them was that Nightwing wanted it badly enough to kill for it, while Star—he'd accepted his fate. Still, he thought he understood now what was happening. Nightwing was stealing foals to create a new herd, one that respected him. Star peered at the pregnant Wind Herd mares, which included Frostfire's mate, Larksong. Once Nightwing had enough steeds to start a new life, what would he do with the adults? Star shivered. All of Wind Herd was in great danger, more than they knew.

"Morningleaf must dig that tunnel quickly," Star said, his panic rising. Just then a small pebble bounced off Star's forehead. He looked up, but the darkening sky was empty. The patrol had moved on. Another pebble stung his neck. He turned in a slow circle. Frostfire became alert, noticing Star's flexed muscles.

"Someone's trying to get our attention," Star whispered. He lowered his neck and crept toward the direction of the flying rocks, with Frostfire following him. He crested the hill and walked down the back side, which was hidden from the valley. Two pegasi stood in the shadow of a small cottonwood tree. Star recognized Hazelwind's wide blaze. Brackentail stood beside him. Star signaled to Frostfire to remain silent. "What are you two doing here?" Star whispered.

Hazelwind glanced down at a steed lying at his hooves.

Star followed his gaze and recognized Bumblewind stretched on the grass, but something wasn't right. Star dropped his nose toward his friend and touched his shoulder, which was as cold as snow. Sadness drove him to his knees. "It can't be."

"I'm sorry," said Hazelwind, and his grief emanated from him in waves, like summer heat.

Star's soul groaned, and his throat closed. "He—he's been gone too long. I can't save him."

"We're not here for that," said Hazelwind, touching Star's shoulder.

Star looked up at Hazelwind. "Then why have you come?"

"To bury him," said Hazelwind, and he explained their idea of hiding Bumblewind in the tribute.

At first Star balked. The idea seemed backward and wrong, but as the thought sank deeper into his brain, he understood the gesture. He would be building the monument for Bumblewind, not for Nightwing. And this knowledge would give Star the strength he needed to finish it. Each and every stone would mark his love for his friend. "Leave him with me," said Star, agreeing. "As the tribute rises, it will stand for Bumblewind, and our freedom. Our future freedom."

Hazelwind and Brackentail nodded, looking relieved.

Star drew closer to Hazelwind. "Petalcloud is with foal."

Hazelwind pinned his ears. "I wondered. I saw signs . . . ," he said, trailing off.

Star continued. "Nightwing is creating a new herd out of the stolen weanlings, and I think he'll take the coming foals too. He's just using the Wind Herd steeds, but eventually he won't need them anymore. Do you understand? You must work faster."

Hazelwind arched his neck. "I understand. We'll increase our shifts." He and Brackentail retreated, skirting the back side of the hill, remaining low and hidden from the valley as they returned to the den.

Star and Frostfire stared at each other, thinking.

"I want Larksong and our colt to be the first ones out of that valley when the tunnel is finished," said Frostfire.

"That's a long ways off," said Star, distracted. "Look, we need to bury Bumblewind by morning. You might have to help me."

Frostfire nudged Star hard with his chest. "Not until I know you've heard me. I helped you find your friends because I need your help rescuing Larksong. Don't forget what you promised me, Star. She gets out first."

"Yes, I remember," said Star. "I'll save your mare."

"And my colt."

"And your colt." Star sighed. He could promise Frostfire the moon too, but right now he didn't know how he was going to rescue anybody.

The two stallions waited until the final glow of evening had faded and it was true night. Then Star turned to Frostfire. "Help me lift Bumblewind."

They carried the pinto's cold body up the hill. Star broke apart the stones he'd spent all day placing and mudding together, and then he dug a shallow grave.

When it was ready, the two stallions stood over the body, and Star spoke. "Bumblewind, colt of Stormfire and

Crystalfeather, lover of milk and friend of all friends, you will be missed. You may have died in a den of wolves, but you have risen to the golden meadow, where you will always be free." Star took a ragged breath. "Fly straight and find your rest."

"Fly straight and find your rest," repeated Frostfire.

Star placed Bumblewind in the depression on the hill. His stiff body had already softened into death, and Star was able to shape him as though he were sleeping, curling his head toward his hooves and wrapping his black tail toward his nose. Star scrubbed away the loose dirt that marred Bumblewind's white-splotched hide. He tucked errant feathers into place and then dropped his muzzle to Bumblewind's one last time, as though they were exchanging breath. His tears dripped, and white flowers grew between his friend's hooves. "Good-bye," he whispered.

Star spent the rest of the evening in toiled frenzy, diving into the river and feeling for appropriate rocks, trotting them up the hill, and slathering them in clay. Bumblewind's body had to be completely hidden before sunrise.

Since it was dark, Frostfire helped Star. If they were caught, a walker would be killed, but Star needed assistance. His heart pounded throughout the night, and he shed black feathers all over the hillside.

When the first sunrays broke the horizon, Star sat on his haunches. His wings slung to his sides and his hide was white with froth, but he'd done it. Bumblewind was buried.

"I saved this," said Frostfire. He held up a long, brown-tipped golden flight feather.

Star took the feather, holding it gently in his wing. He stared at it and then at the secret grave. Building the tribute for Bumblewind was a small victory, but it was *their* small victory. Star climbed out of his mad tangle of anger and hurt, and lifted the feather over his head, letting his heart lift with it. "For Bumblewind," he said.

"For Bumblewind," Frostfire repeated.

23

STEALTH

AFTER BUMBLEWIND'S BURIAL, THE DAYS marched past, each the same as the last. Star settled into a pattern of moving stones from the river to the monument while his friends in the forest dug the tunnel.

Summer brought warm rains and belly-high grass. Star toiled in the middle of the day because the burning sun best illuminated the underwater stones. Next came autumn, which was hotter but drier. The tree leaves exploded with color and then drifted off the branches like molting feathers. Star's hooves wore down the fading grass, creating many paths from the river to the hill. Frostfire stayed close to him, but the two spoke little. The magnitude of Star's task became more obvious each day.

After three full cycles of the moon, he was still constructing the base of the tribute.

Winter began with a gentle snowfall that floated from the clouds in fat, soft flakes and flecked the trees. But this mild beginning was a trick, because the wispy snow did not stop falling, nor did it melt. The gray clouds that rolled in had come to stay, and they blocked out the sun. Soon the delicious grasses were covered in deep snow, a vague memory. Buffalo, land horses, moose, and other antlered creatures pressed closer, digging at the buried foliage with their hooves, their hunger consuming their shyness. And the dire wolves grew bolder.

Star and Frostfire spent the cold nights curled in their separate snow shelters, but Frostfire often inched closer, attracted to the heat that radiated off Star's hide. Often, by morning, he was snoring in Star's ear. Star rarely slept, watching instead for predators.

This particular winter morning, Star yawned as the rising sun turned the sky from soft black to pale orange. It had snowed again, and the fresh white crystals padded the world, making it feel smaller and quieter. Overnight, the clouds had drifted apart, allowing a rare glimpse of sunshine. Star and Frostfire slept on the eastern side of the swells, out of sight of Wind Herd, but if Star listened carefully, he could hear the soft snorts and muffled hoof-beats of the pegasi in the valley.

The herd had also settled into a familiar pattern. They marched onto the Flatlands each morning and returned to the valley each night. Black pillars of smoke rose each time a steed disobeyed, but those pillars were becoming fewer, especially since the last escape attempt. A group of young stallions and mares, all from Desert Herd, had flown off and raced for the jet streams, hoping to blast away before Nightwing could stop them.

Star shook his head, hating the memory of what had happened next—the silver fire, the rain of ashes, the screams. They had been free, but only for a moment, and now they were just . . . gone.

Star thought often of Morningleaf. He hadn't seen her since summer, and he missed her and Brackentail and Hazelwind. He missed Bumblewind too. Frostfire had saved the pinto's long flight feather. They kept it tucked in the tribute, out of sight, but Star often pulled it out at night and sniffed it, remembering his friend. Bumblewind had always treated Star like a regular pegasus, but he'd also accepted that Star wasn't a regular pegasus. The rest of his friends, even Morningleaf, focused too much on his black hide and his golden starfire. But beneath it all, Star was just like Bumblewind: a young stallion who wanted to play, learn to fight, and sleep at night without regrets. But those days were over, and not just for Bumblewind. Today was Star's birthday. He was two years old, an adult stallion.

It was Morningleaf's birthday too. They'd been born on the same night, a full moon earlier than the rest of the Sun Herd foals. Star wanted to visit her, but Petalcloud's Ice Warriors, led by the big gray named Stormtail, flew the sky day and night, watching for deserters and trouble-makers. Star's black coat contrasted with the snow and the gray sky, making him stand out wherever he went. He dared not use his starfire to turn invisible, but his thoughts traveled to the den each night, just before sleep.

Star shook off his gloom and stood, rousing Frostfire. The stallion stretched and peered at the sky. "Today is the shortest day of winter," Frostfire said.

"I know. It's my birthday."

"You're a yearling no longer!" whinnied Frostfire.

Star couldn't believe twelve moons had passed since he'd received his starfire, and twenty-four moons had passed since he was born. "I'm an adult."

Frostfire snorted. "Every two-year-old thinks that. Talk to me about being an adult when you're ten."

Star nickered. "I would be finishing flight school right now."

"Yes. And then training for the army."

Star swung his thick forelock out of his eyes. "I don't think I would have chosen the army. Maybe I'd be a scout."

Frostfire played along with Star's imaginings, but they both knew that this idea of a normal life was impossible for the black foal of Anok. "You're too large to be a scout," said Frostfire, looking him up and down.

Star nickered. "But I can disappear." Just saying the word caused Star to blink out and turn invisible, startling Frostfire.

"Come back," the stallion warned.

Star hadn't meant to do it, but in a streak of rebellion, he took advantage of it. He scooped a hunk of snow and lobbed it at Frostfire, hitting him on the rump.

Frostfire whirled. "Not fair, Star."

The sun rose higher, casting shadows. Frostfire flicked the snow off his rear with his tail, scooped up a wingful of snow, and tossed it where he'd last seen Star. He missed.

Suddenly, Star heard wingbeats behind him and turned, his heart racing at unexpected company. Nightwing soared over the tribute and landed next to Frostfire. *No*, he thought. *Nightwing must have felt me use my power.*

Star cringed but remained invisible, dreading what was coming next.

"Where's Star?" Nightwing asked.

Star froze, holding his breath. He was standing just a winglength away from Nightwing. How did the Destroyer not feel him or sense him? Star waited and watched.

Frostfire knew how close Star was, and his pulse throbbed in his neck, but he smoothed his expression and lied. "Star is at the river."

Nightwing nodded, looking right past Star. Was Nightwing pretending to be unaware of him, or could he really not sense him? Star still wasn't sure, and he dared not move.

Nightwing turned and flew up the hill to inspect the tribute. "When will the base be finished?" he asked.

Frostfire leaped at the chance to distract Nightwing. He flew to the black stallion and toured him around the massive stone base, which so far consisted of more than four thousand river rocks. "By spring the base will be finished," said Frostfire, "and then the tower will rise much faster." He led Nightwing to the other side of the tribute, gesturing with his wings and explaining the construction.

When they were out of sight, Star lifted off and flew quickly to the river. He landed on the shore and then reappeared, listening intently and ignoring his surrounding.

He heard Nightwing's voice. "Take me to Star."

Star relaxed. Nightwing had not been pretending. He really hadn't sensed Star, and now Star was at the river where he was supposed to be, so Nightwing couldn't get angry and kill a walker. As Star contemplated this, he became aware of heavy breathing behind him and then a quick, sharp growl.

He sprang into the sky just as sharp claws raked down his flank and became entangled in his tail, yanking Star down onto the icy mud. He smelled wolf, and then one landed on his head. The long claws cut his flesh, and sharp fangs pierced his neck. Two more wolves ripped at his wings, and one pounced on his flank, latching his jaws into the meat of his leg. Star kicked wildly, his vision blurred.

They dragged him through the snow.

Star bit into a wolf's paw. The wolf snarled and snapped at him, biting his muzzle. Star squealed, the pain as hot as blood, but the wolf let go.

The others pulled harder, sliding him down the muddy shore and into the river. Star's blood streamed, mixing with the water.

A black wolf clamped his jaws on Star's neck and shook him hard, shoving his head under the water. Star's jaw smacked against the rocks at the river bottom. He twisted as another wolf bit into his neck and yet another snatched his tail and yanked on it.

Star dug his hooves into the mud and pushed himself up, flinging the wolf off his neck. It splashed into the water. Star spun in a circle. He was surrounded.

Then a giant white she-wolf, the one whose attack had killed Bumblewind, launched out of the water and onto Star's back. Her claws dug into him; her snarls filled his ears. She crawled up his neck, her jaws snapping.

He bucked and spread his wings, but her pack mates snatched his feathers and held him down. Star blinked and saw the she-wolf's huge white fangs driving toward his throat—a killing bite.

Star clenched his muscles and let his starfire explode. But instead of fire, out came noise—a loud, blaring alarm that rose from his throat—and bright flashes of gold light sprang from his eyes and hooves.

The wolves whined and blinked rapidly, letting go of him. The alarm pulsed in a steady rhythm, and the pack shrank farther away from him, their tails tucked between their legs.

Star faced them, bleeding in a dark gush. The wolves licked their muzzles and paced, wanting more of him. He heard the whoosh of wings and turned to see who was coming. The wolves leaped at him again. Star ejected more golden light and loud noise, a supernatural scream of alarm, and the wolves backed off, whimpering in frustration. Nightwing and Frostfire crested the hill, and the wolves saw them and then galloped away.

Star crawled to shore and flopped on its slick bank, gasping for air. Far away in the valley, he heard the concerned whinnies of the Wind Herd pegasi, who must have heard the awful alarm.

Nightwing and Frostfire glided to Star's side and landed. Frostfire saw the bites. "Dire wolves?" he asked, his eyes scanning the woods.

Star nodded, his sides heaving.

Nightwing's nostrils widened, drinking in the scent of Star's blood. He pranced with excitement, and his hooves turned silver. Star lurched upright and leaned into Frostfire, ready to protect them both if Nightwing attacked.

"You used your power," said the ancient black stallion.

Star froze, wondering if he was referring to the invisibility or to the noise.

"You look surprised," continued Nightwing. "You didn't

know you had an alarm, did you?"

"I didn't," admitted Star. "It just came out of me."

Nightwing huffed. "Your golden starfire is weak, Star. It's for healing—it's not for killing, yet you continue to rely on it. Why scare the wolves off with an alarm when you could have killed them?"

Star met the Destroyer's gaze. What answer could he give that Nightwing would understand? None.

Nightwing snorted at him and lifted off the shore. "I want my tribute finished. Heal your wounds and get back to work." He hovered a moment, shaking his head in disgust. "And the next time you're attacked by wolves, don't let them get away. They stalk my foals, you know. You couldn't protect a herd if you had one, Star. You can barely protect yourself." Nightwing took off and flew back to the valley.

Star dragged himself out of the water and collapsed with a groan, his red blood vibrant against the white snow. "Hurry," Frostfire urged him. "Or you might bleed out."

Star closed his eyes and sent his golden healing fire through his injured body. He was out of practice, but he knew to heal his worst wounds first, then the bruises and the scrapes from the claws. When he was finished, he stood.

Frostfire whistled. "That's amazing."

Star stood with his wings dragging and his head low. "Yeah, but he's right. An over-stallion, or *any* stallion, would have killed the wolves so they wouldn't turn and hunt the herd. I only protected myself, and not very well."

Frostfire pinned his ears. "So what? They weren't threatening anyone else. I'm not wrong about you, Star, and that wolf attack brought out a new power."

Star folded his wings. "Yes, and did you notice that Nightwing couldn't sense my presence when I was invisible?"

"I did," said Frostfire. "But how is that possible? Don't you and he have the same powers?"

"We do, but now I know that the invisibility power goes beyond mere disappearance," said Star. "It's . . . how do I explain? It's like an *inversion* of power, not a projection. The shield and the alarm and the healing light—they blast out of me—but this power closes around me. It hides me *completely*—and Nightwing can't feel it. It's . . . privacy, I guess. And you saw how well it worked."

"So Nightwing can use it too?"

"I'm sure he can, but why would he? He's got no reason to hide." Star's eyes brightened. "But I do."

"That's good news, Star—you can walk among the

pegasi now, the ultimate spy." Frostfire glanced at the sky where the Hundred Year Star had transferred its power to Star exactly one year earlier. "Happy birthday."

Star glanced at the forest in the south, toward the den. "And now I can visit my friends."

24

THE VISIT

STAR DECIDED TO VISIT THE DEN THAT VERY EVE-
ning. "You keep watch while I'm gone," he said to Frostfire.
"But we'll need a signal in case Nightwing comes and I
need to return quickly."

"What sort of signal?"

"The call of a hawk will work well."

Frostfire snorted. "Do I look like a hawk?"

Star explained. "When I was in the Trap, the Desert
Herd captain named Redfire taught my army how to imi-
tate bird calls. Just think about how a hawk screeches
and copy it. It's like whistling."

Redfire's system of animal calls was complicated, but
Star and Frostfire had simpler needs than an army. They

required one sound, one alarm that would call Star back, and they spent the afternoon perfecting it while Star worked on the tribute.

Star repeated the same steps over and over again. He crushed the thin river ice with his hooves, sorted through the rocks until he found a flat one, loosened it from the cold mud, and dragged it out of the river. Then he carried it up the hill to the tribute, leaning forward with the stone cradled in his wings. The base was taller than his shoulders now and it spread across the entire top of the hill, consisting of over four thousand river rocks, but it wasn't finished. The base needed one more full layer, according to Frostfire, before Star could build it higher.

Star lifted the stone over his head and then set it in place. He flew to the river for clay, returned, and wiped the clay around the new rock. Frostfire followed him, making horrible sounds, none of which sounded like a hawk. "More like a whistle," Star reminded him.

Star returned to the river. He'd worked his way farther and farther east of the hill because he didn't want to strip the riverbed of rocks completely. As he kept moving upstream—farther away from the tribute—each trip took longer. Soon he would be harvesting rocks from miles away.

Frostfire watched Star lift the stone as high as he could and set it down. "How are you going to build this thing once it's taller than you?" he asked.

Star had wondered the same, but he had an idea. "I'll ask Morningleaf to weave me a basket."

"She doesn't know how," said Frostfire. "That's a Mountain Herd secret."

Star explained to Frostfire how Morningleaf had taught herself to weave by taking apart a basket in the Trap, while the herds were living together. Star marveled at the things his friends had learned from the other herds: weaving, animal calls, rock throwing, riding jet streams, sky herding, and egg hunting.

The herd of Star's birth had lived in a territory that had a mild climate and plentiful grass and water. Because of the rich grasslands there, the Sun Herd army was the largest in Anok when Star was born. The other four herds faced harsh challenges from stronger enemies, vicious predators, long droughts, and voracious overgrazing, but Star now understood how their challenges made them smarter, more inventive.

Frostfire halted and screeched, sounding somewhat like a hawk.

"I think that's good enough for our purposes," said

Star. "As soon as it's dark, I'll go."

Star finished his work at dusk and pranced next to Frostfire, waiting for the orange glow of the sunset to fade.

"What if I call and you don't hear me?" asked Frostfire.

Star tensed, hoping Frostfire wouldn't try to change his mind about the visit. "If someone comes and I don't hear your call, just say I've gone for a flight. Nightwing didn't say I couldn't fly. But you can't stop me from seeing my friends tonight."

Frostfire pricked his ears. "I'm not trying to."

The two waited in silence for the sky to blacken, in case a patrolling Ice Warrior flew overhead. The heavy cloud layer blocked the moon and stars, and when the last trace of light vanished, Star unfurled his wings. "I'll return in time for you to get some sleep."

Frostfire nickered. "Don't worry about me."

Star kicked off, turned invisible, and flew southwest, toward the woods and the den, his heart soaring. He glided over the snow-flecked cottonwood forest, his sharp eyes looking for landmarks. When he spotted the tallest elm, he knew he was close. He landed and trotted to the low ridge and fallen tree that hid the den. He hoped his friends were inside and hadn't traveled yet to work on the tunnel.

He swept aside the dried branches and ducked into the first chamber. It was empty, but still warm. He'd just missed his friends. Star checked the second two chambers; each was empty of pegasi, but not empty of their presence. Feathers littered the packed soil, and pretty stones were piled against a wall.

Star cocked his head, eyeing the stones. They were stacked exactly like his monument. His friends were making a miniature replica of the tribute! They'd also saved a feather from Bumblewind, and it was tucked into the stones, standing upright. His friends hadn't forgotten him; they were keeping track of his progress. It was a good sign, a hopeful sign. He guessed it was Echofrost who'd built this replica when she visited the den so that Morningleaf and the others could see what Star was doing, and also to remember her twin brother.

Star exited the den and made himself invisible again. He flew toward the blind that hid the tunnel and landed when he finally found it. It was difficult to spot because it blended so well with the forest.

Star entered and dropped his invisibility, shocking Hazelwind and Dewberry, who were just popping out of the tunnel. Hazelwind reeled backward, blinking hard. "Star? How did you do that?"

"It's a new power." Star disappeared again to show them.

"That's incredible," said Hazelwind. "But won't Nightwing track you here if you use your power?"

Star reappeared. "No. He can't sense this one. It's pure stealth, as Frostfire calls it."

"How is the captain?" asked Hazelwind. "Causing you any trouble?"

Star shook his head. "No, he's been helpful." Star paused.

"What is it?" asked Hazelwind, suddenly alert.

"Probably nothing," said Star. "Frostfire's nervous about his coming colt. He's asked me to make sure that Larksong and his son are the first two out of the valley when the tunnel is finished."

Hazelwind flexed his wings, thinking. "Well, it all depends," he said. "I'm not opposed to it, but I don't want to make any promises."

Star stared at the soil.

"Did you . . . make him a promise?"

"I think so," said Star, trying to remember the conversation. "Frostfire brought me here to help him save his family. We have an agreement."

Hazelwind met Star's eyes. "Then I will honor it, if I can."

"Thank you."

"We heard a terrible noise today," interjected Dewberry, "and we saw bright flashes of light."

Star nodded. "I was attacked by dire wolves at the river, and I discovered another power, which is that noise you heard. It scared the wolves away from me." Star peered at the dark hole in the ground. "How's the tunnel coming along?"

Hazelwind answered. "It's slow going. We work every night, but I feel like we're getting nowhere fast."

"I know how that feels," said Star, thinking of the tribute.

"Morningleaf and Brackentail are hiding dirt, but they'll return soon. Go on inside the tunnel and see it for yourself."

Star ducked his head and entered. The dank smell of worms and mulch reminded him of the wolf den. The passageway angled downward, toward the valley far away. Star walked for what seemed a long time in the blackness, and then he reached the end.

Hazelwind's voice drifted to him from the surface.

"The dirt is packed tighter the deeper we go, but there are fewer tree roots, so we're leveling off and digging straight. I hope this speeds things up."

Star twisted his head around and squeezed his body into a turn so he could walk back to the surface. He emerged from the tunnel to see that Morningleaf and Brackentail had still not returned.

Hazelwind read his expression. "They have to travel farther and farther away to hide the dirt."

Dewberry swiveled her ears, listening. "But they should be back by now."

That was all Star needed to hear. "I'll go look for them." Without waiting for a response, Star blinked out and trotted into the forest, completely invisible.

"I wish I could do that," nickered Dewberry.

Star kicked off and glided over the treetops, eyes down since he knew the pair wouldn't be flying. A snowfall began, light and fluffy, and excitement reared in his chest—he missed Morningleaf and he would see her soon. Star spotted two dark shapes walking beneath the cottonwoods, and their whispering voices drifted up to Star. He dropped closer and hovered over them, about to interrupt.

"Why are you walking so slow?" Brackentail asked Morningleaf.

She trekked ahead of the young brown stallion, placing her hooves carefully so as not to slip on the frozen ground, but at Brackentail's words she swished her long tail across his face. "So I don't lose you," she answered.

Brackentail nudged her flank. "You couldn't lose me if you tried."

Star grimaced, hating that their friendship irritated him so much.

Morningleaf's carefree expression evaporated. "Right, of course. I couldn't lose a one-winged butterfly." She ruffled her ruined feathers, shaking off the fresh snowflakes.

Brackentail halted. "I didn't mean it like that."

She halted too. "I know you didn't. But I can't fly . . . and when this is all over . . . you'd be wise to forget about me." She turned and walked on, her breath drifting toward Star like smoke, and he felt awkward. He should have announced himself right away.

Brackentail cocked his head. "Don't do that," he said to Morningleaf. "Don't shove me off."

She exhaled. "I'm sorry. It's just . . . I know Hazelwind ordered you to protect me, and I appreciate it, but I don't need the extra . . . help."

"He didn't," rasped Brackentail. "Is that what you think?"

"Yes."

Brackentail flinched, and Star saw the hurt in his golden eyes. "If you don't want me here, I'll go. I'm not under orders to do anything except hide dirt. Tell me what you want and I'll do it."

Morningleaf faced him, blinking as though waking from a bad dream. "Hazelwind really didn't ask you to watch me?"

"The only steed who ever asked me to watch over you is Star, and it was a request, not an order."

"He did?" Morningleaf's eyes softened. "When?"

"It was before he took off to save the walkers. But it doesn't matter—that's not why I'm here either." He stepped closer to her, then halted, his body tense. "I follow you because I want to. It's my choice."

Star jolted as if struck, and he soared higher, away from them. He should go, but he couldn't look away.

Morningleaf trembled softly and lowered her muzzle to Brackentail's.

Brackentail inched closer, then slid on the ice, falling at her hooves.

Morningleaf stifled a loud nicker and helped him up.

Brackentail wiped the frost off his knees with his wings. "Anyway, if a wolf comes, I'm counting on *you* to protect *me*."

Morningleaf pricked her ears. "Is that so?"

"Yep, it's why I stay behind you. I'm hiding."

Star watched Morningleaf's amber eyes flicker and her jaw relax as she resumed walking.

Brackentail trailed her, looking pleased. "You know what today is, right?" he asked her.

Morningleaf exhaled. "Of course I do; it's Star's birthday."

Brackentail snorted. "It's *your* birthday too."

She halted again, and Brackentail almost bumped into her. Star, who was hovering a tree length above them, accidentally struck a branch with his wing, making it whip back and forth. Morningleaf's head snapped upward and she stared right at him, but through him. "I heard something," she said to Brackentail. "We better hurry back."

Star watched his two friends trot away, his thoughts tumbling. Even though he'd accepted Brackentail, Star's original dislike for the brown steed returned in full force, shocking him. He was over the past, wasn't he?

Star shook his head. *No, he wasn't over it.*

And now, like daylight, it was clear to him. Star had never been angry at Brackentail for calling him a horse or harassing him when they were foals—that was not at the root of it. Star's dislike of Brackentail had been because he'd tried to keep Star and Morningleaf apart when they were young. Star thought it was because the brown colt had feared him, but it was because he was in love with Morningleaf, had *always* been in love with her.

Star faltered, dipping toward land. How had he lied to himself for so long? And why did he care? He and Morningleaf were just friends. No—not just friends—they were *best* friends.

Star wheezed, trying to breathe, and his chest tightened, hurting him. This must be how Nightwing felt about him—*threatened*.

It made Star want to rip Brackentail's wings off his body.

But he liked Brackentail. And Brackentail liked him.

Star flew faster, swiping at his thoughts, trying to untangle them, but new understanding slammed him. Morningleaf was two years old tonight. Someday she might want foals, and someday she might choose a stallion. Things between her and Star would never be the same. She was mortal and so was Brackentail—they would grow old, and he would not. They would die, and he would not. It struck him that he and Morningleaf could not—would not—be best friends *forever*.

Star gulped, overwhelmed. He shed invisible feathers, turned, and fled. He would not let Morningleaf see him this way.

He left the forest and returned to the swells, sick and confused, and feeling exactly as he had when Silverlake had hid him on the coast as a weanling and left him on his own—alone. *No*. Abandoned.

25

STARFROST

STAR COASTED ACROSS THE FOOTHILLS, RETURN-
ing to Frostfire, and landed beside the white stallion. "I'm
back," he muttered.

Frostfire heard him but couldn't see him. "I don't like
talking to you when you're invisible, Star."

"Sorry." He retracted his power.

His uncle studied him. "Why don't you look happy,
Star? What's wrong? Is it the tunnel?"

Star plunked onto his haunches in the snow, mentally
exhausted by his visit. He glanced up the hill to the tribute. "No, I think they've made more progress than I have."

"So what's wrong with you then? You were as excited
as a spring filly before you left."

Star shrugged his wings. He didn't want to explain what was wrong with him.

Frostfire pawed the snow, crunching it under his hoof. "All right, don't tell me."

"Was it quiet here?" Star asked, glancing at the heavy layer of clouds.

Frostfire's eyes shifted quickly toward the valley, but he didn't answer. That's when Star noticed the hoofprints. They were small and didn't belong to him or Frostfire. "You had a visitor," Star said, pointing at the prints.

"It was Larksong," the stallion admitted.

Star bristled. "We're banished, Frostfire. We aren't allowed visitors."

The white stallion erupted. "You saw *your* friends!"

"That's different. I—" Star stopped. It wasn't different. He'd also taken a risk. "What did she say? Does she have news from the valley?"

"Yes, she's afraid for our foal, for all the coming foals. She thinks Nightwing and Petalcloud will steal them." The stallion paced, his anxiety building.

"Look," said Star, stopping Frostfire with his wings. "They might take the newborns when they come, I don't disagree, but they can't do it until they're fully weaned. By then the tunnel will be finished, and I spoke to Hazelwind tonight. Larksong will be the first steed out."

"He said that?"

"He did."

"What if he was lying?"

Star jerked up his head. "He wouldn't do that. He would just tell me no."

"It's that simple, is it?" said Frostfire with a huff, and Star remembered how easily the captain had lied to him in the past. How could he convince his uncle that he and his friends were different, that they were trustworthy?

But Frostfire's throbbing pulse slowed, and his wings relaxed. "I have no choice but to continue to rely on you," said Frostfire. "Don't let me down."

"I won't."

"Larksong told me the name of our colt," he said, changing the subject. "She's going to call him Starfrost, after you and me."

Star blinked, letting the name settle into his heart—*Starfrost*. He and this colt shared the same grandsire, Iceriver, and this colt would carry Star's name, Star's blood. They would be cousins. He turned his face away, hiding the tears that threatened to fall. "Why would Larksong do that?" Star asked. The mare had been part of the Black Army that had tried to kill Star.

"It's obvious, don't you think? You saved her and our colt's life in the Trap when you could have let them die."

Star turned to his uncle. "And you still don't trust me?"

Frostfire stiffened. "I don't trust your friends."

The two stallions fell into silence for a long while, and they dug at the snow, hunting for grass to eat. Star's thoughts ventured to his adoptive mother, Silverlake. Now that he could turn invisible, he could visit her too.

"I'm going to visit the valley. I need to speak to Silverlake." Star exhaled, and his breath curled like smoke in the cold air. "The herd is depressed. I want them to know this won't go on forever."

Forever . . . the word bounced through Star's mind like a falling rock, reminding him that he was immortal and Morningleaf was not. It wasn't a concept he'd thought much about until he inherited the starfire, but could anything really last forever? Star shook off his thoughts. "It's almost dawn," he said to Frostfire. "I'll visit Wind Herd tomorrow night. Why don't you sleep for a bit?"

Frostfire peered at Star, curious. "Tell me what happened at the den, Star. Does it have to do with Morningleaf?"

"Nothing happened," Star snapped. His loud denial shattered the winter hush.

Frostfire spread his wings, looking innocent. "I pressed; you flinched."

"What?"

"It's how we find injuries on our warriors. We press on them until they react."

Star's head was so full he didn't understand what Frostfire was getting at, so he ignored him, shooing him off.

Frostfire strolled away but said, "*You* sleep, Star. You'll feel better if you do."

Star sank into the snow, right where he sat, not caring about finding his shallow bed. *I don't need sleep*, he thought, closing his eyes.

26

NEWS

WHEN STAR OPENED HIS EYES, IT WAS PAST dawn. He lurched to his hooves and shook off the snow-flakes that had floated down from the clouds and stuck to his black hide.

Frostfire cantered toward him, his breath stream-ing from his nostrils and blowing away in the blistering winds. The fresh snow deadened his hoofbeats. He halted next to Star and blinked the snowflakes off his lashes. "This place is worse than the Trap," he grumbled. "Too much shelter there, not enough here. I can't stay dry." He shook hard, flinging melted snowdrops off his body. "Are you feeling better?" he asked.

"Yes," Star admitted. He imagined Morningleaf and

Brackentail in his mind's eye, walking together through the cottonwoods, and then he stared up at the tribute. He had to let Morningleaf go, let her live her life. He'd known this for a while, but now that he'd seen how much she'd grown without him, he was certain.

Feeling resigned, Star toiled, working harder than usual, clearing his mind of all thoughts except his tasks: chipping ice, finding and lifting stones, carrying them up the hill, placing them, and then setting the rocks with clay. He could move about forty stones a day now, but he had to travel farther downriver each time. The river ice and the deep snow also slowed him.

Nightwing and Petalcloud soared overhead while he worked. The ancient black stallion liked showing Petalcloud his monument and taking her into the storms when they came, especially the lightning storms. Nightwing encircled Petalcloud in his shield, keeping her safe from the electric power of the sky. He flew her through blizzards too, shining his starfire ahead of them—and her happy whinnies reverberated through the sky, a sharp contrast to Wind Herd's utter lack of joy on the ground.

When night came, Star was anxious again to leave, this time to visit the Wind Herd steeds. The dark clouds had returned, threatening more snow. He drew his power, vanished, and flew toward Wind Herd. Soon he crested the eastern swells and dropped into the shallow valley. It stretched for miles in each direction but was still inadequate for twelve thousand pegasi.

Nightwing and Petalcloud slept at the western edge of the valley, under a large sycamore tree. Petalcloud's guards patrolled each grouping of pegasi, but they'd relaxed since the early days. Each Wind Herd steed had learned that disobedience led to immediate execution, and disobedience had all but disappeared.

Star landed near the elder mares and lurched across the pitted soil and crushed, dirty snow. A few eyes peered his way, attracted by the soft noises he made, but since he was invisible, the concerned mares went back to dozing. Silverlake and Sweetroot stood huddled together with their heads low and their eyes closed. He lowered his muzzle to Silverlake's ears and whispered, "Wake up."

Her nostrils flared, and her eyes opened. She yawned and nudged Sweetroot. "I dreamed that Star was here."

Star greeted Sweetroot, and she gasped. "He *is* here."

"Shh," said Star. "Follow me."

Sweetroot and Silverlake gaped at each other. "How come we can't see you?" asked Silverlake.

Star didn't want to talk with them near other mares.

"Let's go to the pond," he whispered. "No one is there right now."

Silverlake trotted to the lead Ice Warrior guarding her group and requested permission to drink, then returned. "Okay, let's go," she said.

Star followed the mares to the pond, and they did their best to look bored and depressed, but Star noticed their excited panting breaths.

When they reached the pond, they halted. Sweetroot and Silverlake stood on each side of him and lowered their heads to drink. Star nuzzled Silverlake, inhaling her familiar scent. She was Dawn Meadow to him, the place where he'd been born. She was sweet milk, lazy days, and cool nights under the blinking stars. But when he opened his eyes, he saw that she was bone thin and weak of muscle, and her once thumping heartbeat now limped in her chest. Star held back his tears, grateful to have good news for her. "Morningleaf and Hazelwind are alive."

Silverlake's head flew skyward.

Across the snow, only a mile away, Petalcloud craned her neck and stared at them, attracted by the sudden movement.

"Don't react to anything Star says," whispered Sweetroot.

Star held his breath as Petalcloud squinted at them, but then she resumed her preening of Nightwing's feathers.

"I'm sorry," said Silverlake. She dunked her nose in the pond again, then lifted it, letting the water stream off her muzzle. "Where are they?" she asked, her voice trembling with excitement.

"They're hiding in the southern woodlands with Brackentail and Dewberry. They wanted to tell you, but your sadness helped convince Nightwing that Morningleaf was truly gone, and that has helped keep her safe. You must continue to act sad."

"I will."

Star watched the mares make a show of drinking the water. They had little time and he had lots to say. "Morningleaf and the others are digging an underground tunnel from the forest to the valley. They're going to smuggle out a group of pegasi to cross the Dark Water and start a new herd on a new continent."

"How many?" asked Sweetroot.

"I don't know yet, but it has to be a number that Nightwing won't notice. We need to spread our kind out of Anok . . . in case I fail."

Silverlake ruffled her plumage, looking concerned.

Star continued. "The tunnel will reach this pond soon,

by late spring before the coming newborns are weaned. Be ready. Morningleaf will need help choosing the steeds who go."

"Does Frostfire know about this plan?" asked Silverlake. "I don't trust him."

"Yes, he knows the plan."

"He lied to us once before," Silverlake reminded Star.

"I can't explain now, but I've grown to trust him, and I think he's starting to trust me." Star glanced at Nightwing and Petalcloud. The gray mare was looking their way again. His voice quickened. "Listen closely—I need Wind Herd to know that I'm not building that tribute for Nightwing."

Silverlake turned her eyes to the hills where Star had constructed the base. "For who then?" she asked.

Star tensed as Petalcloud stood and stretched, scanning the valley for anything amiss, then her black eyes settled again on the two mares.

"Start walking back," Star urged.

They turned and he followed them, continuing in a low whisper. "The tribute is for Bumblewind."

Silverlake spread her wings to balance herself as she wobbled across the bumpy terrain. "For Bumblewind? Why? What happened to him?"

"He made it to the interior, but then he lost a fight with wolves. He's in the golden meadow now," said Star, his breath hitching.

Silverlake faltered, almost falling over, and Star saw her eyes brim with tears.

"I'm sorry to tell you that," Star said. "We buried him beneath the base. But with each stone, know that I honor Bumblewind, not Nightwing. Spread the word. The tribute belongs to us."

Sweetroot's chest swelled, and her eyes watered as she gazed at the four thousand stones he'd already moved. "Thank you, Star. Wind Herd needs this, something of our own. Nightwing's taken . . . everything else from us."

"For Bumblewind," whispered Silverlake, also gazing at the tribute.

The beating of wings interrupted them, and Petalcloud landed in front of the mares. Silverlake and Sweetroot halted and dropped their heads. Star froze, holding his breath. "What are you two talking about?" she asked.

"The coming foals," Sweetroot answered quickly.

Three of Petalcloud's Ice Warriors glided toward her and landed next to Petalcloud. They were hairy and muscle-bound and fat with grass. Next to them, Petalcloud sparkled like a beautiful crystal, exquisite to look at, but also hard and cold. They stood out in the herd of pegasi who were dull coated and thin. Petalcloud peered at the old pinto medicine mare. "What about the coming foals?"

Sweetroot glanced at Nightwing, who watched them from a distance. "Is he going to take them too?"

Petalcloud snorted. "It's not your concern. You're both too old for newborns."

Silverlake set her jaw and lifted her chin, looking exactly like her filly, Morningleaf, and Star's heart ached for them being split apart. "I was once lead mare of Sun Herd," Silverlake said. "What you're doing is wrong."

Star, who was still invisible, tensed. *Don't press her too hard*, he thought, staring at his adoptive mother.

Petalcloud huffed. "Is it wrong to save them?" She lashed her shining tail, and her swollen belly glowed in the moonlight. "Because that's what I'm doing. Come next winter, you'll all be dead. But the foals, and me, we'll live on, because we know how to cooperate. If you had any sense, Silverlake, you'd have executed Star yourself when he was born. *He* woke the Destroyer. *He* brought destruction to Anok. Don't blame me for making the best of it." Petalcloud turned to her warriors. "Let's go!" She lifted off and soared over their heads, kicking snow off her hooves that fell on Silverlake's ears.

Star saw the fury in Silverlake's eyes, but she flung off the snow and folded her silver wings across her back, walking with her neck held high.

"Stay calm," Star warned her.

"She'll be fine," said Sweetroot. "You've given her hope, and her family is alive. We'll endure what we must as long as you and Morningleaf and Hazelwind stay committed. Build that tribute for us, Star, and I'll make sure every steed knows that it's for Bumblewind. When you finish, it will mark the end of the reign of Nightwing. Forever."

Star huffed. "I didn't promise that."

"No, you didn't. I did."

"But how can you?"

Sweetroot's eyes filled with tears. "Because we have a plan of our own."

Star's blood chilled at her words. "What plan?"

"Remember when your friends ate the death berries in the Trap?"

Star nodded. How could he forget? The toxic berries had poisoned them instantly. They'd be dead if Star hadn't healed them.

Sweetroot nodded toward the flat grassland. "I found a grove of them. Enough for all of us."

Star reeled. "No, please, you can't do that."

She stared toward his voice and through his invisible body, spreading her wings. "You heard Petalcloud. Once the next batch of foals is born and weaned, he's going to get rid of the adults. This isn't living, Star. This is waiting to die, but it will be on *our* terms, not his."

Star turned in a circle, taking in the herd of twelve thousand pegasi who stood under the drifting evening clouds. They weren't allowed to fly, their families were ripped apart, and they were guarded night and day. They had no future, no hope except for him . . . and the death berries. "I understand," he said. "But please don't eat the berries. Wait until the tunnel is finished, and wait for me. Let me try to defeat Nightwing."

They reached the group of elder mares. "We'll wait for you, Star, but if you fail—we'll eat the berries. One way or another, we'll be free. Now go," said Sweetroot.

Star rose into the sky and flew back to Frostfire with renewed energy and determination. He would not let his cousin Starfrost be stolen by Nightwing, and he would not let Sweetroot feed Wind Herd the death berries.

He soared over the tribute and landed next to it. When it was finished, the tunnel would also be finished. Hazelwind and Echofrost would free enough pegasi to cross the Dark Water and establish a new herd on another continent, in case Star failed. And on that day he would stand on top of the tribute, raise Bumblewind's feather into the sky, and trumpet an over-stallion's challenge to Nightwing. It was Star's right to request a battle to the death. It was how leadership changed hands in every herd except Desert Herd, where leadership was inherited. Nightwing would be forced to attack Star with all his strength, and then Star would learn if Frostfire was correct, if Star's defensive powers would react with greater strength. If Star failed, the Wind Herd steeds would consume the poison berries. One way or another, it would be the last day of his friends' captivity in the valley.

27

THE NEWBORNS

SPRING ARRIVED QUICKLY IN THE FLATLANDS.
The snow turned to slush and then to mud. The plains
grasses reached for the sun, succulent and sweet, and
warm rains shed from the clouds. Like Star's tears, the
raindrops caused bright flowers to spring from the soil.
The insect population erupted, filling the sky with black
hordes of swarming bloodsuckers, and the first of the newborn pegasi buzzed over their dams like fattened bees.
Otherwise, the shallow sky was empty. The rest of Wind
Herd—having no territories to defend, no predators to
kill, and no wars to fight—had no purpose at all, except to
watch Star build the tribute.

A few mothers were still round with foal, and one of

those was Petalcloud, but the rest had dropped their young. Star studied Petalcloud as he worked on his tribute. She was acting strangely today, pacing and gripping her belly with her wings, her expression twisted with pain. "Something's wrong with Petalcloud," Star said.

Frostfire trotted to Star's side and watched, looking curious.

A shadow passed over them, and Star saw Nightwing soaring overhead, but when he noticed Petalcloud on the ground, he landed beside her. She halted, and they whispered together. Then she leaned against him, and Nightwing brayed for Sweetroot, who was known for her vast birthing skills.

Sweetroot immediately galloped to the groaning mare, and they retreated to the shade tree where Petalcloud and Nightwing often slept. Star could no longer see them.

"Is Petalcloud going to be all right?" Star asked.

Frostfire flattened his neck. "How should I know?" he grumbled, and walked away.

His own colt had been born two days earlier, and Frostfire was beside himself with desire to see him up close. From a distance, Starfrost was a fine foal, compact and muscular, pure white with pale-yellow, white-edged feathers, and a short, curly tail. He flew just moments after his birth, and Frostfire had gasped with pride. Star too felt the pull in his heart for his young cousin.

Star lifted the stone he'd put down and returned to work. Silverlake and Echofrost had spread the word that the tribute was for Bumblewind, and a seed of hope had bloomed in the hearts of the pegasi. Star saw them watching him from the distant grassland, encouraging him with their eyes, and he worked harder, faster.

But as the monument rose, it became more difficult and tiresome to build. Morningleaf had woven a large basket over the winter, which Star used to carry stones to the top of the monument. But lifting and setting the flat rocks and wiping the clay while trying to balance on the tribute—it all took a heavy toll on Star's legs and wings. His end feathers had eroded into bloody nubs; his flying muscles often seized, causing him to crash; and his back ached between his shoulder blades. It hurt him to fold his long wings when resting, so he let them drag on the ground. When Star looked at his reflection in the river, it was like traveling back in time, to when he was a dud foal in Dawn Meadow.

But Star was not that foal any longer, and he was not discouraged. He'd asked permission to heal his wings several times so he could work faster, but Nightwing had refused. The sight of Star's low-slung head, exhausted body, and sagging wings delighted the Destroyer. He often pointed at Star and whinnied to Wind Herd, "Look at your black foal now. He's nothing but a broken-down horse."

So Star threw his energy into building the tribute, while his friends built the tunnel, knowing these were the two things keeping the steeds' hearts aflame. And both were almost finished. Star had become adept at counting, and today when he made his tally, he was pleased to note there were only seventy stones left to move.

Several hours passed, and the spring sun rose, glinting off Star's black hide. He dripped sweat but kept working.

"What's that?" neighed Frostfire.

Star lifted his head. He heard it too: a wild roaring sound that filled the sky like whistling winds. It was coming from the shade trees where Sweetroot had gone with Petalcloud and Nightwing. He looked in time to see Sweetroot limping out of the shade with a huge welt on her right leg. Someone had kicked her! Star lunged forward, his heart racing. From across the valley, Sweetroot caught sight of his sudden movement and shook her head. She stumbled back to Silverlake, and all the mares gathered around to hear what had happened.

Star halted, his pulse thumping in his neck. The

wailing continued, and Star recognized the sound as grief. But it wasn't Petalcloud's voice. It was Nightwing's. Frostfire flew across the grass and hovered near Star, his eyes round and wild. "Who died?" he asked, also recognizing the sound of mourning.

"I don't know." Star watched the darkened area under the trees, then a black figure emerged—the Destroyer, carrying a newborn pegasus in his wings. Nightwing was shedding feathers and trembling violently. The colt looked asleep, but no newborn pegasus was born sleeping. The colt's hide was black, and his long wings hung limply to the ground. Star staggered, and tears sprang to his eyes. It was like looking at himself, except this foal had a wide blaze and violet feathers, just like his dam.

"Born dead," said Frostfire, shaking his head. "It's Petalcloud's curse that she inherited from Rockwing. All his colts were stillborn and so are hers. I'm the only living male in her line, and now another colt is lost."

"No," said Star. "You're not the only male. Now there's also Starfrost."

Frostfire grunted, looking pleased but also concerned. "You're right."

Nightwing placed his son in the grass and reared, throwing back his head. Silver starfire crackled across his glossy hide, and every pegasus in Wind Herd stared at him, their eyes round.

"Get back," Star whispered to Frostfire, even though they weren't anywhere near the ancient stallion, but Star saw what was coming.

Nightwing swiveled his head and locked his eyes on the Wind Herd steeds. "Are you laughing at me?" he brayed. "At my son?" He lifted off, tucked his wings, and hurtled toward them, panting starfire. Sparks flowed off his hooves.

Star leaped into the sky and soared toward the pegasi in the valley. "Run!" he screamed to them.

The Wind Herd steeds bolted, galloping in every direction. Nightwing shot starfire in random bursts. He aimed at anything that moved, and several pegasi exploded into flames. Star brayed new instructions. "Hold still!"

Then Petalcloud stepped out of the shade with a tiny piebald filly nursing at her side, flying like a hummingbird. Star cocked his head. "They had twins," he said to himself.

Petalcloud halted near her stillborn colt's body that was curled in the grass and whispered a few words over him, and then she turned her back, returning to the shade with her healthy filly.

Nightwing dived toward his colt as the Wind Herd pegasi collected and stood shivering, afraid and confused. The Destroyer landed and pulled the limp foal into his wings. Black flowers sprang out of the soil around them.

Star pricked his ears, stunned. The Destroyer was crying.

Then Nightwing inhaled deeply and attempted to heal his son, coughing golden starfire on him. He did this repeatedly, but the starfire swirled in weak bursts. The colt didn't move. Nightwing didn't have enough experience with healing to help him.

Without thinking, Star glided across the valley and landed next to the pair. He understood that Nightwing's dark thoughts were stifling his healing power, but Star was well practiced with it. "I can save him," he said. "Let me try."

Nightwing didn't move, didn't seem to hear Star at all.

"Please, let me help."

Nightwing inhaled again, taking a long, slow breath. Star moved closer, expecting agreement. Nightwing drew his face level with Star's, and their eyes connected. Star was bigger, taller. He looked down at Nightwing and was overcome by sympathy for him. Hope rose in his chest. Maybe if he healed the son, he could befriend the father—or at least soften his heart.

Nightwing blinked, and his eyes darkened.

Too late, Star saw his intention. The Destroyer hissed like a snake and shot quills of silver light at Star. They punctured his hide in a dozen places. Star cried out in shock. Nightwing let loose more deadly quills, and Star threw up his shield, protecting himself from the second attack. "Go," roared Nightwing. "Leave us."

Confused, Star lurched across the valley. Halfway, he collapsed, unable to breathe. The light quills had punctured his lungs and his legs, and pierced his gut. Star quickly pushed starfire throughout his body, healing himself. He glanced back at Nightwing, but the Destroyer ignored him, too lost in his grief.

Then Petalcloud marched out of the shade and confronted Nightwing. The two argued, and Petalcloud pointed across the valley—at her grandson, Starfrost.

Frostfire saw this from afar. "No . . . no! She wants my colt." He flew off the grass at the same time as Nightwing. They each hurtled toward Larksong and Starfrost. "Fly!" Frostfire neighed to her. Larksong shielded Starfrost, shaking her head. A newborn could never keep up with her if she fled, and Star saw she wouldn't leave her son.

Nightwing reached her first. Larksong flew up to fight

him, her teeth flashing, but Frostfire knocked her out of the way just as a burst of silver starfire flew past her head. Frostfire pinned Larksong to the grass to protect her while Nightwing picked up their perfect white colt in his wings.

Larksong screamed, "Let him go!" She tried to break away, but Frostfire held her back. With a hiss of sparks, Nightwing cantered back to Petalcloud, carrying Starfrost in his wings. The newborn colt bleated loudly for Larksong, and she answered him with shrill whinnies.

When Nightwing reached Petalcloud, he laid the colt at her feet, and then he walked away, returning to his son who'd died.

The valley was still. Not a single pegasus moved. Stealing a newborn from its mother was unheard of in Anok—weanlings, yes, but not newborns. Star's gut twisted, and he felt sick.

Petalcloud nuzzled her new colt Starfrost and then lifted her head, gazing at Frostfire, her eyes hard and black, but pleased. She shrugged her violet wings, almost as if in apology, then turned and took her two foals beneath the sycamore tree to rest.

Larksong melted into the grass, crying. Frostfire swept his wings over her, trying to calm her. Nightwing took his dead colt to the river and buried him under stones. And Star flew back to the tribute, swallowing waves of emotions. Why hadn't Nightwing let him help? He could have saved the foal! Fury, sadness, and grief pulverized Star from the inside out.

Long hours passed this way, and the herd returned to grazing. Eventually Frostfire left Larksong's side. He flew to Star and landed in front of him.

"I'm sorr—" Star began, though none of it was his fault.

Frostfire flattened his ears. "Don't."

Star closed his mouth. He could think of no words to soothe Frostfire.

His uncle pushed past him and stalked into the woods to be alone. Sweetroot limped to Larksong's side, feeding her calming roots.

Nightwing returned from burying his colt and joined Petalcloud. They nuzzled their foals and comforted Starfrost.

And Star watched it all, studying the Destroyer and wondering how it felt to have a family and a herd of his own, but at what cost?

Petalcloud ordered the Ice Warriors to take the herd out to graze. They obeyed, and Star watched the pegasi of Anok stomp onto the grassland because they weren't allowed to fly—and he realized they were the band of horses that he'd feared they'd become when he was in the Trap. Silverlake had asked him to leave Anok and to come back when he was stronger. He'd told her he wouldn't go because he was afraid of what he'd find when he returned: *I'll find a herd of dull beasts, slaves of Nightwing, pegasi afraid of their own shadows. You'll be turned into a herd of horses—mindlessly following one stallion.*

Star gazed over the valley at the pegasi of Anok and saw that his fears had already come true. "It's time," he said to no one. "It's time to end this."

28

WISHES

THE NEXT DAY ECHOFROST GAVE THE SIGNAL. THE tunnel was finally finished.

At dusk, Frostfire trotted down from the hillside, his wings flared.

"What is it?" Star asked.

"Larksong is planning to ambush Petalcloud and take Starfrost back." He rattled his feathers. "Nightwing will kill her for it, but she doesn't care. She'd rather be dead than without our colt." Frostfire wrung his wings, pacing. "What are we going to do?"

"The tunnel is finished, Frostfire. We can get Larksong out."

"But what about Starfrost? Can you get him out too?"

Star blinked at him, feeling helpless. "Petalcloud is nursing your colt, Frostfire. We can't just take him without her noticing. And if he goes missing, Nightwing and the Ice Warriors will turn the forest upside down searching for him. They'll discover the rebels, the den, and the tunnel. Everything we've worked so hard for will be destroyed."

"But you *promised* me," said Frostfire.

Star backed away, his heart torn for his uncle. "I said I'd save your mare, and I will, but you'll have to be patient about Starfrost. Now is not the right time, but Nightwing isn't going to hurt him; your colt is safe."

"Safe," rasped Frostfire. "He's anything *but* safe!"

"Listen, I'm going to the den tonight. I'll talk to Hazelwind about it. I want Starfrost away from Nightwing as much as you do."

Frostfire whipped his heard toward Star, looking furious.

Star shut his mouth. He wasn't the colt's sire; he couldn't know how Frostfire felt. "Just wait, please," said Star. The way Frostfire was pacing and rattling his feathers, Star knew he was asking a lot from the stallion. Frostfire wanted blood in exchange for his son, and so did Larksong. She was a sky herder, a highly specialized battle mare, and Frostfire was a captain—they were steeds who made decisions and took action. Asking them to wait was like asking the sun to shine less brightly.

Frostfire folded his trembling wings. "All right, I'll wait." He exhaled and peered at Star, his pale, mismatched eyes glinting like ice. "But if I had your silver starfire, I'd use it. I'd save my son with it."

"It's not that simple," explained Star.

Frostfire shook his head slowly. "I think it is that simple."

Star saw the conviction, the desire in Frostfire's eyes. He *wanted* Star's power; he *wished* for it. Star recoiled but tried to hide his reaction. There was darkness in his uncle, deep in his core. The kidnapping of his colt had awakened it.

"Save my family," Frostfire ordered. It was a command and not a request.

Star nodded. "I'll try."

Frostfire turned away and flew up to the hill to keep watch over his family, and Star's thoughts returned to Morningleaf. Over the past winter, he'd tried to let her go, and living apart from her had helped him with that, but every time he visited the den, he was crushed by how much he missed her. And as close as she was to Brackentail, she was brighter, more alive when Star was near. He didn't think he was imagining that, and tonight he would see her. The section of his heart that was reserved for Morningleaf thumped to life.

As the sun completed its descent, Star slid his power across his dark hide, vanishing from view. He flew to Frostfire and reminded him, "Make the call of the hawk if Nightwing comes."

Frostfire nodded, but his eyes remained trained on his abducted son.

Star flew to the den. The dire wolves had dug a new one farther away, and they menaced the pegasi less often. Nightwing had turned several members of the wolf pack to ash, and that had helped deter them from hunting pegasi in general, but they refused to vacate the Flatlands. Star landed at the tall elm and then walked to the rounded berm and the fallen tree that hid the den. He swept aside the branches and ducked inside.

"Star!" Morningleaf rushed into his open wings. "We did it! The tunnel is finished."

Hazelwind, Dewberry, and Brackentail greeted Star with soft nickers.

"The tribute is almost done too," said Star. "I can slow down, to give you time to transport the pegasi out." They had spent many hours discussing this already. They'd decided to take two hundred pegasi, approximately forty from each of the original five herds. Two hundred steeds would be enough to found a new herd on another continent, but not so many that Nightwing would notice they were gone. Hazelwind, Morningleaf, Brackentail, Dewberry, and Echofrost would lead the new herd as a council.

Sweetroot would not go. She planned to administer the death berries if Star failed, and Silverlake would not leave either. "I'm too old," Silverlake had said, but Star didn't think that was the reason. Anok was her home, to her core, and that's why she couldn't—wouldn't—leave it. But Star and his friends hoped that two hundred pegasi, in a herd of thousands, could escape unnoticed, fly south across the Dark Water, and begin new lives. There were eight continents in total, according to the legends, and it would take Nightwing a small eternity to search an entire planet for two hundred escaped pegasi.

"We'll sneak out twenty per day," said Hazelwind.

"How long will that take?" asked Brackentail.

Morningleaf quickly figured the numbers. "Ten days, and then we'll need an extra three days to get a good head start."

Star had seen the edge of the southern continent on

his high flights, but what his friends would find there was a mystery—Landwalkers, more dire wolves, something worse? No one knew.

"Where will you hide them until all are out?" asked Star.

Hazelwind answered. "We'll fly them several hours south, to a forest almost as thick as the Trap. Dewberry scouted it for us. They'll wait there until all two hundred are free."

"Remember," said Star, "Larksong must be in the first group. I promised that to Frostfire."

"I'll let Echofrost know," said Hazelwind. "Did you promise the captain anything else?" Hazelwind looked irritated, and Star didn't blame him.

"I told him I'd talk to you about getting his colt out too."

"The colt Petalcloud took?" said Dewberry, snapping her head toward Star. "I'd as soon steal a bear cub from its mother."

"Dewberry is right," said Hazelwind. "The colt is too young to leave her side, and if we did get him away, she'd notice immediately. She's claimed Starfrost as her own and so has Nightwing—they would search the woods. They'd find us."

"I know," said Star. "I explained this, but I'm afraid Frostfire will try to save the colt himself. He's not thinking straight."

"Let him get himself killed, then," said Dewberry. "We have our mission."

Star's friends dropped the subject. They had no idea how to rescue the foal and neither did he, but the time had come to execute their plan. Star glanced at Morningleaf, thinking of the dangerous journey ahead. They were only two years old, but they had lived a lifetime, and soon she would be gone.

Morningleaf nudged her brother. "I'll show Star the tunnel. Okay?"

It was obvious to everyone that she wanted to be alone with Star. Hazelwind nodded, and Morningleaf turned, leading Star out of the den. His throat closed, and he couldn't breathe. It was time to say good-bye.

The night air was chilly, a fading memory of winter. Star and Morningleaf walked side by side, like when they were foals.

She inched closer to him. "What's going to happen?"

Their hooves slurped on the muddy path. "I don't know," Star admitted. "When the tribute is finished and the two hundred are safe, I'm going to confront Nightwing. He can't kill me since I have the shield, and Frostfire thinks that if he attacks me, I'll become stronger in response. He says I'm a defender, not a warrior. Do you think that's true?"

She nudged him, sniffing his mane as they walked. "Warriors are terminators. They attack without thinking; they don't regret their mistakes. So, yes, I agree that you're probably a defender."

"But I felt my warrior blood in the battle against Frostfire's Black Army," said Star, feeling suddenly embarrassed. "The Jungle Herd mare, Ashrain, told me I would like it, and I did."

Morningleaf swiveled her ears forward. "Just because you're not a warrior doesn't mean you're not a *stallion*."

Star nickered.

"Look at us," said Morningleaf. "We've grown. We're adults." She shook her long, flaxen mane. "But I don't feel like an adult."

"Neither do I." The two fell silent, thinking.

Soon, they reached the blind, which hid the entrance to the tunnel. Morningleaf entered first, followed by Star. "This goes all the way to the pond?" he asked, examining the dark passageway.

"Yes. We dug into the pond at an angle so the tunnel

wouldn't fill with water. The steeds will swim through the hole we made and then walk up the tunnel, above the water level, and there the passageway straightens and levels. Do you want to look inside? I'll wait here if you do." She stared into the tunnel. "I don't like it in there."

Star guessed that the black passageway reminded her of the lava tubes where Frostfire had once imprisoned her. "No. I don't need to see the whole thing, and besides—I don't think I'd fit." He peered into the round black hole. The soil had either contracted over the winter or else he'd grown larger.

Morningleaf dragged her eyes across him, from his tail to his mane, pausing over his wings and chest. "You're right, you wouldn't fit."

Star lowered his neck, feeling self-conscious under her stare.

She sensed his unease and nickered. "Be proud, Star, you're . . . really incredible to look at."

"What?"

"It's just that . . . seeing you full grown, you're . . . perfect."

Star felt more like a buffalo than a pegasus. He was the largest steed in Anok—larger than Nightwing. Many moons of lifting the heavy stones had developed muscles like boulders across his chest. His haunches were thick and defined from walking up the hill to the tribute, and the crest of his neck curved in a tight arch from carrying the heavy basket in his mouth while he flew. Even Petalcloud's gigantic stallion Stormtail walked in Star's shadow.

Morningleaf's eyes shone with pride as she looked at him and continued explaining their plan. "Echofrost and Shadepebble will send messages to the separate divisions in the valley."

"It's all so dangerous," breathed Star. "If Nightwing catches on . . ."

Morningleaf nodded. "If he becomes suspicious, we'll leave Anok immediately, with whoever we have. We won't risk the new herd for the old one. We can't."

"But you must wait here, so I can heal your feathers. Otherwise, how will you cross the Dark Water?" asked Star.

"My wings don't hurt anymore. If we have to leave early, the others will carry me."

Star's throat tightened. "If I can help it, I won't let that happen. It's too dangerous."

Morningleaf pressed against him, lifting her muzzle to his, breathing out and then inhaling his scent, and she relaxed. "Do you ever wish things had been different? That you were born a regular pegasus and not the black foal?"

"Of course, that's all I ever wanted," said Star, then he thought about it some more. "But I've done amazing things." And it was true. He'd turned enemies into friends, brought the dead to life, and healed Larksong's unborn foal—he enjoyed his gifts.

"You're our defender," said Morningleaf, her amber eyes glowing.

"Maybe," said Star. "But mostly, I'm just a healer, like Sweetroot."

"Only taller," nickered Morningleaf.

"And better looking," said Star.

The two friends nuzzled each other. They'd grown up together, but they were trapped in separate currents, heading in separate directions. Morningleaf and the two hundred pegasi would carry their bloodlines out of Anok, and they would start a new herd far away. It comforted Star to know that even if he failed, the pegasi would live on.

"You'll soon be free," Star said, and he couldn't stop himself from staring at her. Morningleaf had transformed into a beautiful mare with a shining chestnut coat, a mane and tail as light as oat grass, and powerful muscles—made stronger by all the digging and walking. Her burned feathers lay dry and curled across her wings, adding to her legend. Morningleaf's feats of bravery floated around her like fireflies, setting her apart from other pegasi.

But to Star she was more than her beauty, and she was more than a vessel to carry her pegasi lineage. Morningleaf was a story holder. She'd memorized pegasi legends and history as told by the elders, and Star considered this her most valuable accomplishment, because she could pass the knowledge on to the foals in her new herd. He caught her gaze. "Teach the stories you learned from Mossberry and the other elders so the pegasi don't forget where they came from, or what happened here. Will you do that? Promise me you'll do that?"

Huge tears rolled from Morningleaf's eyes and streamed down her chestnut face. She wrapped her wings around Star and sobbed, and he cried too, leaving white flowers all around the tunnel. With a deep throb in his chest, he realized the flowers would be the first thing the two hundred pegasi would see when they emerged from the dark, and so he didn't stomp them out but left them growing there.

Star and Morningleaf returned to the den where he said good-bye to Dewberry, Hazelwind, and Brackentail.

The plan was set. Hazelwind would send a signal, three caws of a crow, when the two hundred were out of the valley. Then they would fly south. Star would wait three days, finish the tribute, and then confront Nightwing. What happened next depended on the outcome of the battle, and that was yet unknown.

Star left his friends and returned to Frostfire feeling hopeful. They couldn't take Starfrost through the tunnel, but Larksong would soon be free and safe. Surely Frostfire would understand. But Star would not give up on freeing the colt. He landed by the tribute. "Frostfire?"

The white stallion emerged from behind the monument.

"I talked to Hazelwind," said Star. "Larksong will be in the first group out, but everyone agrees that Starfrost will have to wait. There's no way to get him away from Petalcloud without someone getting killed."

Frostfire's eyes turned cold. "Then it's not going to work. Larksong won't leave the valley without him."

Star didn't know what to say to that.

Frostfire bobbed his head as though coming to a decision. "I get it," he said.

"You get what?"

The ex-captain folded his wings and lifted his head,

meeting Star's gaze. "I mean to say that I understand Hazelwind's decision, but it changes nothing. Larksong won't leave without Starfrost."

"I'm sorry," said Star.

Frostfire snorted bitterly. "So am I."

29

STAMPEDE

SEVEN DAYS LATER, THE PLAN WAS UNDER WAY
and going well. One hundred and forty steeds had been
removed from the valley without Nightwing or Petalcloud
noticing. Silverlake chose the steeds, and Echofrost's
growing network of spies informed them and then helped
them escape at night, while drinking at the pond. The
Ice Warrior named Graystone helped her communicate
between the groups.

All winter, the captured pegasi had created the habit
of drinking in large numbers, so the practice was not suspicious to Nightwing. A few chosen pegasi from each group
slipped under the water and swam to the tunnel. The rest

returned to their section as though nothing unusual had happened.

The pegasi who weren't escaping didn't resent it. Each knew what was at stake, and why they couldn't all leave the valley, and many didn't want to leave. A trip through the tunnel was a one-way journey to another land, across a dangerous ocean. Finding two hundred steeds who *wanted* to leave had been the challenge. The remaining pegasi watched Star build the tribute, hope glittering in their eyes.

On the morning of the eighth day, Frostfire leaped in Star's path. He was upset, twitching. "Larksong changed her mind. She wants out tonight."

"Without Starfrost?"

"She's trusting me to save our son," said Frostfire, arching his neck.

"But how—"

"Let me worry about that," interrupted Frostfire.

"Okay, I'll ask Echofrost to put her in tonight's group."

"Don't *ask* her, *tell* her. The time has come for you to fulfill your promise to me. I've been patient, and I want Larksong rescued before she changes her mind again."

Frostfire's expression was tight, his eyes desperate. Patches of feathers were missing from his wings, and Star saw that Frostfire had reached the end of his endurance with waiting. "I understand. I'll tell Echofrost."

Frostfire dipped his head, then stared into the distance, seeming to consider more words. Then he glanced at the dark clouds overhead and said simply, "A storm is coming."

"I know. I feel it," said Star. Just then a blast of wind blew his mane straight off his neck.

Frostfire flared his wings and trotted away.

Star decided to visit Echofrost right away while she was grazing on the open plain, because the valley was no longer safe. The spring mud had pushed the segregated pegasi groups closer together as they attempted to share the driest land, and it was possible his voice would be overheard if he visited her there. On the grazing lands, the pegasi were spread far enough apart that he could speak without detection.

Turning himself invisible, he flew toward Wind Herd. Below him, Petalcloud napped under her shady sycamore tree, and Nightwing stood beside her, head to tail, so they could swipe the flies, mosquitoes, and gnats off each other's faces. Her filly, who she'd named Riversun, and Frostfire's colt nursed side by side while Nightwing watched over them.

The trampled valley was vacant during the day, and Star coasted over it on the way to the grasslands. The winds raced unencumbered here, and they hit him hard, knocking him sideways. He rolled, wing over wing, before regaining his bearings. The gusts howled in his ears like dire wolves, and the rushing air blew the grazing steeds' tails toward their heads. They walked with their backs to it, and Star knew how much they hated the wind. The clouds closed over the sun, leaving the interior dark but warm and alive with static. The sky spit rain and threatened lightning.

He landed, out of breath from fighting the current. The pegasi grazed in their separate groups. Stormtail and the Ice Warriors patrolled them, but after several moons without an escape attempt, they looked bored.

Star quickly spotted Echofrost grazing with the adult mares and darted across the grass, flying low. He landed next to her and nickered a soft greeting.

"Hello, Star," she whispered, keeping her head down so no one would notice her seeming to talk to herself.

"Hello." He gazed at his friend, wondering if he'd see her again after she left with the two hundred pegasi to cross the ocean. She was tall, lean, and solemn, but not unhappy. Bumblewind's death had cracked her, but

Echofrost was too strong to crumble. And after helping organize the rescue mission to save the pegasi from extinction, she was days away from freedom. But there was a reason he was here, and he didn't have much time. "Larksong's decided to leave; Frostfire just told me. He wants you to get her out tonight."

"Who is *he* to demand anything?" asked Echofrost with a snort.

A distant guard glanced in Echofrost's direction. "Shh," Star warned her. "Relax your wings."

Echofrost took a deep breath and pretended to preen her feathers. "I already have tonight's group chosen; I'll take her tomorrow."

Star shushed her again, beginning to regret coming to the Flatlands. "If you don't do it tonight, Frostfire won't trust me. Just send her, please. I promised I'd help her."

Echofrost chewed her lip, thinking. "But why the sudden change? I see how she pines for Starfrost; I can't believe she'd leave without her colt. Did you ask him about that?"

"No," Star admitted. "He said he'd worry about Starfrost himself."

"You see, I don't like this, Star. It sounds like he's making his own plans."

"Maybe he is, but can you blame him? Nightwing took his son."

"Right, that's the problem. Frostfire is desperate. He can't be thinking straight."

Star nodded. "Well, getting Larksong to safety will ease his mind, don't you agree?"

"I don't know, maybe. Let me use the tunnel to speak to Hazelwind and the others about this, but no promises. I won't make this decision on my own."

"Thank you."

Echofrost scowled. "No promises," she repeated.

Star returned to Frostfire and gave him the news. "Echofrost will try to get her out tonight, but it's up to Hazelwind and the others."

Frostfire narrowed his eyes. "Don't they obey you, Star?"

"Obey me? No. We work together."

Frostfire leaned closer, his muscles quivering, his eyes glinting. "So all along you've had no authority to promise me *anything*?"

Star balked. "No, that's not it. You know my friends and I work as a team. We want to save *all* the pegasi, including Larksong; nothing has changed. Hazelwind is committed to saving her."

"All the pegasi?" snorted Frostfire, shaking his head and backing away from Star as if seeing him for the first time. "You're no warrior, no defender. You're a *dreamer*." He spat the word like he tasted something nasty. Then he gnashed his teeth, lifted off, and flew away.

"Where are you going?" called Star, panic rising in his chest. He was about to follow Frostfire when he froze, feeling quick vibrations under his hooves.

He waited, swiveling his ears, then the ground shook harder, and the soft soil conducted odd vibrations that were somehow familiar to Star. He closed his eyes, tracing his memories until he found it. On his first migration, a grass fire had sent a herd of land horses galloping out of the forest and into the herd of migrating Sun Herd walkers. The fire had killed Mossberry and almost reached Star, and it was a terrible memory, but he knew the cause of the strange vibrations. "It's a stampede," he whispered to himself.

Star peered at the dark clouds that threatened rain—there was no smoke in the sky, no drifting flakes of ash. It wasn't a fire causing this panicked run.

Then the near horizon blackened, and a wave of frightened creatures blasted into view, seemingly out of nowhere. Panic shot through the Wind Herd steeds on the plain. Some pegasi rocketed toward the clouds, and others froze. Nightwing didn't allow them to fly without permission, and this had been deeply ingrained in them.

But they had to do something, because these weren't stampeding horses.

They were buffalo.

Giant, panicked buffalo.

30

ALARM

STAR DARTED BACK TO THE OPEN PLAIN, SHED his invisibility so they could see him, and neighed to Wind Herd. "Get away! Fly!" Thousands of buffalo plowed toward him and the pegasi, their eyes bright with fear.

Some jetted off the grass, some stood frozen.

Star whirled and galloped through Wind Herd, ordering frightened steeds to take flight. The younger pegasi spiraled across the grassland, tossed by the violent winds. Stronger pegasi tore after them, trying to catch them.

The buffalo pounded the soil, their eyes narrow, their sides heaving. They cut long trails through the grass, mowing it down with their hooves and leaving hundreds of injured pegasi sprawled behind them.

Sharp screams whistled through the currents, and Star's mane whipped his eyes. Hoofbeats rumbled like thunder, confusing his ears. He glanced upward. The clouds swirled in opposite directions and began to spin. *How was that possible?* Star heard heavy breathing. He turned just as a thick-maned bull buffalo roared past, slamming Star's shoulder and sending him spinning. Star landed on his side, rolled onto his hooves, and leaped into the sky, his wings clamoring for the heights.

The buffalo herd sped across the plain faster than Star imagined such large beasts could run, and he still wasn't sure what they were afraid of.

Star dived toward the pegasi, leveled off, and flew over their backs, neighing to the steeds who were still on the ground to get up. "Fly," he whinnied. The pegasi obeyed. Behind the buffalo lurked the dire wolf pack, sensing a feast.

Star trumpeted the alarm of an over-stallion, calling the pegasi to him. The old habit of instant obedience sent steeds flying his way.

Then a black shadow dropped from the clashing clouds. Nightwing.

Star's pulse thundered in his ears, deafening him, and

the cries of the injured pegasi ripped at his heart. He drew on his power and turned himself invisible before Nightwing spotted him.

"Who called?" boomed the ancient stallion.

Below Star, the wolves realized the wounded pegasi were easier prey than the fleeing buffalo. They spread out and crept toward the fallen steeds.

Ahead of Star, the Desert Herd stallion named Redfire brayed the call to battle and dived on the wolves. Thousands more pegasi dropped onto the pack, kicking and biting them. The wolves snarled, frustrated but thwarted.

Star exhaled. The herd could handle the wolves.

Nightwing flew above the melee, his nostrils filtering the wind. Star hovered near him, invisible, holding his breath and glad the ferocious currents masked his wingbeats.

Petalcloud darted out of the throng and joined Nightwing. Star dropped to a lower altitude, but he could hear them speaking. "What is it?" Petalcloud asked, studying Nightwing's expression. Over the winter, Nightwing had fully recovered from his long hibernation. His muscles had rounded, and his once brittle coat was as glossy as northern ice.

"Where are our foals?" whinnied Nightwing.

"Riversun and Starfrost are with Stormtail," she said. "What's wrong; who's calling the herd?" She scanned the sky.

"Star is here," said Nightwing. "He sounded the alarm."

"What? Where?" Petalcloud craned her neck. "I don't see him."

Nightwing pinned his ears but said nothing, his forehead tight.

Star watched the last of the buffalo pass by just as thunder cracked and the rain fell, drenching the pegasi as they battled the wolves. But the black clouds tumbling overhead cycled in ways Star had never seen, and the wind shoved him like it was angry.

"We should take our herd into the cottonwoods," Petalcloud said to her mate. "The lightning will strike them if they stay out here, and the young ones can't fly in this."

Not the woods, thought Star. That's where his friends were.

Nightwing turned his glowing silver eyes on her. "No. A storm like this will rid us of the weakest steeds."

Wicked delight flickered across Petalcloud's face.

"Good thinking," she said.

Star felt sick listening to them, but then the sky stole back his attention. The winds crossed their currents, and Star braced as he was pushed higher. The air thickened, dripping moisture, and the clouds collided, forming a monstrous, swirling funnel. The wolves whined and bolted, vanishing like shadows.

Star soared toward his friends, realizing it was the *storm* that had caused the buffalo to stampede, not a distant fire or the pack of wolves.

An elderly pegasus was snatched by the wind and thrown hundreds of winglengths across the sky. "Land!" Redfire bellowed to all of them.

The flying pegasi dived toward land. Star opened his mouth, ready to trumpet another alarm, but then the cloud mass dropped toward him, sucking the winds into a faster spiral. Star flung himself backward and plummeted toward the grass. The circling cone followed him, roaring like a lion.

Star banked and flew away from it. Nightwing sprang his shield around himself and Petalcloud, winging her to safety.

Star swooped over the pegasi, directing them to the

area of lowest ground. "Head to the valley!" he whinnied.

Nightwing retracted his shield and flew toward Star's voice. "I hear you, Star," he brayed, his eyes glowing brighter. "Show yourself."

Fear shot through Star's veins. He didn't answer.

The funnel cloud touched down and ripped at the land, tearing up small trees and brush and sucking them into its blustering center. *The sky is alive*, thought Star, his heart thudding.

Nightwing shot silver fire in the direction he'd heard Star's voice. "Come out," he warned, scanning the elevations between the ground and the clouds. Star considered escaping through the storm, knowing that if he flew high enough he would encounter a safe blue sky. Lightning crackled, followed by thunder, and the wind blew harder, faster, but Star couldn't leave Wind Herd. He turned and flew after the pegasi who were heading toward the valley.

The twisting cloud retracted briefly, then dropped down in a new place, on the tails of the herd. Sweetroot and Silverlake galloped with the elder mares, afraid to fly in the gusting winds. The cone cloud followed like it was hunting. They weren't going to outrun it.

Star hurtled toward them. Silverlake slipped in the mud, giving the cloud the split second it needed to gain on her. Star gasped as the ravenous funnel snatched her up and swallowed her.

Star dived after Silverlake, suddenly remembering the word for this spiraling wind: *tornado*.

31

TWISTER

THE TORNADO SUCKED STAR OFF HIS WINGS AND knocked the breath out of him as it whipped him sideways. He curled into himself to protect his long neck and wing bones. Small trees and shrubs slapped his hide, leaving long trails of blood. Dust filled his throat and choked him. Roaring wind assaulted his ears, deafening him. The cone of air dragged him up through it, higher and higher, and ahead he saw Silverlake's white tail.

Star sprang his shield and was immediately encased in peaceful silence. He rolled through the tornado in his orb, watching the chaos, but he could breathe and open his wings. He scanned the debris for Silverlake.

She was above him. Her eyes were closed, and she was

curled tight like a newborn, her wings covering her head. He flew toward her, but she spiraled up and away. He flattened his neck and flapped harder, finally catching her. Her lips were moving, and Star guessed she was calling the Ancestors to help her. Star pushed his shield out, projecting it around them both.

The second his golden orb sealed around them, Silverlake crashed to the bottom of it, lying on her side with her chest heaving. The power of the twisting cloud multiplied as they rose, spinning them around and around. Star lost control of their direction. Silverlake opened her eyes wide. The world around them was a blur.

"Am I dead?" she whinnied, staring through him.

Star realized he was still invisible. He shed that power and reappeared. "If you're dead then so am I," he said.

"Oh, Star!" Silverlake tried to stand but couldn't.

They stared at the funnel cloud, each of them pinned to Star's spinning orb, their wings plastered against the side of it, their lips rippling. It was almost impossible for a pegasus to feel dizzy, but soon Star was light-headed, and his gut had lost its bearing on whether he was upside down or right-side up. The sphere whipped around faster and faster. A buffalo soared by, bellowing and kicking the sky.

"Did you see that?" Silverlake gasped.

Star also didn't believe his eyes.

A large boulder slammed the orb, sending them spinning in the opposite direction. Star forced one wing off the wall, but gravity slammed it right back.

Then the twisting cloud spit them out, and they went blasting across the sky. Star couldn't see, didn't know what to do.

They dropped below the cloud layer. Now Star could see which way was up and which was down, but his gut was still drifting, his brain still spinning.

Wobbling a bit, he flapped his wings, and Silverlake helped him. They synchronized and settled into a fast glide, parallel to the land, slowing their descent. The sky was calmer here, the clouds whiter, and the rain softer. When they were traveling at a safe speed, Star retracted the shield. He and Silverlake coasted onto the grass and landed, exhausted.

Silverlake staggered to keep her balance, her eyes bulging. "We're alive," she said, like she didn't believe it.

Star panted, trying to regain his breath. He saw lakes and a bog, and a beaver dam in a thin river. "Where are we?"

The storm had thrown them miles away.

Silverlake leaned into him and took a long breath, and Star's fondness for her filled his heart. They hadn't always agreed with each other in the past, but they had the same goal: to unite the pegasi of Anok. Silverlake glanced at the clouds, which were clearing. "We must get back," she said.

Star agreed, and they oriented their path with the sun and then flew back toward the valley. It was raining, and the clouds were dark gray but not ominous. The tornado had passed over and moved on. The air warmed, and the bugs resumed their chatter. The worst of the spring storm was over.

Star drew up his camouflage and disappeared against the big sky before anyone could spot him flying back with Silverlake. Large sections of the Flatlands were ravaged where the tornado had touched down, but the rest looked the same. The dire wolves had returned, and Star saw them feasting on a dead buffalo. The Wind Herd steeds stood in the shallow valley basin, and the massive tribute stood tall, reaching toward the clouds. Frostfire's input on how to build a strong base and to reinforce it with river clay had withstood an incredible test of strength.

"I am ten stones short of finishing the tribute," Star said to Silverlake. "Ten stones, and then this is over."

A black shadow flapped across the trampled ground. It

was Nightwing returning to the valley.

"I have to get back," he said.

"Star?" Silverlake turned her dark eyes to his, and Star melted into her warm gaze. "No matter what happens next, know that I'm proud of you." Her voice echoed like a dream, and Star inhaled sharply, overcome by a sudden feeling of dread.

"What is it?" asked Silverlake, her voice rising.

"I don't know. Something is wrong." Star looked into her eyes, and suddenly he was sure with all his breath that he would never speak to her again. But why? His blood turned to ice as the dread washed over him again. He whipped his head toward the valley and the forest, toward his friends. The planet seemed to tilt, and he was certain of one thing: someone was in great danger.

"I have to go!" Star bolted forward, his words flying away with the wind.

32

BURIED

MORNINGLEAF STUCK HER HEAD OUTSIDE THE den. "The tornado is gone," she said to Brackentail. It had ripped across the sky, landed on the plain, and then swept through the forest, touching down near the blind where the tunnel was hidden. Inside the den the walls had shaken and dirt had fallen on Morningleaf's head, but the storm had passed, and the cottonwood forest had burst back to life.

It was the eighth day, and they'd rescued a total of one hundred and forty pegasi. Tonight, twenty more would leave, and then forty more over the next two days. Hazelwind and Dewberry escorted the refugees to the lake many miles away to wait for the rest.

"Hazelwind and Dewberry should be back by now," said Morningleaf, pacing in the small chamber.

"I'm sure they saw the storm and took cover," said Brackentail.

Morningleaf halted. "You're right. It's just . . . we're so close to the final day. I'm afraid everything will go wrong. Many moons of planning will be wasted."

Brackentail pricked his ears. "No, nothing will be wasted. Remember, our true hope is in Star. The tunnel, the escape, it's just a backup plan. He's not going to fail. He will defeat Nightwing."

Morningleaf met Brackentail's gaze and relaxed. His loyalty and devotion had long ago erased her memories of the brutish colt he'd been, and Brackentail had transformed in every way. Always big and gangly for his age, he'd grown into a handsome stallion. A glossy sheen enhanced his dark-orange feathers, long brown lashes bordered his golden eyes, and his handsome, unmarked brown face had become the very trait that made him stand out among the pegasi. "I feel like my whole life has led up to this moment," she said to him.

Brackentail snorted. "That's because it has."

The fluttering of giant wings caught Morningleaf's

attention and blew back her mane, but the approaching winged steed was invisible. "Star!" she whinnied.

Her best friend landed and turned visible, and she flung herself into his wings. "What's wrong?" she asked him. "You're shaking?"

"I don't know, but I have a very bad feeling that none of us are safe."

"We aren't," she said honestly.

"I know, but this is different. You all must leave tonight. Take the one hundred and forty steeds you've already rescued and go, leave Anok."

"Did something happen?" asked Morningleaf.

Star shook his head. "Maybe it's just the storm, but I feel like something isn't right, and I don't think we should wait another day. One hundred and forty is enough to start a new herd, so go."

Morningleaf glanced at Brackentail.

"If Star feels that strongly about it, then I agree. We'll leave now," said Brackentail.

"Not now," said Star. "It has to be tonight. We have one more pegasus we must rescue: Larksong. I promised Frostfire."

Morningleaf twitched, irritated, but said, "Okay, I'll

tell my brother and Echofrost."

"I already told her," said Star. "In fact, she's probably in the tunnel now on her way here."

"We'll meet her at the blind," said Brackentail.

"Then this is good-bye," said Star. He extended his wings, and the three huddled together, with Bumblewind's absence still aching between them. "You aren't just my friends," said Star. "You're my guardians." He gazed at each of them. "No black foal can survive without help, and you two have given me . . . everything." Star pressed his forehead against theirs and then stepped back. "Now lead the pegasi home."

"Home?" asked Morningleaf.

Star nodded. "When I was a foal, I thought home was where you lived. When I was a yearling warrior, I thought home was where you died. But now that I'm an adult stallion, I know that home is where you love. Go find a new home on the southern continent and then spread our kind across the planet." He arched his proud neck. "Make new legends."

Morningleaf's tears rolled down her cheeks. "You'll meet us there, right?"

Star nuzzled her, not answering, and Morningleaf and

Brackentail pressed against him a final time. "I have one more thing to do," said Star. He panted, drawing up his starfire.

Morningleaf watched him, stunned as usual by the glittering power that radiated from his hide in waves of warmth. She'd been healed several times and had grown to love the sensation. She waited expectantly. Then Star opened his mouth and doused her dead black feathers with his golden light. Morningleaf spread her wings as the tendrils of starfire curled around her feathers, healing them down to their roots. With great satisfaction, she watched them grow longer and turn from charred black to shimmering aqua blue.

When he was finished, she rushed to Star's side and wrapped her healed wings around his neck, unable to speak but radiating joy. She sniffed his mane, and it smelled like the grasses of Dawn Meadow. To her, he was home.

"Fly," Star whispered, "and don't look back." His words urged Morningleaf and Brackentail into the wind. They flew fast and low, but Morningleaf, who never did as she was told, looked back.

Star waved, and she saw a waterfall of tears sliding

down his cheeks and a wreath of white flowers growing around his hooves. Her heart squeezed tight. Would she ever see him again?

Then Star lifted off toward the valley, passed through a cloudbank, and disappeared.

When Morningleaf and Brackentail arrived at the tunnel, Morningleaf put her head inside and listened, feeling the same anxiety that Star had described. "Something *is* wrong," she said to Brackentail.

"Shh, I hear hoofbeats coming," he said. "Who's there?" he neighed into the passageway.

A muffled voice answered. "It's Echofrost. I have to get a message to Hazelwind about Frostfire and Larksong."

"Hazelwind's not here," whinnied Morningleaf, "but we know about Larksong. Star told us."

"Okay," Echofrost huffed. "I'm alm—"

The ground rumbled, and then Morningleaf heard the heavy thud of falling dirt. Dust billowed from the entrance of the tunnel. Morningleaf and Brackentail fell backward, coughing and covered in dirt. They scrambled to their hooves and raced back to the entrance. "Echofrost!" screamed Morningleaf.

There was no answer.

Morningleaf gaped at the dark hole, which continued to shudder and exhale dust, wondering how much of the passageway had fallen. "Echofrost!"

All their hard work—and maybe Echofrost herself— was buried.

Brackentail stuck his head inside, neighing for Echofrost, but there was still no answer from her. "I'm going in," he whinnied, and charged into the collapsing passageway.

Morningleaf rushed to follow him but halted at the entrance, her hooves rooted to the ground. "Wait," she whispered, choking on dust. Morningleaf stared at the black tunnel, listening to it shudder, knowing it was caving in, that it was growing tighter and smaller . . . and her mind sailed back to the lava tubes where Frostfire had imprisoned her. She'd hidden in that utter blackness for days, starving and with rats crawling over her hooves. Morningleaf's legs trembled as though she were there again.

These aren't the lava tubes, she told herself.

But her hooves wouldn't budge.

Then Echofrost screamed.

Morningleaf snapped back to the present and galloped into the tunnel. Dust and debris crashed around her as the tunnel crumbled. "Where are you?" she whinnied.

"We're here!" answered Brackentail. Morningleaf reached them at a point in the passageway that was about halfway to the pond. The sky was visible above her where the land had caved in and buried most of Echofrost. "Grab a leg," Brackentail said.

Morningleaf wrapped her wings around one front leg, and Brackentail had the other. They pulled, and Echofrost screamed again. "My back leg is caught on something, maybe a tree root."

"We have to dig her out," said Brackentail.

Morningleaf bit back her terror. She and Brackentail scooped dirt away from Echofrost until they discovered the thick root trapping her. Morningleaf twisted Echofrost's leg to free it. Her friend groaned.

"I'm sorry," said Morningleaf.

They pulled Echofrost upright. The tunnel quaked again, and more dirt slammed their backs.

"Run!" neighed Brackentail.

The three of them galloped toward the light at the forest-end of the tunnel. Echofrost limped badly, but fear kept her moving. Behind them the tunnel slammed in on itself. Field mice and snakes passed them, racing for their lives, and Morningleaf swallowed her screams. A clump of dirt smacked her tailbone—the tunnel was coming down—all of it!

The three friends burst out of the darkness just as the rest of the tunnel collapsed, closing off all escape from the valley. Morningleaf skidded to a halt, almost crashing into a dark-gray mare who stood waiting for them.

It was Petalcloud! Her Ice Warriors stood behind her with their ears pinned and their eyes triumphant.

"No!" Morningleaf cried, confused.

But it wasn't the sight of Petalcloud that shocked Morningleaf the most; it was the stallion standing next to her.

Frostfire.

"Seize her," said the white stallion to the Ice Warriors.

And Morningleaf knew instantly that he had betrayed them all.

33

LIAR

STAR COASTED OVER THE EASTERN SWELLS. THE pegasi were back in the valley, chased there by the storm. They were haggard, windblown, and tired. Sharp peals of mourning lifted into the sky over the pegasi who'd been killed by the stampede, the wolves, and the tornado. Silverlake had made it safely back after he'd left her in the grassland, and she was standing with Sweetroot, tending to distressed steeds. Other than the obvious, nothing unusual seemed amiss.

Star glided to the stone tribute and flew circles around it. From a distance it had looked intact, but up close he saw massive damage. The clay had cracked between the stones, and hundreds of rocks had fallen, leaving a huge chunk open on one side. Dust billowed around him, making him cough. Star landed and whistled for Frostfire. When the stallion didn't immediately appear, Star whistled for him again. "Frostfire?"

There was no answer.

"I'm back!" Star called out. Then he heard hoofbeats behind him. Star whirled around and found Frostfire, side by side with his mother and her guard. Star leaped backward. "What's this?" he asked, looking from the white stallion to Petalcloud to Stormtail.

"It's over, Star," said Frostfire, looking resigned. "All of it: the tunnel, the tribute, the plan."

"What do you mean *over*?" Star's heart thudded hard, sending his pulse racing. And why had Frostfire mentioned the tunnel in front of Petalcloud! He scanned Frostfire for injuries, wondering if her guard had attacked him or tortured him, but he seemed unharmed. "Did they hurt you?" Star asked his uncle.

Petalcloud pranced forward, swishing her tail. "He doesn't get it," she nickered to Frostfire.

"Get what?" Star forced himself to take deep breaths, but he felt his gut twisting like a snake.

Petalcloud gazed up at him, her black eyes shining. "Frostfire has made a deal . . . with me."

Star reared as the ground seemed to swirl beneath him. "Frostfire!" he screamed. "What have you done?"

His uncle flattened his ears. "I made promises too," he said, his voice ragged. "To Larksong. She can't eat or sleep; she's molting. They took our son, and I promised I'd get him back, but I was fair to you, Star. I helped you find your friends, I stayed by your side while you built this tribute, and then you *didn't* save my mare or my colt, did you? And now it's too late—the tunnel is ruined. I had to do something."

"Ruined? How?"

"It collapsed, just a few moments ago."

Star's heart lurched. Morningleaf and Brackentail had just flown there! This explained his feeling of dread— it was about the tunnel! "Was anyone inside?" he asked, afraid of the answer.

"Yes, someone was," answered Petalcloud. "Someone we all thought was dead until Frostfire told us where to find her."

Star grunted. He knew exactly who Petalcloud was talking about, but he lifted his eyes to Frostfire's, hoping he was wrong. "Tell me you didn't," he pleaded, his voice strangled.

"I did," said Frostfire. "I traded Morningleaf for

Starfrost. My colt is being returned to Larksong right now, and Nightwing is setting my family free."

Star saw that Frostfire took no pleasure in what he'd done but that he'd do it again in a heartbeat.

Star faced Petalcloud. "Where's Morningleaf now?" he asked, fearing the worst, that she'd died in the tunnel.

Petalcloud curled her lip, then quickly softened her expression—but not before Star had seen the white flash of her teeth. "She's safe; she's with Nightwing."

Star's veins turned to ice. "Safe?" he spat, and suddenly he understood what Frostfire had been feeling since Nightwing took his son: panicked. "A good lead mare would never allow this—any of this," said Star, his lips trembling.

She snorted, tossing her glossy silver mane off her dark neck. "Do you think I wanted to trade Starfrost for Morningleaf? I didn't, but I can't stop Nightwing, and neither can you. I've chosen his protection."

"You've chosen our *destruction*!"

Star turned on his uncle, his anger bubbling hotter. "And you! Maybe I didn't save your mare . . . yet . . . but I didn't harm her either. Nightwing will *kill* Morningleaf."

Frostfire averted his eyes but remained stoic. "I saved my family, Star."

I'm your family too, Star thought, but Frostfire had made it clear during their travels that he didn't feel the same connection.

Petalcloud fluffed her feathers. "You can't trust a liar, Star."

Star's wings fell to his sides. "You're right," he said to Petalcloud. "But I did."

"Twice," she said. Petalcloud glowed with pleasure over giving Star the news that he'd been betrayed. "Your plan is ruined, the rebels are revealed, and your best friend is captured. What do you have to say about that?"

"Nothing to you." Star lifted off and flapped his giant black wings, heading toward the valley, toward Nightwing.

34

THE TRIBUTE

STAR SOARED OVER THE VALLEY OF PEGASI, hunting for the Destroyer. Below him he saw the collapsed tunnel. It appeared as a long, jagged rip in the green grass, leading from the pond toward the forest in the south. The Wind Herd steeds huddled in their separate groups, confused and with their necks craned, calling to herdmates across the valley, whinnying for news.

Star flew low, just as the clouds parted and the hot sun lit the valley, casting his shadow across Wind Herd. They looked up at him, and their rumblings ceased. Star saw Sweetroot and Silverlake and all the rest who had not left the valley. The sight of Star gliding overhead calmed their panic. *We've come a long way*, he thought, remembering the days when a glimpse of him caused terror.

Star hovered over the heads of the Wind Herd guards. "Where's Nightwing," he trumpeted. He saw no sign of Morningleaf.

The Ice Warriors cast their eyes toward Petalcloud, who had flown to the hill next to the tribute and stood alone.

She glanced at the sky, her eyes triumphant.

Then another shadow passed by the sun, shading the stone tribute and then angling toward Star. It was Nightwing. He circled the valley, his eyes focused on Wind Herd. He opened his mouth and scorched the grass with silver fire. The pegasi galloped toward the woods.

"Hold steady," Star neighed to them, pitching his voice so low his words vibrated their ribs. Only over-stallions spoke this way, and the twelve thousand steeds halted, instantly responding to his authority and standing at attention, ready for his next command. Star sighed, realizing he couldn't change the inherent nature of pegasi. They responded to strength and power, and this kept order in their massive herds, but it was also their greatest weakness when that power was abused.

Star whirled, facing Nightwing. It was time to rid Anok, and the Beyond, of the Destroyer; and it was time for Star to rise to what he believed was his true destiny. It wasn't to unite or conquer the herds, or to heal or destroy the pegasi; it was to *defend* them. Frostfire had been right about that much. "Set Wind Herd free," Star commanded. "Let them go."

Nightwing glided toward him and hovered, his wings creating wind that blew back Star's forelock. Nightwing nickered, and sparks popped between his teeth. "Here we are again," he said. His eyes turned from brown to silver as he opened his mouth and blasted Star with his fire.

Star sprang his shield. The starfire split around it, unable to touch him. Star watched the clouds drift by, waiting until the black stallion shut his mouth. When he did, Star retracted his shield, unharmed. "Let them go." he repeated, keeping his voice calm and steady.

Nightwing roared and dived toward the pegasi in the valley. Screaming erupted as they stampeded, and Nightwing unhinged his jaws to blast them.

Star tucked his wings and tore after Nightwing, flying under him and then darting upward and ramming him in the belly. Nightwing spun across the sky, then fell, slamming into the grass and skidding across it. He rolled to his hooves, his chest frothing. "Anok is mine!" he neighed.

"Anok is theirs," Star answered. He landed and faced

the dark stallion. They circled each other, heads low, ears pinned. Star willed Nightwing to attack him. If Frostfire was correct, Star's defenses would multiply in strength.

As if sensing a trap, Nightwing closed his wings. "I don't have to fight you," he said.

Star's hot blood turned cold. *What did that mean?*

Triumph blazed in Nightwing's eyes. "I have *her.*"

He was talking about Morningleaf, and Star's feeling of dread returned.

Nightwing nodded toward the woods, his expression smug.

Star followed his gaze. Frostfire emerged from the woods followed by two Ice Warriors who had Morningleaf in their grasp. They dragged her by her newly healed wings as she thrashed, trying to get free.

Star bolted toward her.

At Frostfire's command, an Ice Warrior twisted her left wing. Morningleaf shrieked as the small end bones snapped.

Sweat erupted between Star's ears and he halted, choking on the air as though he were drowning. "Let her go," he whinnied to Frostfire, his eyes pleading.

Guilt washed over his uncle's face, but he gave a small

shake of his head. He had chosen sides.

Star turned to Nightwing, begging him. "Please. This is between us." His heart thudded so hard he thought it would break through his rib cage.

"You can challenge me and lose her, or submit to me and save her," Nightwing neighed, his voice floating across the valley. "It's your choice."

Star blinked rapidly, trying to think. The pegasi of Anok stared at him, waiting. He held their fate and Morningleaf's in his wings.

Morningleaf's eyes bored into his, willing him *not* to save her, to save the herd instead. How had it all come back to this, a choice between saving one or all? It was a repeat of the night he'd received his power: when Frostfire had Morningleaf gripped tight in his jaws, and Rockwing had offered to spare her life for Star's. He'd chosen to save her, and then she'd thrown herself into the path of the deathblow meant for him. And she'd died anyway.

Star's feelings twisted, making him dizzy. If Star let Nightwing execute him to save Morningleaf, none of her sacrifices, none of her bravery, and none of her faith would equal anything. He returned her gaze. Understanding flashed between them. Star would save the herd.

Morningleaf would have to save herself.

The pegasi in the valley, Petalcloud, Frostfire, and the Ice Warriors—they all quieted, waiting for his decision.

Star arched his proud neck, flexed the powerful muscles he'd developed building the tribute, and stood to his full height, shadowing Nightwing. "I challenge you," he said, and then he brayed the battle cry of an over-stallion over the valley until it echoed from the land to the stars.

Surprise flickered across Nightwing's face.

Star drew his golden starfire and shot it throughout his body and into the sky like an erupting volcano. His power healed the damage he'd endured building the tribute. As the pegasi watched, Star's battered hooves turned smooth, his dull hide glowed black, and his tattered feathers lengthened into glossy plumage.

The pegasi in the valley cried out as one, in an ear-jarring cheer for Star. They rattled their feathers and grouped into the formation of an army—all of them—down to the elders and the walkers. They splayed their wings, and ferocious energy blazed through them.

Nightwing shook his head as though he didn't believe his ears. "Break her wings and drop her from the clouds," he ordered.

The two Ice Warriors darted into the sky, with Morningleaf dangling between them.

"No!" whinnied Silverlake. She and Redfire and their friends rocketed after Morningleaf.

But Star kept his eyes trained on Nightwing, even as his heart broke into a thousand pieces for Morningleaf. "You will never win this," Star said; then he lifted off and glided to the top of the tribute. All eyes followed him.

Star found the special feather he'd tucked into the rocks—a long and beautiful flight feather that was golden in color, with a dark-brown tip. It still smelled of his friend. Star lifted the feather over his head and trumpeted across the valley and the grassland, his voice carrying for miles and miles. "For Bumblewind!" he brayed.

Sweetroot trotted forward and raised her wing over her head. "For Bumblewind!" she whinnied.

Behind Sweetroot, the nearly twelve thousand pegasi all raised one wing over their heads and repeated her words. "For Bumblewind!" And Star's heart pounded at the sight of them spread across the green valley, their bright feathers fluttering in the wind, crying out the name of their fallen friend.

Nightwing choked on his silver fire and whirled, facing

Star. "What is this? Are you mocking me?" he neighed.

"This is freedom," Star answered.

Then the nearly twelve thousand pegasi lifted off, in battle formation, and swarmed Nightwing's army of Ice Warriors.

35

TOPPLING DOWN

THE DESTROYER WOULD NOT BE DISTRACTED from his rival. He wove out of the advancing army of pegasi and hurtled toward Star. Petalcloud sent her newborn filly, Riversun, into hiding with her guard, Stormtail, and then she tucked herself against the side of the tribute, watching as the Wind Herd steeds overwhelmed her warriors. The pegasi tore apart the clouds as they drove her Ice Warriors out of the sky.

Silverlake, Redfire, and their friends attacked the two stallions holding Morningleaf, kicking them in the legs and wings. From the corner of his eye, Star saw Morningleaf break free. She spread her aqua feathers and caught the wind, flapping erratically because of her broken end bones.

"You've doomed your friends," brayed Nightwing, charging toward Star. Bright sparks shot from his mouth.

Star sprang off Bumblewind's monument and soared toward the Destroyer. They clashed over the heads of the battling pegasi. Nightwing shot a stream of fire, but Star deflected it with his shield. "You can't hurt me," Star reminded him.

Nightwing snorted, his eyes glinting. "Maybe not *you*." He turned and sailed toward Wind Herd.

"No!" Nightwing was supposed to attack *him*, not his friends.

The pegasi met Nightwing head-on and surrounded him, their teeth bared. The Destroyer stalled in midflight and dropped beneath them, then he flew circles under them, panting, and drawing up his silver fire. It streamed behind him, growing in power the faster he flew. He was spinning it into a tornado, inspired no doubt by the recent storm. The pegasi stared, shocked. And then Nightwing released the supernatural twister.

Star gasped as hundreds of pegasi were whipped into the cone of fire and did not come out the other side, their souls cast into the Beyond.

Star dived toward Nightwing, avoiding the silver cyclone. "Get out of here!" he called to the herd.

"No. Don't flee!" neighed Silverlake. She soared toward Nightwing, and Star wondered what had happened to Morningleaf. Knowing Silverlake, she'd ordered her daughter to hide, and maybe for once Morningleaf had obeyed her mother.

Silverlake raised her wing over her head, fanning her flight feathers. "For Bumblewind!" she blared, glancing at Star.

Wind Herd saw her and rallied, re-forming their battle lines.

Star exhaled. Silverlake was right. The time for running was over.

Nightwing vanquished his tornado, his expression nasty. "For Bumblewind? What does that mean?"

"The tribute is ours," answered Silverlake. "Our friend is buried under it. And you . . ." She paused, lifting her chin and setting her jaw. "You don't deserve honor. You're a coward."

Nightwing reared back, his fury rippling in waves, and he exhaled a puff of silver steam, so light and gentle it seemed harmless, but it was starfire. The mist enveloped Silverlake.

"No!" Star cried.

The gray mare folded her wings, looking apologetic,

and then she transformed into dust. Star darted to where she had been, but Silverlake was gone, banished to the Beyond, where her mate, Thundersky, was also trapped.

Star stared. He didn't believe it. Silverlake, his adoptive mother, was dead.

Nightwing nickered as though amused and glided toward the tribute. "I'll show you a coward," he rasped. Then he inhaled, and Star thought Nightwing was going to use his fire, but he didn't. Instead he faced the tribute and ejected a powerful noise, like the noise Star had used to scare off the dire wolves at the river, only louder. The sound vibrated the ten thousand stones and rippled through the sky, knocking all the pegasi to the ground.

Star slammed onto the soil, his head spinning. All around him pegasi fell like hail, smacking and bouncing off the grass. Star pressed his wings against his ears, trying to block the awful noise.

He staggered upright, and his vision sharpened. His friends' bodies littered the valley in broken heaps, their legs twisted, their wings bent in half. They were screaming; he knew that by their open mouths, but he couldn't hear them over Nightwing's blaring. Star remembered when he'd healed the entire Black Army at once, and he drew his golden fire up his long neck and shot it in a wide beam. He doused the fallen steeds in healing light, setting the meadow aglow.

Behind him the tribute began to crumble.

Star ignored it and focused on the pegasi. His starfire licked across the grass, healing bones and wounds, and staunching the flow of blood. The Wind Herd steeds lifted off the ground and tumbled in the light. Star saw Petalcloud, who was still hiding at the base of the tribute, watching him—terrified.

Nightwing continued his assault on Bumblewind's monument, breaking the clay and splitting the stacked rocks with his horrible noise. The tribute swayed.

When all the pegasi were healed, Star uncovered his ears and crawled toward Sweetroot. "It's coming down," he cried. "You all must leave. Now! Forget the berries, forget fighting him—just go. I need him to attack me, not you, and he won't do that while you're here."

Sweetroot flared her pink feathers. "We won't abandon you, Star."

"Please go."

"No. We're seeing this through, for better or for worse. We're your guardian herd."

Just then Nightwing paused his attack, and the terrible noise evaporated, leaving Sweetroot's last words ringing across the valley: *We're your guardian herd.*

The pegasi of Anok, nearly all twelve thousand of them, charged toward Star and slid to a halt, bowing their heads to him. "We're your guardian herd," they whinnied in unison.

Star's throat constricted, and tears stung his eyes.

Nightwing threw back his head. "No, you belong to me!" He turned on the tribute and hurled twisting spheres of silver light at it, over and over, blasting rocks and causing explosions of dust. The tribute quaked, and the staggering mountain of rocks leaned toward the valley as the hard clay at the base cracked, creating fissures like spiderwebs that raced up the sides.

Star heard a scream, and he saw Petalcloud dart out of the billowing dust. She bounded like a deer, leaping over boulders, her black eyes bulging, but she was too late. The tribute quaked and toppled toward her with a mighty groan.

"Mother!" Frostfire whinnied.

Petalcloud threw out her wings as though someone might pull her to safety, but no one was there. Star scrunched his eyes as the almost ten thousand stones tumbled over the gray mare, squashing her flat.

The dust billowed and swelled toward the clouds.

Nightwing soared through it, landing where Star had last seen Petalcloud, but she was deeply buried. Nightwing faced Star. "You killed her," he raged, spitting his words.

Star didn't answer, for he had done no such thing.

Nightwing reared and slammed the grass with his hooves, conducting starfire through the soil. The valley floor rolled and broke open, creating huge rifts in the grass. Some pegasi fell in, but they quickly opened their wings and flew out of the crevasses and up toward the clouds. Nightwing stamped his hooves again, and the land rippled out from under him, knocking down pegasi and felling trees in the forest.

Star reeled from the explosions, trying to keep his balance. Around him, the lush green grass caught fire, and several fallen pegasi exploded into flames. The rest bolted toward the clouds. Nightwing followed them, sending silver starfire after them, the flames licking their hooves. He flew around the pegasi, herding them into a tight group with his fire. He was going to kill them all.

Star charged Nightwing, his ears pinned, his breathing heavy, and his heart beating faster, for this was the final hour.

Time slowed as Star rocketed toward Nightwing in the sky. Nightwing tossed his mane in a wild arc and swung his head like a snake. His jaws gaped open, and starfire roared from his mouth. His eyes gleamed, mad with fury, and his ribs vibrated.

Star's golden fire responded, surging through him, crackling along his hide and heating his bones. Sparks tingled his tongue. Maybe Star wasn't being threatened, but his guardian herd was, and he would defend them.

36

DESTINY

AFTER MORNINGLEAF BROKE FREE OF THE ICE
Warriors, her mother had ordered her to hide. "Go into
the forest," Silverlake had said.

"But I can help you."

"It's for me that I want you to go!" cried Silverlake. "I
caused all this when I chose to protect Star as a foal. He
woke the Destroyer when he received his power, putting
you and the herds at risk. I need to see this through, but I
can't focus if you're near. You must hide. Please."

Morningleaf gazed into her mother's gray face and
saw her determination, and her love. It was Silverlake's
quest to protect Star to the end, a quest that Morningleaf had adopted. But maybe Dewberry was right; maybe

Morningleaf had a destiny of her own. "Okay, Mama, I'll go."

Silverlake had exhaled in a quick, relieved sob. "Thank you."

Morningleaf had fled to the woods where she'd last seen Brackentail. He and Echofrost had fought to protect her when Frostfire and the Ice Warriors seized her at the tunnel, but the guards had slammed Brackentail into the ground and knocked him out. Echofrost had fled, at Morningleaf's insistence, to find Hazelwind, Dewberry, and the hundred and forty pegasi waiting on the coast. It was time for them to go, to leave Anok for good.

Now Morningleaf landed at Brackentail's side, and when he saw her, he whinnied, "You're safe!"

She nodded, flinching at the pain in her wings. She had three broken wingtips, and her injuries throbbed, but they weren't serious, just uncomfortable. "You're bleeding," she said, noticing a wound behind his ear.

"I'm fine," he insisted. He glanced toward the valley. "What's happening?"

"Star is fighting Nightwing. I escaped."

"What do we do?" he asked her. "Help Star or leave Anok with Echofrost?"

"We can't help Star," said Morningleaf.

Brackentail turned his gaze south, toward the Dark Water, and then looked back at her. "I can't leave."

Morningleaf exhaled with relief. "Neither can I. Let's go to the blind; we can watch the battle from there."

They lifted off and flew through the trees. "I can't believe Frostfire betrayed us," said Brackentail.

"Oh, I knew he would the moment I saw him in the den."

Brackentail snorted. "Then why didn't you tell Star?"

She paused, thinking. "Star knew I didn't trust him."

"But if you'd pressed him, he would have gotten rid of the stallion."

Morningleaf glanced at Brackentail. "You're looking at this all wrong. You think Star's at fault for trusting Frostfire, but that's his nature, and it's what I love most about him. Yes, I could have planted fear and suspicion in Star's heart, but it doesn't belong there. The pegasus at fault here is Frostfire."

"You're right," said Brackentail, sounding surprised.

She flicked her tail at him. "I know," she nickered.

They reached the blind and stood together, peering beyond the leaves of the cottonwood forest to the valley. Pillars of smoke drifted up from countless small fires that spread across the grass. The tribute Star built had collapsed, and the almost ten thousand stones—some shattered, some intact—had tumbled across the valley like eggs spilled out of a nest.

Nightwing and Star faced off beneath the cloud layer, each drawing up his starfire—one silver and one gold—and Morningleaf caught her breath, stunned—not by the smoke, debris, and violence, but by Star's beauty. His hide glistened like a stone underwater, his hooves and eyes beamed yellow light, and his long mane fluttered across his muscle-bound chest. He held his head high, his neck curved in a tight arch—not with pride but with confidence.

Morningleaf gasped. "*This* is his destiny." And her gut flipped, making her feel weak. "Everything we've done has brought him to this moment."

Brackentail watched her, his golden eyes warm and sad. "This isn't the end, Morningleaf; it's the beginning."

She leaned against him, and they gazed through the leaves, watching Star's final battle together.

37

STARFIRE

STAR LOWERED HIS NECK AND CHARGED THE
Destroyer. Nightwing flashed his teeth and flew to meet
him. They collided over the heads of the Wind Herd steeds,
fighting with hooves and teeth. Star bit into Nightwing's
neck, tasting blood, while the Destroyer tore into Star's
chest with his hooves. They battled each other through
the clouds, twisting and kicking, flying higher and higher.

But Nightwing's muscles were weak. He'd spent his
time in the Flatlands eating and playing with Petalcloud.
Star had spent his time lifting and carrying heavy stones.
He reared back and struck Nightwing, sending him hurtling across the sky.

The Destroyer twisted around and returned, hissing

starfire. This is where *he* was stronger—with his powers. Nightwing sucked in a huge breath and then shot hundreds of silver light quills at Star. They arced across the sky with ferocious speed, trailing sparks.

Star threw up his shield and watched the sharp quills bounce off.

Then Nightwing circled closer, blasting him with star bombs. Star ducked and twirled as they exploded against his shield, over and over, lighting up the clouds and sky. Silver smoke billowed, and shocked screams erupted from the watching steeds. The fiery bombs knocked Star's golden orb toward land, and he struggled to right himself.

Nightwing roared in frustration.

Star hovered high above the Flatlands, his thoughts tumbling. He'd once asked his mother in a vision, *"What if I can't defeat him? What if he's stronger?"*

"Maybe you're not stronger," his mother had answered, *"but you're better, Star. Follow your love, not your fear."* What did Star love? He loved the pegasi of Anok. What did he fear? That Nightwing would destroy them. But Star didn't fear the Destroyer himself, and suddenly Star had an idea.

All that mattered was *them*—the pegasi of Anok. And since Star couldn't project his shield around the nearly twelve thousand steeds, he would project it around one—Nightwing.

But first he would have to get close to him. Star dropped his shield and faced Nightwing with his hooves down, his mouth closed.

"Are you surrendering?" asked Nightwing.

"In a way I am," said Star.

Nightwing flew closer, studying Star's expression, noticing that he wasn't poised to fight. "What are you playing at?" he asked, spitting sparks. They landed on Star's hide and sizzled through it.

Star winced as the cold embers burned through him, not like fire, but like ice. "I'm not playing," he said.

Nightwing clacked his teeth in Star's face, close enough to feel his hot breath. Star didn't flinch.

Triumph bloomed in Nightwing's eyes. He inhaled sharply, unhinged his jaw like a viper, and roared starfire, thinking to end Star for good. Star faced it, his heart thrumming, and he sprang his shield, but not to protect himself. He snapped it around them both, sealing their fates together.

The starfire filled the sphere, burning both stallions.

Star gasped and clamped his jaws, biting back his screams.

Nightwing threw out his wings, touching the sides of the golden orb. "Let me out!" he brayed.

Star's teeth rattled, and the burning fire scorched his flesh and feathers, and reached into his bones, but he focused all his energy on keeping his shield intact.

Nightwing panicked and attacked Star harder, burning them both worse.

Star trained his eyes on his enemy, watching Nightwing's flesh blister with his own.

Nightwing withdrew the fire and kicked Star in the knee. The orb fell toward the valley with the two stallions battling inside. Star reared, striking Nightwing across the jaw with his hooves, but kept his attention on projecting his shell and keeping them both trapped inside.

They crashed onto the grass, scattering the Wind Herd steeds into the sky. Star and Nightwing bounced across the Flatlands until the orb rolled to a stop. Star felt his rear leg snap, so he balanced on three.

The Destroyer roared at him. "You're killing us both!"

Star shook his head. "No. *You're* killing us both."

The Wind Herd pegasi dropped from the clouds and surrounded the two stallions who were trapped inside Star's golden shield. Star saw their terrorized expressions, but also saw that they were safe.

Nightwing lashed his tail. "This just makes you easier to destroy," he said, and then he re-created the thin beam of silver light that had pierced Star's chest in the Sun Herd lands. He shot it at Star, in the exact same spot, and Star's eyes popped as he felt the power press through his hide, through his chest bones, and into his thumping heart.

Not again, he thought. Then a soothing voice filled his head: *Don't fight him.* And Star relaxed as peace washed through him. He accepted Nightwing's power and let it spread into his heart and throughout his body, absorbing it as his own, and it didn't kill him.

But with the Destroyer's silver fire came his dark feelings of destruction. They cycled through Star's mind, poisoning his thoughts. He bucked and twisted as his mood blackened. *The world was hateful, despicable. He was despicable.* Star slammed into the side of his shield, every piece of his soul begging him to release Nightwing and fly away.

Nightwing saw Star's agony, and he pressed his hatred deeper and deeper into him.

Star glanced at the Wind Herd steeds surrounding him, gaping at him, and he wanted to destroy them all. But he also knew these weren't *his* feelings but Nightwing's. How the ancient stallion had lived with this poison in his heart for so long, Star didn't know. He bucked again, and the orb spun around the field.

Nightwing touched Star's neck with his wing, trying a new tactic, appealing to Star as a fellow black foal. "Don't fight me, Star; join me." His voice was low and tantalizing, as though he were offering Star something delicious.

Star felt how easy it would be to give in. . . .

Then Star's eyes rolled back in his head, and he saw white light—his mother.

Lightfeather roared her secrets into his ears—no, not her secrets, her *instructions*, repeating words he'd heard before: *Don't fight him. Heal him.*

Star shook his head. No, that wasn't what she'd said to him on the night she died. She'd said: *Don't fight* them, *heal* them.

The image of Lightfeather appeared, and she pressed her forehead against his. "It was never about *them*," she said. "It was always about *him*. Nightwing is the Killer of Light. He is Fear. He is Hatred. Don't fight him, Star. *Heal* him."

Star shuddered, and his eyes flew open. He stared into the empty eye sockets of Nightwing's skull. *Heal the Destroyer, could he?* He had nothing to lose by trying.

"Destroy me if you must!" Star brayed. He would need

all Nightwing's rage and hatred directed at him if he was going to heal it.

Nightwing's eyes widened, and he gleefully accepted the challenge, blasting Star with the full strength of his powers, and Star absorbed it all and let it fill him, taking four hundred years of Nightwing's hatred into his gut.

The pain of it shredded Star's thoughts and rattled his bones; but he held it inside, and he seared it with his golden fire, cleansing it and turning it back on Nightwing, soaking him in healing light.

The Destroyer froze, stunned. The starfire repaired him. Star watched Nightwing's black heart soften, his injuries heal, his coat turn glossy, and his eyes shine with hope. Star held out his wing, offering Nightwing an opposite truce. "Don't fight me, Nightwing; join me."

Nightwing stared, his jaw hanging slack. A single tear fell from his eye, landed at the base of the shield, and a white flower blossomed between them. Star's heart pounded with excitement.

But Nightwing groaned like a whale, holding his head and staring at the white flower in awe, then horror. He reared and crushed the flower under his hooves, and then he bellowed at Star. "NEVER!"

Nightwing shut his eyes and squeezed his muscles,

ejecting Star's power from his body. The golden light flashed and disappeared, leaving Star empty. It was all the starfire he had. He'd given it all away. And now it was gone. The shield evaporated, and Star saw Sweetroot fly off to retrieve the death berries.

"I failed," Star whispered.

Nightwing pounced on Star and blasted him with renewed power.

Around Star the valley burned and the pegasi trembled, watching the two black stallions destroy each other.

Star grit his teeth against the astonishing pain, and the agony of losing. But then he saw an aqua feather floating over his head, and Morningleaf dashing across the sky, rocketing toward him, with Brackentail at her side. Star realized that everyone had been wrong—including her. *Heal him. Embrace him. Fight him.* Star had tried it all. But only one pegasus in Anok had the power to destroy Nightwing—and that was Nightwing himself.

"You don't fight a pegasus on the terms he sets," Morningleaf had warned him once, when they were still weanlings. He remembered the conversation in a blur.

"It has to be on his terms, Morningleaf. Otherwise it won't mean anything," Star had answered her. And with a ragged breath taken through shredded lungs, Star

exhaled and relaxed. He knew exactly what to do, and he'd known it all along. He had to beat the Destroyer on his own terms.

As Nightwing poured all his hatred into the silver fire and blasted it at Star, Star let it fill him. When the weight of death and suffering, guilt and grief all but crushed him, Star faced Nightwing, opened his mouth, and gave it all back.

The Destroyer hid his face and bellowed in terror as his own silver fire blazed from Star to Nightwing, in one colossal burst, and then the ancient stallion's body exploded.

Purple and silver smoke drifted upward and away, revealing one neat pile of black ash.

The Destroyer was dead.

38

WINDBORN

"YOU DID IT, STAR," CRIED SWEETROOT. **"IT'S OVER."**

The pegasi folded their wings and sobbed, overwhelmed.

Silver sparks crackled in Nightwing's black ashes, spooking the pegasi. Then his dust caught fire and vanished in a puff of smoke. And just like that, the Destroyer was gone, borne off by the wind.

Star stared at the singed grass, at the toppled monument, and at the pegasi who sagged with relief. It was over, not just for him, but also for them. "You're free," he said, and he collapsed, out of breath.

Quick movement caught Star's eye. Morningleaf and Brackentail dropped out of the sky and landed beside him.

Morningleaf sank to her knees, stroking his smoking back and staring into his eyes. "You beat him. I knew you would." She threw her wings around his neck. Star stifled a moan.

"I'm sorry; you're hurt!" she cried, stepping back.

Star's hide was burned, his chest bruised and bitten, his back leg broken. "Just a little," he said. He drew on his power and then paused, remembering it was gone.

Sweetroot galloped to him. "Your power?" she asked, sensing the problem.

Star shrugged one wing. "I guess I used it all," he said.

Sweetroot's eyes flew wide open. "Oh no!"

Star turned his mind inward, feeling into his gut, which was empty of the golden embers that had burned there since he'd turned one and received his power from the Hundred Year Star. Without the embers, he couldn't produce new starfire. He felt heavy and cold, and hungry too. He felt like a normal pegasus.

"Maybe it will return," said Sweetroot, looking hopeful.

"Maybe," said Star. "Or maybe it's gone forever." *Forever*, there was that word again. What did it mean? He'd been immortal, and now he was not.

Suddenly the sky lit up with color, and all the pegasi

lifted their heads. Beautiful lights burst down from the blackness of space and rushed toward them. "It's the Ancestors," whinnied Sweetroot. The living pegasi couldn't see their ethereal bodies, but the streaks of color from the Ancestors' feathers whirled and twisted around them as if they were celebrating.

But it wasn't just the Ancestors. The Beyond was destroyed with the death of Nightwing, and the pegasi who'd been stuck there were released. Some had been trapped for four hundred years, and now they sailed with their herdmates from the golden meadow, reunited and free, and finally at peace.

But Star could see their translucent spirit bodies clearly, perhaps because they'd visited him before when he'd been thrown into hibernation by Nightwing during their first battle, many moons ago. Star saw Hollyblaze, the ancient Ancestor filly whose weanling army had protected Star in the past. Her eyes glimmered at him with pleasure and approval. And Bumblewind glided overhead, streaking the sky in shades of gold and brown, joyful that his friends were safe. And Star's adoptive mother, Silverlake, played with a crimson-winged stallion: her mate, Thundersky.

"Those are my parents," said Morningleaf, in a choked

breath, recognizing the colors of her parents' feathers.

Her body shook as she burst into tears, and Star wrapped his wing over her back. They curled together on the grass, watching the Wind Herd steeds lift off and fly with the Ancestors. Beautiful lights illuminated the clouds in every hue of color found in Anok. The spirits of the dead danced higher and higher and then disappeared.

Then pegasi all over the Flatlands met in groups, reunited. The grieving dams found their kidnapped newborns and weanlings, and happy nickers filled the valley.

Star glanced around him, and he saw how his huge herd was really made up of thousands of tiny herds called families. And he thought about his birth mother, Lightfeather. When she'd died, he'd felt alone, but now thinking back, he'd never been alone. Family wasn't just who made you; it was who loved you. It was who raised you, protected you, and believed in you. And Star had been greatly, deeply loved by Silverlake, Sweetroot, Grasswing, Bumblewind, Echofrost, Brackentail, Morningleaf, and finally, his guardian herd. As he gazed about him, he realized that he'd had all along what he'd wanted since he was a dud foal in Dawn Meadow: a family.

Then Star caught sight of Frostfire sneaking away with Larksong and their colt, Starfrost. Disappointment reared within him. They had unfinished business. Star had one broken leg, but his wings were fine, so he scooted away from Morningleaf, lifted off, and flew to Frostfire, landing three-legged in front of him.

The white stallion froze, and the two faced each other.

"I told you I'd rescue your mare, and I did," said Star, his hide still steaming where Nightwing had burned him. "All of you are truly free."

Larksong cringed, and Frostfire just stared, speechless.

Star lowered his muzzle to their young colt. Starfrost trotted bravely closer, exchanging breath with Star and flicking his short, curly tail. Star looked into his light-green eyes, which were shining with curiosity, and his heart opened wide to the colt. "You're my cousin," he said.

Starfrost bleated and lifted off, hovering over Star like a bumblebee. He tugged gently at Star's mane with his small teeth, enticing him to play. Star's throat closed. He wanted to play with Starfrost, teach him to fly, and watch him grow up, but Frostfire was taking the colt away. He looked at his uncle and understood that he couldn't force Frostfire to accept him any more than he could force Nightwing. He had to want it, and he didn't. "Take good care of him," Star said to Frostfire and Larksong.

The buckskin mare reached out to Star with her dark-blue wings and burst into tears. "We will. Thank you."

Frostfire opened his mouth to say something, but at the last moment he turned away. "Come, Starfrost," he said to his son. And Star watched his uncle walk out of the valley with his family, and he doubted he would ever see Frostfire again.

Morningleaf trotted to his side. "Someday he'll come around," she said.

Star nodded, but he didn't think so. He turned to Morningleaf, wincing at the pain in his leg and the burns across his black hide, but noticed also her bent wing. "I would heal the two of us, but my starfire is gone," he whispered.

Morningleaf stared at him. "You mean you're not immortal anymore?"

"No, I don't think so."

"And you can't fly around in tornadoes?"

"No." He noticed her amber eyes shining mischievously.

"And you can't go days and nights without eating or sleeping?"

"I don't think so," said Star.

Morningleaf dropped her wings, looking relieved.

"Good. Because it was getting really hard to keep up with you."

Star nickered with relief, because he thought she'd be disappointed. "I don't think I'll be going anywhere for a while." He stared at his broken leg, which throbbed, making him feel sick, and at the burns on his black hide that would leave scars. It would take time to heal.

"Well, you know what this means, don't you?" she asked.

"What?"

"Now we can be best friends forever."

"For *our* forever," he clarified, because he was mortal now, and he would one day die. A tear rolled down his cheek and mixed with the burned soil.

He and Morningleaf stared at the ground. Not a single flower appeared. "My power is really gone," he said, finding it difficult to believe.

"But you're not."

Star exhaled. "No, I'm not."

Brackentail joined them, and Star saw how happy Morningleaf was to see him. "The future is ours to create," said the brown stallion.

"It is," Morningleaf agreed, and she leaned toward Brackentail, and Star noticed how they'd grown together, like two trees sharing the same light. And he realized that he was that light, and for once he was pleased instead of jealous.

"What about Echofrost and Hazelwind and the one hundred and forty pegasi?" Star asked his friends. "We need to find them and bring them back."

Morningleaf shook her head. "They won't come back. We talked about this in the den and decided that, win or lose, we need to spread our kind out of Anok. The pegasi who left are excited; they want to explore and find a new home. But I—I decided not to leave," said Morningleaf. "I love it here."

Brackentail gazed at her. "Me too."

The tip of a loose feather flapped in the breeze, catching their attention. It was trapped under the remains of the tribute—golden in color, with a brown tip. Morningleaf pulled it loose. "This is Bumblewind's feather, isn't it?" she whispered.

A hush fell over the pegasi in the valley when they saw Morningleaf holding the special feather. Star watched her face brighten. "I have an idea." She galloped away, leaving Star and Brackentail standing in her dust.

Morningleaf flew to the hill where the tribute had stood, and she lifted the feather over her head, waiting for everyone's full attention. "We're going to rebuild the tribute," she neighed, her voice ringing clear across the Flatlands. "To mark the day of our freedom."

The pegasi murmured, staring at the stones strewn across the valley. "Each able adult will take a stone," she continued. "We'll build our new tribute in the west, at Crabwing's Bay, where the birds don't fly." She glanced at Star, and he nodded. She was referring to Star's bird friend who'd died there—Crabwing the seagull—and Star was glad she remembered him. Morningleaf continued, her voice quaking. "The monument will stand for Bumblewind, my mother, my sire, and for all the pegasi who gave their lives to free us."

"But we can't fly if we're carrying stones," said Sweetroot.

"We should walk anyway," said Morningleaf, "so we can stay together. I don't want the walkers migrating alone. We'll leave as soon as our injuries are healed."

After their long captivity in the valley, the pegasi leaped on the idea of returning to Western Anok, where the wolves were smaller and the wind gentler.

They spent the following moon strengthening their flying muscles and eating their fill. Sweetroot dug for herbs and healed the pegasi, doing what she did best. And Star enjoyed letting her care for him. She set his leg with a straight branch and fed him yarrow for his pain, and he marveled at her knowledge.

"You kept me out of work for a long time," she said to him, nickering.

On the last day of spring, the nearly twelve thousand pegasi each lifted a stone in their wings, and they trotted out of the Flatlands, the place of their enslavement, that very day.

Star wasn't blind to the group of steeds who refused to join them, mostly Ice Warriors and some weanlings who'd grown to adore Nightwing when he was alive. Stormtail led this herd, and he kept Nightwing's and Petalcloud's orphaned filly, Riversun, close to his side, protecting her as he'd once protected her mother.

"Do you think Riversun has the starfire?" Morningleaf had asked him. "Since her sire is Nightwing."

"I guess it's possible," he'd answered.

"That could be a problem."

Star sighed. "Let's not worry about what *might* be." Then he'd watched as Stormtail's forces, defeated and angry, traveled north, heading back to the cold region.

Some pegasi wanted to stop them, but Star argued against it. "Freedom isn't just for my followers," he explained. "It's for everyone." Since his birth in Dawn Meadow, Star had learned that no pegasus could be forced to accept a leader—they followed who they chose, and Anok was big enough for all of them. It was when pegasi forced their will on others that Anok became too small.

As they traveled through the fractured grasslands, walking like horses, Star watched Morningleaf with sidelong glances, and noticed how the herd quieted when she was near, how they listened to her, and how they loved her. The vision he'd had of her in the Trap had come true: she was a legend, a living one.

Star walked at her right flank and Brackentail walked at her left, and for the first time in many moons, Star relaxed and enjoyed the shining sun, feeling content. He was just a regular pegasus, he belonged to a giant herd, and his best friend was leading him home.

ACKNOWLEDGMENTS

MY HEARTFELT APPRECIATION GOES TO RICHARD Bach and Sabryna Bach for allowing me to use a quote from *Jonathan Livingston Seagull* as an epigraph in *Windborn*. Mr. Bach's inspiring novel about a seagull named Jonathan carried me through some hard and lonely times in high school. I moved often, which meant I changed schools often, but my books moved with me and became friends. So when I decided to create a special friend for Star on the coast of Anok, it was no accident that I chose a bird— a seagull I named Crabwing. And their scenes together remain some of my favorites. Thank you, Richard Bach, for creating the wonderful character of Jonathan Livingston and writing about him.

I'm thankful to have such a wonderful and dedicated team at HarperCollins Children's Books. I offer huge applause to each person who has helped these books soar. And without further ado, may I introduce you to the hard-working and passionate folks who turn computer files into full-fledged, hold-in-your hands, see-them-in a bookstore, bona fide, made-in-the USA books:

Rosemary Brosnan, Editorial Director

Karen Chaplin, Senior Editor

David McClellan, Illustrator

Heather Daugherty and Erin Fitzsimmons, Book Jacket and Interior Design

Alexei Esikoff and Jessica Berg, Production Editors

Andrea Curley, Copyeditor

Oriana Sisko and Tina Cameron, Production Managers

Kimberly VandeWater, Marketing

Andrea Pappenheimer and Kathy Faber, Sales

Patty Rosati and Molly Motch, Library Outreach

Olivia Russo, Publicity

Andrew Eiden, Audio Book Narrator

Deyan Audio, Audio Book Producer

Special thanks goes to my agent, Jacqueline Flynn. She's my friend and advocate, and I appreciate her strong and knowledgeable support, not just for my books, but also for me as an author. Thanks also to my family: my husband, Ramon, and my three children. My family is patient and encouraging, and I hope they are as proud of me as I am of them.

I also want to express special appreciation for Karen Chaplin, my primary editor. When it comes to my writing, there is no relationship more important to me than the one with my editor. I trust Karen completely and without reservation. Any story faults and writing flaws—they are mine. Karen doesn't fix my work for me. She guides me. She points out what is confusing and what doesn't belong. She's very good at doing this and then she leaves me to my revisions. She helps me discover the story within the story, she helps me clarify the world I've created, and she sticks up for the characters when I write over them. And where I don't succeed, we start again. We keep revising until I've reached the end of my abilities. A great editor is a gift, and I'm blessed to have a great editor. Thank you, Karen Chaplin.

TALES FROM

THE
⇐ GUARDIAN HERD ⇒

"Across the Dark Water"

By Jennifer Lynn Alvarez

Four hundred years before the birth of Star, a special black foal named Nightflame was born to Jungle Herd. After receiving the starfire power on his first birthday, Nightflame vanished for many moons. He returned a changed pegasus. He had become Nightwing the Destroyer, and he terrorized the herds, seeking followers through intimidation and cruelty.

Soon after his return, a great and deadly rebellion against Nightwing swept through the herds of Anok. The uprising stretched all the way to the interior of the continent, to the reclusive Lake Herd pegasi, and straight into the heart of a brave and romantic young stallion named Skyblaze. This is his story.

SKYBLAZE GALLOPED TOWARD THE FLATLANDS with his wings arched and flowing behind him. His heart sped as he neared his friends, the two-year-olds. They reared and stomped in the distance, neighing at the sky. Around them, the ferocious spring winds bent the long grass in half. He raced past his dam, Mistflower, who was sheltering in the valley with his new sister. Mistflower pinned her coppery ears at Skyblaze as he tore past. "Please don't fly in these winds," she whinnied.

"Stop worrying," he nickered. "I know what I'm doing." He lifted off, and a powerful gust sent him cartwheeling head over tail.

His little sister, Seabrook, waved one pale-turquoise wing at him, and Mistflower shook her head. "You always say that!"

"And I'm always right, Mother," he neighed as he righted himself. With the afternoon sun warming his feathers, Skyblaze soared into the Flatlands toward the Lake Herd gathering of two-year-olds.

His friends stood in rows, legs flexed, uncertain when to leap into the roaring currents overhead. Their manes and tails lifted and railed against their glistening hides. Free from the plagues and famines that often ravaged Western Anok, the Lake Herd pegasi thrived in their isolation from the other herds. Healthy and strong, stuffed with grass and sturdy with muscle, they played in winds that would devour most winged steeds.

But soon there would be no more plagues! This century's black foal had been born to Jungle Herd, and he was the first one known to survive his birth. The over-stallion of Jungle Herd had sent a messenger to Lake Herd, assuring them that Nightflame would use his power to become a great healer. So on the night that the Hundred Year Star blazed out in the sky, Lake Herd had rejoiced. The black foal had received his incredible power.

But after several moons without news, concern blossomed in their hearts. The elders began to fear the starfire—yes, it could heal, but the prophecy said it could also destroy. Unable to wait another day, Lake Herd's over-stallion, Thornwing, had sent an envoy to Jungle Herd to inquire about the black foal. Those pegasi had not yet returned.

Meanwhile, two-year-olds like Skyblaze had more pressing matters to consider, like showing off, flying in storms, and learning to fight. Skyblaze curled one wing and rolled again, coasting upside down over his friends. "What are you?" he whinnied. "A herd of land horses? Get up here!"

Three young mares squealed at him, pretending anger, but they were the first in the sky. The others followed, bursting into fast gallops and then shoving off the grass. The screaming winds slammed against their tails, hurtling them after Skyblaze. His large eyes rotated back and he could see them—over a hundred youngsters, their paths shaky and their muscles tight. He snorted. They thought riding the winds was about power, but it wasn't. It was about submission. The best fliers let the wind do the work.

The only two-year-old who understood windsurfing as well as he did was Willowsun. His eyes sought her now—her golden hide, her midnight-black mane and tail, her dark-blue eyes—but the sky was empty of her.

"Who are you looking for?"

Startled, Skyblaze rolled his eyes toward the voice, careful not to move his head lest he throw himself out of the current. It was Ashleaf. Lithe and graceful, she powered closer to him; the wind pushed her yellow forelock off her face, exposing her bold cheeks, fine muzzle, and luminous green eyes. "Well?" she pressed.

"I'm not looking for anyone." The lie was out before Skyblaze could stop it.

Ashleaf clenched her jaws and stared straight ahead. It was obvious she didn't believe him, and tension filled the air, making Skyblaze uneasy. "Want me to chase you?" he asked.

Sensing his guilt about the lie, Ashleaf pounced. "Race me to Boulder Creek!"

Skyblaze groaned inwardly. Boulder Creek was deep in the cottonwood forest. If they raced to it, they'd be alone together, which was exactly what she wanted. But he just wanted to find Willowsun. "All right," he said.

With a triumphant expression, Ashleaf wrapped her wings around the current, flattened her neck, and tucked her hooves, gliding ahead of him. Skyblaze remained relaxed, in no hurry to catch her; and he resumed his scan of the Flatlands, looking for Willowsun. The other two-year-olds avoided Willowsun, thinking the dun mare odd. And she ignored them right back, including Skyblaze. It was why he found it so difficult to say no to Ashleaf, because he knew how frustrating it was to be ignored.

As Skyblaze and Ashleaf angled toward Boulder Creek, a flash of white-tipped blue feathers caught Skyblaze's eye and he lost his breath—it was Willowsun, foraging in the trees! Just then, Ashleaf whinnied in joy as she reached the tip of the creek, thinking he was still chasing her. But Skyblaze had turned his head toward Willowsun, a painful error. The movement caused his body to twist, and the brunt of the wind struck his shoulder, knocking him sideways. He tumbled across the sky like a loose weed and fell toward land. Willowsun, who'd been grazing alone, jerked up her head and spotted him.

Skyblaze threw out his long, cherry-colored wings and braked hard, slowing, but not enough. He slammed onto the grass and rolled onto his back.

Ashleaf and Willowsun flew to him, arriving at the same time. "Are you hurt?" Willowsun asked. Skyblaze stared up at her dark-blue eyes, struggling for breath.

The palomino, Ashleaf, stomped her hoof and glared at the other mare. "You distracted him."

"I did not," sputtered Willowsun.

"You made him fall." Ashleaf bent over Skyblaze and fanned him with her violet feathers.

Willowsun raked her eyes over the tangle of hooves that was Skyblaze. "Whatever happened here—he did it to himself." She turned to trot away.

"Wait," Skyblaze gasped. "Don't go, Willowsun."

Ashleaf marched between them, addressing Skyblaze. "We're playing chase, remember?"

His chest tightened. All this had gone on far too long. Ashleaf outshone the other mares, it was true, and she regarded Skyblaze as a stallion worthy of her status; but did that mean they belonged together? He eyed the palomino and braced himself. "Ashleaf?" he said.

The mare kept one green eye on Willowsun. "What?"

His next deep breath tingled his bruised ribs. "I lied. I *was* looking for someone. I want to be with her." He pointed at Willowsun.

Both mares gasped.

He flinched, waiting for Ashleaf to blast him, but it was Willowsun who reared and bit his flank.

"Hey," he whinnied.

Willowsun galloped away on hoof, neighing over her shoulder, "Both of you, stay away from me."

Damp soil kicked up by Willowsun's fleeing hooves filled his mouth. "What happened?" Skyblaze muttered, coughing.

Ashleaf whirled on him. "What do you see in that dud-born mare?"

"Don't call her that!"

"Both her parents are walkers," she spat. "And they raised her like a land horse. She's weird. No one likes her."

"*I* like her."

Ashleaf drew back, squinting at him. "You two deserve each other." She lifted off and soared away.

Skyblaze watched Ashleaf disappear, but his thoughts remained on Willowsun. She didn't pursue him like the other mares did, but she didn't pursue *any* stallions. Still,

Willowsun was the only pegasus in Lake Herd who made him laugh, the only one who stood up to him, and certainly the only one who'd ever bitten him.

He opened his eyes and noticed that Ashleaf had found her friends. They whinnied and squealed to one another, making a strong point of turning their rumps toward him. Skyblaze stood alone, abandoned. The winds blew stronger as evening descended, and he decided to walk back to the valley rather than fly so he could think.

Halfway home, he stopped. *I want to be with her.* Had he really said that? He'd arrogantly assumed Willowsun wanted the same thing, but maybe she didn't. And he'd also made her his excuse to ditch Ashleaf. No wonder both mares had stormed off. He lifted his head and swiveled his ears. He had to find each of them and apologize, but first Willowsun.

Just then a loud whistle pierced the wind. It was Thornwing, the over-stallion of Lake Herd, sounding an alarm. Skyblaze crouched, hiding himself in the tall grass. Were the dire wolves hunting again? Was a lightning storm burgeoning? His nostrils filtered the scents of the Flatlands—sweet growing grains, crisp cottonwoods, buffalo scat, stagnant lakes, and land horses—but nothing seemed amiss. He lifted off and soared toward where he'd last seen Willowsun. Then he spotted her, gliding toward him. "What's happening?" she whinnied.

"I was going to ask you that."

She flapped past him; her blue eyes round with panic. "Have you seen my parents? Have you seen any dire wolves?"

He caught up to her. "I haven't, but I don't smell them."

She snapped her head his way. "You wouldn't if they were hunting, would you? They'd be downwind."

"Right," he said, feeling stupid.

She spoke with patient fury. "Your type can fly, so you have no idea how the wolves plague us."

"Plague *us*?" he asked, baffled. "You can fly too."

She fluffed her plumage, sailing easily on the wind. "What good are these wings when the ones I love are grounded?" Willowsun didn't wait for a response. She reared midflight, surveying the Flatlands. "There they are!" She struck hooves to grass and galloped toward her parents with the practiced grace of a land horse. Skyblaze landed and followed. Long ago, a tornado had injured Willowsun's sire, grounding him forever, and her dam's wings had not grown since her birth. The tiny appendages fluttered on her back, useless.

"Willowsun!" whinnied her mother. "Where did you

go?" She eyed her daughter and Skyblaze with undis-
guised curiosity.

"Off to be alone," said Willowsun, rolling her eyes at
Skyblaze.

Looking confused, her dam continued. "Thornwing
is calling us; let's hurry." She and her mate whirled. All
four cantered toward the sheltered valley with their wings
tucked high on their backs.

Skyblaze watched Willowsun's black mane ripple as
they loped toward Thornwing. She glanced at him. "It's
rude to stare."

He arched his neck. "Not when I do it."

"Ah, you think that highly of yourself?" she asked,
humor flickering in the question.

"No, I think that highly of *you*."

She blinked in surprise as they entered the valley and
skidded to a halt. The entire herd was gathered around
the three scouts who'd been sent to Western Anok a moon
earlier.

"They're back," nickered Skyblaze. "Finally we'll have
news of the black foal." He and Willowsun pushed through
the throng to hear the scouts, their earlier spat forgotten.

". . . fires everywhere, pegasi turned to ashes," a gray
stallion, one of the scouts, was saying.

"Nightflame is not a healer," said another, a chestnut. "He's Nightwing the Destroyer."

Skyblaze felt his heart stutter at the word *destroyer*.

"Treachery and death have invaded the herds," the chestnut continued. "No one can tell us exactly what happened. Some say an over-stallion tried to make a pact with Nightwing and failed. Now traitors and rebels are battling one another; it's pegasus against pegasus. But Nightflame, now Nightwing, is loyal to no one."

"What's his purpose?" asked Thornwing.

"Revenge, punishment, I don't know," answered the gray scout. "His starfire is like a snake; it slithers from his mouth and hunts pegasi, choking and burning them."

"Revenge for what?" asked an angry mare. "The Jungle Herd steeds protected the black foal."

"Rumors tell the story," said the gray. "Some say he murdered a filly named Hollyblaze and his guilt is driving him. Others say that this has been his plan from the beginning—to rule the herds alone. But of one thing all are certain, he's the Destroyer."

The word dropped on the Lake Herd steeds like a deathblow, crushing their spirits. "He's healed no one?" asked Brightstorm, who was Willowsun's dam.

The gray stallion shook his head.

Brightstorm glanced morosely at her mate and Sky-blaze reeled. It had never occurred to him, the hope that must have blossomed in the hearts of the walkers when Nightflame survived his birth and received his power—hope that he'd heal them and they'd fly again. All throughout Lake Herd, the disabled steeds grumbled, and Skyblaze felt their despair. Anguish for his herdmates enveloped him. "We have to join the fight!" His voice slaughtered the silence.

"Who speaks?" asked a Lake Herd captain.

The pegasus herd parted, revealing Skyblaze, who shrank beneath their urgent stares. "I do," he murmured.

"Skyblaze is right," said Thornwing. "The Destroyer must be stopped."

"But how do we fight his starfire?" asked a battle mare.

"No, this isn't our problem," argued a brown steed. "We're not his guardian herd. Nightwing is Jungle Herd's responsibility."

The chestnut scout interrupted. "There's no one left to stop him. *All* the over-stallions of Anok are dead, except ours."

Frightened murmurings shot across the valley.

"A yearling stallion is leading the rebels," the scout continued. "His followers call him Spiderwing, even though he's no over-stallion."

"A yearling?" sputtered Thornwing.

"Yes. He's the brother of Hollyblaze, the pegasus Nightwing is accused of murdering."

Skyblaze listened, his heart thudding. *A yearling colt leading a fight against a destroyer?* "Spiderwing." He whispered the name. "I want to help him."

"So do I," said Willowsun, her eyes smoldering with anger.

"I think we *have* to fight," said the gray scout. "Nightwing will come here next if we don't. He wants all of Anok, not just the west."

Thornwing nodded. "I'll speak with my captains and think on this overnight," he said. "Gather at dawn to hear my instructions." The powerful over-stallion clapped his wings, dismissing the herd.

"There hasn't been war between pegasi in eighty seasons," said Willowsun.

"I don't think that's right," Skyblaze nickered, following her as she headed to Crooked River, the eastern waterway that fed the pond in the valley. Her parents and the other walkers lived there, segregated from the herd by their own choice.

Skyblaze continued. "There was that battle between

13

Sun Herd and Snow Herd over the western beaches, about whether they counted as neutral territory or not. And Snow Herd has raided Mountain Herd more than once."

"Those were just skirmishes," Willowsun argued. She reached the Crooked River and lowered her muzzle to drink.

Skyblaze joined her, lost in thought about Spiderwing. How could a yearling lead a rebellion? The young stallion had to be special, extraordinary. When Skyblaze lifted his head, a hundred pairs of eyes stared back at him. He'd followed Willowsun straight into the center of the walker encampment. "Hel-hello," he stuttered.

"Greetings, Skyblaze," nickered an elder hollow-backed bay stallion.

"How do you know my name?" he asked.

The bay steed exhaled patiently.

Willowsun interrupted. "We might live separately, but we're still members of Lake Herd. We know our herd-mates . . . even if they don't know us."

"I—I know that." But Skyblaze cut his words short before he said another stupid thing, like claiming he knew who the walkers were. Truth was, he recognized the steeds, but their names eluded him.

"Since you're here, follow me," said Willowsun. She

broke into a trot and led him upriver to a small cascading waterfall. Mosquitoes swarmed up at them and he lifted off, flying over her head.

Willowsun halted and stared at him with a disappointed expression that was becoming far too familiar.

"What have I done now?" he whinnied.

She snorted. "Nothing. It's just, I don't fly in front of the walkers unless there's danger." She lowered her voice. "It doesn't seem . . . right."

"I see," he said, and landed beside her. Willowsun grunted approval, and her blue eyes reminded him of the Dark Water ocean, opaque and full of mystery; and he decided to speak plainly. "All my efforts to impress you have failed."

She jerked up her head. "You've been trying to impress me?"

He flexed his wings and cocked his ears. "The fact you haven't noticed proves my point, don't you think?"

She nickered at his exaggerated display, but her dark-blue eyes swept across his wingspan. He knew it was remarkable for a two-year-old, so he puffed his chest, adding to his width.

She shook her head. "You're going to pass out."

Skyblaze exhaled, quickly shrinking to his regular

size. "See, nothing works with you." He leaned closer to her, his gaze drifting toward her muzzle. It looked so soft, like antler velvet.

Willowsun dipped her feathers into the river, scooped a wingful of water, and dumped it onto his head.

"Hey!"

Nickering, she bolted into the water and he chased her, winging water at her. They galloped downstream, splashing, rearing, and bucking. They played until Willowsun slowed and popped to the surface, floating like a duck. "Truce please, I'm hungry."

He was starving too, so he ceased harassing her, and they grazed on the water reeds growing near the rocky banks. The sun dropped, smearing the sky in shades of pink, crimson, and gold. Willowsun's reflection shimmered on the flowing water, and her glossy mane rippled down her neck as she plucked at the most tender shoots. He didn't realize he was staring until she stopped and lifted her head. "Why me?" Willowsun asked. "I see how the other mares treat you. They all like you."

He tossed back his forelock. "Nah, the buckskin twins can't stand me."

"Two mares out of sixty!" she huffed. "That leaves fifty-eight who are in love with you, Skyblaze. Anyway, you didn't answer my question. I want to know what you're up to."

"Up to?" He squinted at her. "I'm offended, Willowsun."

She balked. "What?"

"Let me ask *you* a question. Why *not* you?"

She stammered. "I'm—I'm not like the other mares."

"I *like* that about you. Try again."

"Your friends think I'm strange."

"So what? Give me a better reason."

"I'm . . . I'm not beautiful."

"Wrong. You're not *objective*, that's all. What else you got?"

Willowsun looked around her as though for inspiration. "My parents are . . . walkers."

"You say that like it's a bad thing."

She rattled her feathers. "It's not a bad thing!"

"Right, so try again. Why *not* you?"

She struggled, thinking and stamping. Finally she gave up. "I don't know. I guess there's no good reason."

Skyblaze stepped closer to her, meeting her where the river touched their bellies. He dipped his muzzle to hers and exhaled. Willowsun flinched, then softened, and inhaled his scent, drinking deeply. The crickets began their evening song, and the breeze fluttered through their tails, still cool from winter. Fireflies gathered around them like golden stars, and overhead, the clouds churned, cast aglow by the setting sun. Her wide-set blue eyes met his, and even though a destroyer reigned in the west, Skyblaze felt as content at this moment, standing in the river with Willowsun, as he ever had in his life. "When I look at other mares, I know exactly what will end us. But with you, I can't see an end. That's why you."

"You make a convincing argument," she nickered softly.

Skyblaze flexed his wings again. "You'll get used to me being right."

Willowsun laughed and cantered downriver, splashing him, and he chased her toward the vanishing sun, joy swelling in his heart. *She likes me!*

The following morning, the Lake Herd steeds, including the walkers, gathered around Thornwing. Without ceremony, the over-stallion spoke his decision. "After a night of consideration and counsel, I've decided we've no choice but to help our western allies."

Rattling plumage and battle cries met his announcement, for many pegasi had come to the same conclusion.

"But not all of us will fight," he added. "I'm dividing

the herd. Our strongest warriors will travel west to war. The rest will travel south to the Dark Water ocean, and you will cross it. I won't risk losing the entire herd should the Destroyer prevail."

The Lake Herd pegasi twirled and pranced as anxious whinnies arose at the idea of being separated.

"Flee?"

"Never."

"To where?"

Thornwing reared and leaped off his hind legs, hovering above them. "Silence!" His voice roared over them, quelling their panic. "Nightwing is *supernatural*." He let the word settle before continuing. "He's come to conquer Anok, to murder all leaders and everyone opposed to him. But our fight isn't *against* Nightwing—it's *for* freedom!"

"Freedom!" repeated the pegasi with their eyes turned up to their over-stallion, their devotion to him spilling from their hearts.

"My army and all volunteers will head west today to join the rebellion. My mate will lead the refugees south. After we defeat Nightwing, we'll come for you and bring you home."

"Why so far?" bleated a nursling filly with pale-turquoise wings.

Skyblaze jerked his head toward the voice. It belonged

to his new sister, Seabrook, and it was her first full sentence, spoken perfectly.

"You'll be safe there," Thornwing blared.

Tension whipped through the herd, but no one spoke. Willowsun staggered, her legs trembling. "What is it?" Skyblaze asked her.

She straightened, her expression hardening. "Nothing." Tangy sweat dripped down her brow.

As Thornwing continued his instructions, Willowsun bolted away, cantering to her parents and leaving Skyblaze on his own. Then the herd was dismissed to prepare for departure. He tore after her, but a voice stopped him.

"Skyblaze!" A Lake Herd captain glided across the sky and landed beside him. "You're our biggest, strongest two-year-old. Choose ten steeds your age, the best, and meet me at the west end of the valley."

Skyblaze opened his mouth, questions brewing.

"Now!" neighed the captain.

The other two-year-olds had collected by the cattails at the pond's edge. Skyblaze coasted to the group and explained his task, quickly regretting it when every single two-year-old volunteered to fight. "I can only bring ten."

"Why?" Ashleaf whinnied. "More warriors are better than less."

"We're not warriors," he countered. "We're untrained, but I don't think that's why we're not all going."

His friends stared at him, waiting for an explanation. Skyblaze exhaled, feeling mournful because he'd guessed right away why the captain wanted him to choose only ten of the hundred and thirty youngsters. Skyblaze gestured toward the army. "If they fail, our herd will be gutted. Only elders, new mothers, a wingful of warriors, and nurslings will make the journey across the Dark Water. So he needs the rest of you to help settle and protect the herd once they land." He swept his wing over the two-year-olds. "You're the future."

"Well, I'm going with you." Ashleaf said this with such authority that the pegasi around her nodded in assent.

But the idea of founding a new herd on a new continent excited some steeds enough that they withdrew themselves from consideration. Skyblaze sorted through the rest and chose ten, including Ashleaf, eschewing the strongest for the bravest. None of them could defeat the starfire, so he wanted steeds by his side who could face it without falling apart.

When finished, he flew to his parents and sister. Seabrook plunged her muzzle into his mane, bleating sadly. His mother spoke. "Thornwing has asked us to fly to the new lands to help lead the herd. We can't go with you, Son."

"I understand," Skyblaze said, feeling glum. Then the captain whistled for him. It was already time to go. "Take care of Mama," he nickered to Seabrook. His sister reared, standing on her tiny hooves, and her lean body was like a shadow as she rammed into him playfully. Then his family cantered away to organize the departing herd.

Skyblaze threw back his head and whinnied for Willowsun, not caring how pathetic he sounded, but no one noticed him. Many steeds were doing the same, seeking out their families, foals, mates, and friends to say goodbye.

Hearing him, Willowsun answered, and he flew toward her. "I've been assigned to fight," he said.

She met him midair, tears streaming down her face. "I'm leaving Anok." They landed and touched muzzles.

"I feel like we just started," he whispered, "and now we'll be apart."

She pressed her sky-blue feathers against his cheeks. "I know, but I can't leave my parents. I'm going with them."

His heart stalled and dread oozed—the walkers! He hadn't considered their needs until just now. "How will they cross the Dark Water?" he asked.

"The herd has offered to carry them."

His wings drooped in relief. "Good, that's good. Then you'll all be safe."

"Safe," she echoed.

"I know; that's not saying much, is it?" He pressed harder into her. His throat squeezed and his breath came fast. Was the reason he couldn't see the end with her because they had no future? Were they both going to die? Her name drove up from his lungs in a halting whisper. "Willowsun." Then the Lake Herd captain's sharp summons broke them apart, and Skyblaze wiped his eyes. "I'll come back from this war," he promised. "I'll find you, wherever you are."

"Just be careful." Willowsun tore a white-tipped feather off her wing and tied it into his mane, using her dexterous wingtips.

He ripped out one of his feathers and tied it to her shining mane. Studying her, Skyblaze memorized her dark-blue eyes, tear-stained face, glimmering dun hide, and midnight-black hair. And then, before anguish could steal his nerve, he galloped into the sky and soared toward the army.

Seven captains pranced at the head of their formations with their wings splayed and their hooves tearing into the soil. The warriors also danced, blowing hot breath and snorting. They jostled one another, some rearing and some kicking out. The wind scattered their whinnies across the plains where the long grasses rippled toward the horizon. The journey to Western Anok would take half a moon at minimum; there was no time to spare.

Skyblaze landed next to the chosen two-year-olds, and Ashleaf bowed her neck, her pulse thumping. "Where's Thornwing?"

Just then the over-stallion of Lake Herd sailed across the grass and the army quieted. As the warriors trumpeted to him, he rode their adoration like a wind current, letting it carry him to the front of the battalions. He hovered there, but only for a moment before braying the call to battle. Then Thornwing whipped around, faced west, and flew forward. Behind him, the army lifted off, and a mighty hum filled the sky as eleven hundred battle steeds flapped their wings in unison.

Rocketing after the army was Skyblaze and the two-year-olds. His friends had created their own formation, and they followed closely behind the army. Without anyone saying it outright, they'd adopted Skyblaze as the captain of their squad.

The graveness of it sobered the young stallion. He was

in charge, and he was only two years old. His thoughts turned to Spiderwing, the yearling leader of the rebellion. Skyblaze rattled his feathers; perhaps soon, he would meet him.

The journey to Western Anok passed uneventfully. Predators avoided the large army, and since it was late spring, the forage was plentiful. The scouts had said the battle was taking place south of Dawn Meadow, in the Vein. Thornwing's army glided along the coast of Turtle Beach, skimmed across the emerald ocean, and then cruised up the Vein between the territories of Desert Herd and Jungle Herd. But long before they arrived, they noticed the smoke.

"By the Ancestors," whispered Ashleaf when they got their first long look at the sky over Western Anok.

"It's like a volcano erupted," said Skyblaze. Ash and dust veiled the sun, and a fine spray of gray silt flecked the trees, shoreline, and grass, looking very much like dirty snow. They flew up the coast toward the Vein located south of Sun Herd's territory. The silence was preternatural, and Skyblaze noticed that dead birds littered the forest floor and bloated, decaying fish fouled the creeks.

His own lungs burned as they inhaled ash and noxious vapors.

Thornwing ordered them to land just southwest of the Blue Mountains. "Listen," he commanded.

Pricking his ears, Skyblaze listened and heard the neighs and trumpeting calls of battle, but other noises too: explosions and the crackling of flames. Heat swelled toward him, and Skyblaze began to sweat.

Thornwing pointed toward the noise. "We're heading into the battle but with caution, in single file, until I know what's happening."

The army fell into line, with Skyblaze and his squad taking the rear. They tromped forward, subdued by the increasing devastation. When the march suddenly stopped, tension wove from the front of the line to the rear, reaching Skyblaze and his friends. "What is it?" he asked the battle mare in front of him.

"Shh, I don't know."

Then it happened—an explosion. It was so close to them that it rocked their ears and shook their ribs. His squad gathered closer to Skyblaze, their feathers rattling.

Screams erupted in the line of pegasi ahead. Then the soil sparked below their hooves. Skyblaze and his team lifted off the ground as a long ripple split the forest floor, shaking it apart. Several pegasi fell into the chasm and then flew out, panting and shocked. There was another explosion. "I can't see through these trees," Skyblaze whinnied to his squad. "Stay here; I'm flying up."

He surged out of the tree line and lifted into the smoke. Through the smoldering forest and billowing ash, pegasi lay strewn by the thousands, all of them dead. He recoiled, stunned. His eyes found the front line of the Lake Herd army. Over a thousand piles of ash stood where Thornwing and his battalion had once been. "No!" he cried. His breath stormed through him, choking him. "It can't be." His army hadn't had a chance to fight. They hadn't helped at all. They were just . . . gone, burned up in an explosion of starfire. The only survivors were the two-year-olds. They stared up at Skyblaze, their bravery lost.

Beyond the dead warriors, living pegasi from the other herds battled one another out of sheer terror. The fires prevented stampeding, so they threw their energy into senseless aggression, and the rest trampled one another in futile attempts to flee. And worse—this group included mothers, newborns, and elders. Tears etched their ash-coated faces. Some huddled together, spending their last moments gripped in tight-winged embraces.

Skyblaze groaned. *Why don't they fly away?* he wondered.

A moment later he knew why when a bay stallion

tore toward the clouds, bent on escape. That's when the Destroyer appeared. Nightwing soared out of the smoke, vibrant, his eyes and hooves glowing silver. Sparks shot from his nostrils and sparkled down his tail. Larger than any pegasus stallion in Anok, his wingspan scattered the airborne ash. Nightwing charged the escaping stallion, opened his mouth, and roared starfire at him. The silver flames engulfed the bay, and he was dead before he could scream. His body shifted into dust and swirled off in the breeze.

Nightwing chomped his jaws, and sparks popped across his tongue. The Destroyer took a satisfied breath, and his eyes shifted toward Skyblaze.

The two-year-old pinned his wings and dived back into the trees, landing and holding his breath. His friends surged toward him. Skyblaze's heart hammered, drowning out all other noise. Had Nightwing seen him? "Thornwing is dead, along with our army," he reported in a whisper. Sorrow stung his heart and weakened his legs, but now was not the time to grieve. "We have to go," he sputtered. "There's nothing we can do here."

They turned tail and fled, back the way they had come. Horrific images crashed through Skyblaze's mind, so he turned his thoughts to home, feeling grateful that

Thornwing had had the foresight to send half of Lake Herd across the Dark Water to the southern continent. Whatever they found there, it had to be safer than Anok. His sire, dam, sister, and Willowsun were safe. All he wanted now was to join them. Anok could not be saved.

His group cantered southeast, using the Vein out of habit; but in truth, no herd would take offense at trespassers today. Skyblaze kept his ears pinned, listening for Nightwing, but the immortal stallion did not follow.

Galloping around a bend, the Lake Herd pegasi skidded to a halt when they spotted a bald-faced bay pinto standing with a band of about five hundred pegasi. He was a large yearling with startling blue eyes. "Who goes?" the pinto asked.

"We hail from the Flatlands," Skyblaze answered. "We came to . . . help." His voice weakened on the last, now ridiculous, word.

The bald-faced stallion exhaled, folding his gold-and-green wings across his back. "I'm Spiderwing," he said.

Skyblaze felt the air suck from his lungs. *This was the yearling leader of the rebellion.* He dipped his head. "We're all that remain of our army."

Spiderwing trotted closer, while his small band of rebels murmured to one another about the strangers. "You came to help us?" he asked, impressed. "We're grateful, but as you've seen, the fight is nearly over."

"But you're not fighting," Skyblaze commented, perplexed.

Spiderwing nodded. "I don't know what you've heard in the Flatlands, but our rebellion began against a Desert Herd stallion. He amassed a great army to conquer Anok and make a pact with the Destroyer, a pact that Nightwing has chosen not to honor. But the Desert Herd uprising is over, vanquished. Our fight with that stallion is done." Spiderwing nodded toward the blazing fires. "What you saw back there—that's *not* a rebellion; that's the reign of Nightwing."

"But there are innocents—mares and newborns."

Grief flashed in Spiderwing's sharp blue eyes. "They declined to follow me because I'm a yearling, and now their fates are sealed. I don't blame them, but I can't help them."

Skyblaze dragged his eyes over the band of rebels, five hundred youngsters, a few elders, and a small gang of ferocious-looking, battle-scarred adults. His gaze returned to Spiderwing. The young stallion wasn't extraordinarily large or powerful, but he was extraordinary all the same. From his blinding white-and-bay coat, to his glossy-edged plumage, to his solid round hooves, and up to his handsome wide face, intense blue eyes, and sharply curved ears—his energy fired through him and from him, attracting notice even while he stood perfectly still.

"What will you do when Nightwing comes for you?" Ashleaf asked, trembling.

"He won't," said Spiderwing.

"Why? Is it because of what he did to your sister? Did he kill Hollyblaze?"

The yearling stallion pinned his ears, and anger flashed across his expression. "Fly home, Lake Herd steeds. There's nothing here for you but death, and I can't protect you from Nightwing. My safety arises from his guilt, it's true, but it's a shaky covering at best. Go now, while you still can."

Skyblaze bowed his head and then his group lifted off, one by one, and flew a winglength over the scorched terrain, heading home. He glanced back, once. Spiderwing had rejoined his friends, and the small herd galloped northeast like land horses.

In the distance, explosions and flames engulfed Anok. The grasslands were destroyed, the sky rendered toxic. Skyblaze sent a silent plea to the Ancestors to protect Spiderwing and his band of rebels—the last free pegasi on the continent. Then he turned his face toward home. No, not home, for he would soon be traveling south across the Dark Water, to a new world, one free of Nightwing the Destroyer.

Eleven hundred Lake Herd warriors had flown out of the Flatlands to battle Nightwing; but only the two-year-olds returned. They decided to spend a few days in their homeland to graze and recuperate before undertaking the dangerous journey across the southern ocean. The Flatlands, while full of buffalo, land horses, moose, and wolves, felt empty. Old feathers drifted across the plains, and insects swarmed in greeting; but the forlorn group longed for the contented whinnies, the happy bleating of foals, and the whoosh of wing beats in the air—the signs of a healthy and thriving herd.

After three days of mournful silence, the small group of two-year-olds decided they'd leave Anok the following morning. Now Skyblaze coasted over the long grass, feeling desolate but hopeful.

"I don't want to go," said Ashleaf.

Skyblaze startled, not having noticed her gliding up to join him. "We'll make a new home in the south," he said.

She broke into hard sobs and landed. "Both my parents are dead." Ashleaf stumbled and fell onto her side, wailing her grief.

Skyblaze touched down and curled next to her, stroking her neck with his wing. Ashleaf's parents were both battle steeds from Thornwing's devastated battalion. "They were brave," he said.

"They were, but they didn't get to fight Nightwing. He just—" She couldn't continue.

Skyblaze stayed with Ashleaf until she was calm again, then he lifted off and glided to the walker encampment, where he'd last seen Willowsun. He sloshed through the river, envisioning her golden hide and glossy mane, and the spark that appeared in her deep-blue eyes whenever he was near.

He couldn't wait to see her and his family. His sister, Seabrook, would be taller—that filly grew faster than a stubborn weed. He'd join her on her first high flight. They'd jet to the clouds and back, and he'd watch Seabrook see the world for the first time from the heights. And he'd spend long hours with Willowsun, getting to know her properly. His body shivered with anticipation.

He blinked when a white-edged sky-blue feather floated past him. It looked exactly like Willowsun's feather. Then another drifted past. Skyblaze spun in a circle. Willowsun had left the Flatlands a moon earlier, but these feathers seemed newly shed. They wouldn't just now be drifting down the river—not unless . . . not unless she was still here!

"Willowsun!" He surged out of the water and flew upriver. "Where are you?" There, ahead—he spied shifting wings and legs. Skyblaze blasted through the trees and came face-to-face with the walkers—all of them—and Willowsun was standing with them.

"Quiet," she scolded. "Don't alert the others we're here."

He landed, sputtering. "Why *are* you here? What happened? Where is Lake Herd?"

"The walkers decided to stay behind," her dam, Brightstorm, answered, her voice calm. "The herd offered to carry us, but most of them were mothers, elders, and newborns. Do you think even half of them would have made it across the Dark Water carrying us?"

He shrugged his wings. "I don't know."

"We would have ruined their chances. We slipped away in the night and hid. The Lake Herd steeds searched, but eventually left without us."

Willowsun glowered at her mother. "But none of the walkers told *me* the plan."

Brightstorm sighed, addressing Skyblaze. "Willowsun was meant to cross the ocean with the rest—she's a good flier—but she didn't. She stayed behind until it was too late to go. But tell us, Skyblaze, what happened in the west?"

He shook his head. "Only eleven of us made it back. The warriors were killed."

"Eleven?!" Brightstorm rasped. "Nightwing has won then?"

"He has."

"Then you must go now, and take Willowsun with you. We're—we're staying here. We'll travel farther east, hide in the hills with the land horse herds."

"That's no life," said Skyblaze dully.

"It *is* a life," Brightstorm insisted. "We'll live free there, I think. But please, take my filly with you."

"I won't leave you," Willowsun nickered, and her eyes drifted to each and every walker.

"I forbid you to stay," Brightstorm whinnied.

"Forbid?" Willowsun flared her wings.

"You're not one of us," said a chestnut walker, rattling her feathers.

"You don't belong here," said another.

Willowsun gasped.

Her mother narrowed her eyes. "Your future lies across the Dark Water."

Willowsun grunted and galloped away, her hooves flinging dirt at the walkers.

Brightstorm trotted to Skyblaze and pressed her forehead against his. "Go after her," she said, weeping. "Convince her to cross the Dark Water, and don't leave without her. Please. I'm begging you." She gazed at him, her eyes the same dark blue as Willowsun's. "Please," she repeated.

"I'll try," he promised. Then he galloped after Willowsun, remembering her rule not to fly in front of the walkers.

He chased her until the light seeped out of the sky, leaving only the glow of the moon to illuminate their path. Willowsun finally halted beneath a cottonwood tree, panting and dripping sweat. Skyblaze had kept pace with her, waiting for her to stop. Now he edged closer. "Your parents love you," he whispered, not knowing what else to say. "They're also correct. There are no walkers here your age. Once they all fly to the golden meadow with the Ancestors, you'll be alone."

Willowsun huffed. "Are there no pegasi left in Western Anok?"

He folded his wings, thinking. "Only Spiderwing and his small band of pegasi are still free. They plan to settle, but the Destroyer is a liar. He could change his mind about them at any moment and attack. I'm not sure if Spiderwing's group will survive."

She exhaled and gazed at the stars overhead. "Why would Nightwing turn on his own kind? I don't understand it."

Skyblaze grimaced. "I don't understand it either, but *we* can survive. Please, come with me tomorrow."

He inhaled, preparing a long speech, but Willowsun shushed him. "I'll go with you," she said simply. "The walkers raised me to accept that I'm a flier and to be proud of it. You could say that I'm their future, and I won't disappoint them by staying here. I'm angry about it, but I already know that I must leave." She lowered her muzzle to his, and they softened toward each other.

Willowsun and Skyblaze returned to the walkers and spent the evening sharing stories until they fell asleep. At dawn the two-year-olds woke and the walking herd was gone. Only Willowsun remained.

"It's time," said Skyblaze.

Willowsun nodded, and they flew to meet the other two-year-olds.

Gathered now on the coast of Anok, the small band of pegasi huddled together, ears flat against the wind. The black-sand shoreline stretched for miles, angling toward the sea. Scrub and beach grasses created a desolate plain, and screeching gulls hunted overhead. The pegasi stared at the waves that rippled gently toward the horizon.

"I hate this ocean," said Ashleaf, who was shedding violet feathers on the black-sand beach. "It's so dark that you can't see what's swimming below the surface."

"There's nothing in there that's worse than what's behind us," Skyblaze said, trotting forward and stretching his wings for flight. "Share the currents," he commanded. "This journey is about efficiency, not speed, understand? Otherwise we'll never make it."

Without ceremony, he leaped into the sky, his hooves trailing black sand. Willowsun nickered a broken good-bye to her family that was carried off on the breeze. Ashleaf grit her teeth, eyes rolling toward the opaque water, and the rest of his friends stifled their groans.

Skyblaze led the group to the heights, where they leveled out and then flapped hard for maximum speed. Once they were flying at a nice clip, they flexed their wings and gripped the shifting currents, surfing on the wind. The steeds lost altitude, but slowly. It would be many miles before they'd need to ascend and start over. The wind squalled over the surface, tangy and forceful, speeding their journey. Before long, the coast of Anok dwindled to a thin line and then it was gone.

It was days later before exhaustion took hold. The pegasi landed on the surface of the Dark Water and floated together. Skyblaze flicked his eyes toward Willowsun, but her back was to him. She'd turned quiet since leaving Anok. Was she angry with him? Had he imagined their connection at the river? Doubt crept into his heart and shot through his veins, making him feel weak.

As the herd dozed, Skyblaze drifted in and out of fitful sleep. Images of Nightwing descending from the clouds with sparks trailing from his reddened nostrils ravaged his dreams. Surrounding the Destroyer were piles of ash—pegasi—and billowing clouds of smoke. He jerked fully awake when a burst of starfire exploded near him.

The waterlogged Lake Herd steeds bolted into the sky.

"It's just a whale spouting water," Ashleaf whinnied, glancing down.

Rattled now and anxious, the pegasi rocketed toward the heights, then glided on the wind. Skyblaze followed behind Willowsun, sharing a current with her. She showed no reaction to his presence so he coasted quietly, conserving his energy.

Two more days passed, and the pegasi were in a sorry state. The one night of rainfall they'd experienced had not been enough to quench their thirst. Ravaged by sea spray, biting winds, hunger, sun exposure, and thirst, they powered toward their new home.

Another day passed, and Skyblaze knew he'd reached the end of his reserves. "I'm about finished," he said to no one in particular.

"Good," rasped Willowsun.

He jerked his head toward her and almost fell out of the current he was riding. "Why good?"

"Because look," she said. "We made it." And for the first time since they'd left Anok, her dark eyes brightened.

Skyblaze squinted ahead, spied land. "Praise the wind that brought us here!" he whinnied.

His herd shot forward, bolstered by the sight of

towering trees—the southern continent. They touched down on a black-sand shore, but nothing else about the terrain was familiar. Craning his neck, Skyblaze gazed at the treetops that almost reached the clouds. Birds, monkeys, and insects screamed overhead, making him cringe after the silence he'd endured crossing the ocean.

Willowsun found a bubbling freshwater creek, and the first thing the group did was drink and graze on water reeds. Flying beetles and mosquitoes swarmed the steeds' legs and muzzles. "Just like home," said a pinto pegasus, referring to the bugs.

Skyblaze munched on water plants, edging closer to Willowsun, who grazed with the buckskin twins.

"Can I talk to you alone?" he nickered to Willowsun.

She nodded, and they trotted upstream. There, Skyblaze grappled for words and then dived into his question. "Are you mad at me?"

"Mad? No." Her eyes softened. "I mean, yes, I'm angry, but not at you. Have I been awful?"

"Just distant," he said casually, as if her mood hadn't crushed his soul for the last several days.

"I'm mad and sad." Her breath hitched. "I left my parents behind to save myself. I abandoned them. I'm a horrible daughter."

"No," he nickered. "You *honored* their wishes. You're obedient, not bad."

She sank to her knees and lay in the mud. "I miss them so much, and this place doesn't feel like home."

"I know. It's too bright, too hot. Everything is too big. Like, what kind of animals do you think live in a forest that huge?" He gestured toward the jungle woodland, its treetops disappearing from view.

"Giant animals?" she guessed.

He pawed the riverbank. "Right. See? It worries me." He plucked a flower that had a stem taller than he. "This isn't normal."

"Maybe we shrank?"

He snorted, fanning his long wings. "Maybe *you* shrank."

Willowsun nickered at him, but her eyes seemed to swallow him whole.

"It's rude to stare," he chided.

She arched her neck. "Not when I do it."

Skyblaze trotted to her side and pressed his forehead against hers. "Whatever happens next, let's stick together. You and me."

She exhaled. "Okay."

His heart sang—what a simple and unceremonious

word, *okay*; but it burst within him, sending joy flowing through his veins.

Skyblaze and Willowsun ambled downstream, grazing and drinking sips of water. The small band of pegasi rested until anxiety forced action. "We need to find the rest of the herd," Ashleaf neighed.

The pegasi gathered and flew to the edge of the cloud layer. Even in the heights, the heat stifled Skyblaze's breathing, and sweat drenched his hide. Scanning the horizon, he spotted three active volcanoes, towering mountain ranges, and, between all that, dense palm forests, marshes, and open fields.

"Do you see that smoke?" Willowsun asked.

In the distance, trails of thin gray vapors rose up in the air, hundreds of them. The pegasi flew higher, to see better. Following the lines of smoke down, Skyblaze realized that each led to a fire dug into a pit. But he'd never seen fire like this—fire that appeared tame and controlled. Surrounding the pits were organized structures and stone pathways. Ashleaf gasped. "Look!"

They all spotted the creatures at the same time: skinny, upright beings walking on two legs, poking at the fires, hauling children on their backs, and sharing food. "Are those . . . Landwalkers?" she breathed.

"I thought they lived across the Great Sea in the west," whispered a gray pegasus.

Skyblaze grimaced. "That doesn't mean they don't also live here. And clearly, they do."

Loud banging noises carried from the Landwalker settlement. Felled trees had been stripped of their branches, and the creatures were using them to construct a huge structure.

"I thought the legends of the Landwalkers were just stories," Willowsun nickered.

"Look at all the animals they have," said Lakeheart, the darker of the buckskin twins. "See how they've trapped them."

Skyblaze flew a circle, scanning the terrain and the sky as far as he could see. "Where is Lake Herd? It's been over a moon since they left Anok; they should be settled by now. And why didn't they leave scouts on the beach to watch for us?" His nerves tingled.

"Let's land before the Landwalkers see us," Willowsun nickered.

The pegasi dived toward the jungle. In the distance, shouts arose from the Landwalker camp.

"I think they spotted us!"

"Can they fly?"

"They don't have wings."

The pegasi touched down and slunk into the palm forest to hide. "What is that?" whinnied Ashleaf. She kicked at a giant swell rising out of the soil. It was black but iridescent, reflecting aqua, vermillion, and scarlet colors.

The swell hissed.

The pegasi gaped, their minds racing.

It rose, slowly at first, and Skyblaze stared, transfixed. What sort of hill hissed and moved?

Then a piece of it swung free and swept toward them, knocking the pegasi off their hooves.

Skyblaze rolled and smashed into a tree. *I don't think that thing is a hill,* he thought, shaking his head. The swift shape swung the other way, and he recognized it as a black-scaled tail.

He flew up and over as the tail crashed through the forest. The smaller trees cracked and fell, creating loud explosions. Debris fell on Skyblaze's head, and his heart skittered. He flew to his herdmates. At least three of them were injured or pinned beneath trees. Willowsun and others grappled with the branches, trying to free the flattened pegasi. His ears rang.

Lakeheart stared straight up, her eyes round and white-rimmed. He followed her gaze up the body of the creature they'd mistaken for landscape. Thick muscles bulged from its forearms, large black scales shimmered in the divided light pouring between the leaves, and heavy folds of skin encircled its neck. Atop the body Skyblaze spied the head: wide jaws, serrated teeth, and round, ridged eyes. Long streams of saliva dripped from between its teeth, pooling on the ground in front of the buckskin mare.

"It's a spit dragon," Ashleaf rasped. "My sire told me about these drooling reptiles that live in Jungle Herd's territory, but he never told me they were this huge."

"They usually aren't," said the gray stallion.

The dragon squeezed its ribs and hissed again. Its forked tongue tasted the breeze.

"Fly!" Skyblaze whinnied.

But before Lakeheart could take off, the dragon's body quivered. Its neck shot down in a blur and its teeth found her chest, biting then releasing. The reptile reared back, smacking its jaws, and drool splattered the trees.

Lakeheart collapsed, screaming.

The pegasi redoubled their efforts to free their herd-mates.

The black-scaled dragon stomped its clawed feet, striking two more pegasi, biting and releasing them.

Skyblaze flew to Lakeheart's side and began to drag her away. Her teeth chattered and her eyes rolled back. Blood poured from her wounds.

"The drool is toxic," Ashleaf whispered. "Lakeheart won't survive."

"I can't let him *eat* her," Skyblaze whinnied, dragging Lakeheart faster. Ashleaf and three young stallions shoved over a tree, freeing the trapped steeds. The injured pegasi staggered to their hooves.

The dragon's muscular tail slammed down, crushing a young chestnut stallion.

"More trouble!" Willowsun whinnied.

Skyblaze whirled as shadows crept through the forest toward them, drawing closer and closer. They were Landwalkers riding atop land horses. Mostly hairless, the Landwalkers had covered their bodies in a dark material. Manes of bright hair sprang from their heads, and their teeth were small and white, like baby animal teeth. But the glinting objects strapped to their waists appeared sharp and deadly.

The dragon, excited by blood and fallen prey, ignored them.

The pegasi circled around their injured herdmates and faced the Landwalkers. The creatures yipped to one another, seeming to communicate. "They're hunting us," whinnied Willowsun.

Skyblaze had joined the circle and now stood beside her. "Don't worry; we're bigger and stronger," he said, but as hundreds of Landwalkers drew nearer, rows and rows of them threading between the trees, his confidence melted. The land horses snorted and blew out their nostrils, showing the red color within. Each time the spit dragon took a breath, the horses spooked. Their riders yanked on sinews connected to their mouths, preventing them from bolting.

"Hold," neighed Skyblaze.

Then chaos struck as objects shot through the air. One landed around Skyblaze's neck and tightened, strangling him. He jerked back, and it throttled him harder. Next to him, Willowsun also thrashed. He spied a braided sinew curled around her throat. It was connected to a horse-riding Landwalker, and so was his. The pegasi flew up, but the Landwalkers tied the ends of the tethers to their heavy-bodied land horses. When the flying steeds reached the ends of the tethers, they were jerked back toward land.

Below Skyblaze, Lakeheart gave a final gasp and died. The dragon snatched her up and padded away to consume her in peace.

The Landwalkers turned their horses around and

walked south, dragging the pegasi behind them. Skyblaze ferociously bit at his tether; but before he could free himself, more ropes settled around his wings and legs. All the pegasi were thusly caught, wriggling like helpless flies. No one spoke because there was nothing to say. They were all trapped.

After what felt like a long march through the jungle, the Landwalkers and their pegasi captives emerged from the trees and into their settlement. Bleating animals, small wolf-like creatures, and rough smoke greeted Skyblaze and his companions. The Landwalkers yipped greetings to one another, and their small cubs came galloping out of their dens. "*Kihlari*," they shouted, pointing at the captured steeds.

A short female cub jogged beside Skyblaze. She extended her monkey-like paw and plucked two feathers off his wing. He trumpeted a battle cry at her, but she just skipped away, flapping his two feathers as if they were tiny wings. All the pegasi began kicking at the Landwalkers, and soon the crowd backed away; but the Landwalkers' round, bright eyes followed, direct and fearless, like the eyes of predators.

"Are they going to eat us?" Ashleaf whinnied.

No one knew, but they all fought harder to get free.

The land sloped upward, and the pegasi climbed steps that had been cut into the hillside. A wall of stone loomed ahead, covered in moss and as tall as full-grown willow trees. Four Landwalkers opened a section of the wall, and the pegasi entered. Inside were smaller structures and open-air enclosures. A scent reached Skyblaze that was so out of place, he didn't recognize it at first; but Willowsun placed it immediately. "The Lake Herd pegasi are here! Where are you?" she neighed.

Excited whinnies erupted from a large wooden den within the stone walls. Skyblaze recognized his dam Mistflower's voice, and he surged toward her, dragging the land horse behind him. Then fighting broke out between the pegasi and the horses. The Landwalkers began shrieking.

"Don't fight them!" Mistflower neighed from within the den.

"Why not?" Skyblaze brayed.

"Come inside and see." The authority in her voice quelled the squabbling pegasi. They ceased fighting, and the Landwalkers calmed. Skyblaze moved slowly toward the wooden den, and the Landwalkers approved of this, guiding all the pegasi in that direction. Inside the structure, Skyblaze heard shuffling hooves and soft nickers. A Landwalker female gripped a solid section of wood and slid it open, revealing a warm interior that was divided into many smaller sections. Skyblaze spotted his dam, and she nickered encouragement. "Come inside."

The wary pegasi entered.

Their herdmates were standing or lying on a grass-strewn floor. Many slept, while the others stood watch. Landwalkers moved about, crouching over steeds or prodding their resting bodies. Skyblaze smelled death and sickness.

Ashleaf balked. "What's happening in here?"

"Don't fear," Mistflower murmured. "Soon after we arrived we fell ill. It began slowly, then spread like a grass fire."

Skyblaze and his friends flew backward.

"The contagion is over," Mistflower insisted. "These steeds are recovering, but many have died."

"But why are you in here with *them*?" Skyblaze scanned the enclosed den, his eyes settling on the Landwalkers.

"They found us near the beach," another steed explained. "We were dying and hunted, too sick to fight. They carried us here and healed us. Within two days, I was well again. For our oldest and youngest, it's taking longer to recover."

Skyblaze pricked his ears, thinking of Seabrook, who counted among the youngest. "Where's my sister?" he asked.

"Here." Mistflower swept back her wing to reveal Seabrook lying by her side, taking shallow breaths; but when the filly saw her older brother, she attempted to stand.

"Don't get up." Skyblaze stroked the filly's back with his wing. "Are you in pain?"

"Yes," she bleated, "but the Landwalkers make it go away."

"What's she talking about?" he asked his dam.

Mistflower sighed. "The Landwalkers are more talented than our medicine mares. They give Seabrook strong herbs that comfort her."

Gratitude trickled into his heart, but Skyblaze rallied against it. "Why? What do they want?"

"I don't know," his dam admitted. "They feed us, care for us, and protect us from the dragons."

"There's more than one dragon?"

"Oh yes. The reptiles attacked us while we were sick." Mistflower shuddered. "The Landwalkers drove them off and brought us here. And there are worse creatures in the jungle, Skyblaze."

"We have to go then, find someplace else to settle."

"She can't travel." Mistflower nuzzled Seabrook. "And I noticed injured steeds in your group. The Landwalkers will heal them too. We can't leave yet."

"We shouldn't rely on them, Mother."

"We have to," she countered, gazing at her wheezing filly.

Skyblaze nuzzled his sister then startled when the wooden door of the den slammed shut. "What's that?"

"It's evening," she explained. "We're closed in for the night. They'll bring food and more medicine. You can relax. You're safe."

He trotted out of the small enclosure that held his sleeping sister and joined Ashleaf, Willowsun, and the other healthy steeds. Six Landwalker males walked carefully among the pegasi, removing the tethers, and then they departed the den. The relief Skyblaze felt about this did not lesson his anxiety. "I don't like this," he whinnied to them all. "When morning comes, I think we should go."

"I agree," said Willowsun.

"But the Landwalkers are healers," argued Ashleaf. "And look what they left for us." She trotted to a long bin that was full of delicious-smelling grain. The pegasi, still starved from crossing the ocean, cantered forward.

"Is it safe?"

His dam, Mistflower, answered. "Yes. It will restore you."

The pegasi ate and tried to relax in the strange environment. Skyblaze told the story of their journey to Western Anok and about the death of their over-stallion, Thornwing, and so many warriors. Grief rocked the herd anew. Then Mistflower spoke in greater detail about their journey across the Dark Water, the illness, and their growing bond with the Landwalkers.

Skyblaze and Willowsun drifted away from the storytelling and nestled together. "It's like they've gone mad," Skyblaze whispered. "I won't stay here."

"What about your sister?"

He grimaced. "As soon as she's healed, I want to leave."

"Me too." Willowsun licked her lips. "That grain was pretty good."

He nickered. "Not as good as sweet spring grass."

"True." She yawned and her eyelids drooped. "I'm so tired."

He draped his neck over her back and sighed.

"What are you thinking about?" she asked.

"You," he nickered. "Our future."

"What do you see?"

"I see our herd living in a huge green meadow surrounded by mountains. I see lakes as blue as your eyes and skies to match. I see foals, lots of them, all ours."

"Ours!" she snorted.

"Yes, a million of them—each one looking exactly like you."

Willowsun sighed, pressing into him. "When I imagine the future, I just see us."

He closed his eyes. It was another simple and unceremonious word, *us*, but it filled his heart completely. They were together; that was all that mattered. Skyblaze drifted into a deep and dreamless sleep.

Many years passed after that first night. The pegasi, whom the Landwalkers called Kihlari, did not leave. New injuries and illnesses, the dangers of the jungle, and a growing attachment to the Landwalkers kept them close. The two-legged creatures were clever and generous, and soon they discovered that the pegasi shared their affinity for war. The pegasi and the Landwalkers began to train together, and a new bond was forged between the Kihlari and the clan—the unshakable bond between warriors.

But Skyblaze, Willowsun, Seabrook, and a few others eventually escaped. They fled the clan and glided away into the night, desperate to live free. With their future unknown, Skyblaze flew with a light heart. He and Willowsun were together, and for them, that was enough.

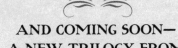

1

THE DEAL

STAR TROTTED THROUGH THE DENSE PINE FOREST, alone. He wanted to practice his flying where the herd couldn't see him. The sharp screech of a hawk drew his eyes skyward in time to see a band of pegasi pierce the drifting clouds. They swooped toward land impressively and then circled around, tapping wings as they passed one another in midair. They were Sun Herd yearlings, out with their flight instructor. Star reared, stretching toward them, trying to fly, but his giant wings hung off him like dead tree branches—useless.

He sagged against a coarse fir tree, already sweating. It was getting hotter each day, and soon it would be time to migrate to the cooler grasslands in the north. He looked up again and watched the yearlings soar in easy loops. They'd been flying since the day they were born. But he— his wings never worked. If he could just tuck them onto his back, he wouldn't look so foolish walking amid the Sun Herd steeds in the grasslands.

Familiar voices pierced the silence, wafting on the breeze from Feather Lake. Star pricked his ears.

"Look at me; I'm a dud like Star."

Star crept to the edge of the trees and peeked through the pine needles. He saw two colts, Stripestorm and Brackentail, playing on the shore. Stripestorm dropped his wings and walked back and forth, imitating and exaggerating the swing-necked gait of a common horse.

Star huffed softly and hung his head. Their joking was why he'd wanted to be alone.

Brackentail snorted. "No, *this* is Star." He collapsed his wings and trotted in a circle, bleating, "Mama? Where's my mama?"

Stripestorm squealed so hard he fell over.

Star turned, galloping angrily out of the forest, ears pinned, and rammed Brackentail. "Don't talk about my mother!" he cried. They tumbled, head over wings.

Brackentail came up with a mouth full of sand. "Get him," he shouted to Stripestorm, choking.

Stripestorm charged, flapping his bright-yellow wings for speed, and Star met him, teeth bared. Stripestorm kicked, smashing Star in the chest and knocking the breath out of him. Brackentail rolled over and took flight, and Stripestorm joined him. They hovered over Star's head and pummeled him from the air.

Star reared, snapping his jaws. Stripestorm lunged, and Star sank his teeth into the smaller colt's leg, tossing him to the ground. Stripestorm tumbled. "Ooof!"

Brackentail flew in, clubbing Star's cheek with his hoof. Lights burst behind Star's eyes, shattering his vision. He shook his head to clear it, wincing at the sharp pain between his ears.

Stripestorm galloped into the sky, then swooped down, gliding toward Star with hooves coiled. Star ducked just in time. "Come and get us," taunted Brackentail as the two flew circles over his head.

Star glared at the colts, who flew just out of his reach. Brackentail harassed all the foals in Sun Herd, but Star was his favorite target—maybe because Star had no mother to protect him, or maybe because Star was a dud, a pegasus who couldn't fly.

Star dodged their hooves as they took turns kicking him. The sharp edge of Brackentail's hoof sliced Star's shoulder, causing bright-red blood to run down his front leg. "Back off," said Star.

"Back off," they repeated, adding a mocking whine to their tone. Stripestorm punctuated their taunting with a kick to Star's flank, causing Star's leg to buckle. Star staggered toward the lake, lost his balance, and fell in.

The two colts landed and hooked their wings around each other, nickering and watching Star struggle.

The shore on this end of the lake was steep, and Star sank when a cramp seized his oversize wings. Bubbles burst from his lips as the spasm rolled from his shoulders to his tail. He drifted helplessly to the bottom, his lungs burning, his black legs kicking.

He was destined to become the most powerful pegasus in Anok, and here he was, sinking to the bottom of Feather Lake. He landed upside down, his legs pointing upward and swaying like reeds. It was dark and cold, like the night. Star tried to flip over, to save himself, but he was running out of air.

Prisms of color exploded around him, and he was sure it meant the Ancestors were here and coming to take him to the golden meadow. As he was accepting this fate, suddenly there was thrashing in the water, and bright feathers surrounded him. They took hold of him and dragged him to the surface. His muscle spasm began to dissipate, and as he surfaced, Star spread his wings, floating and gulping huge mouthfuls of air.

"We've got him," said a male voice.

Star blinked the water out of his eyes, hopeful that he would see his friends, or maybe a regretful Brackentail. Instead he saw four strange stallions looming over him. His heart bucked. The bright feathers he thought were those of Morningleaf or Echofrost were actually of his enemies!

Star quickly twisted out of their grasp and bolted, galloping off an embankment and thundering toward the woods.

Amused nickering followed him. "So the rumors are true," said one of the stallions to another, "the black foal can't fly."

A white steed glided past Star and landed in front of him. He had one blue eye and one brown eye. Star skidded on his haunches and turned, almost crashing into the chests of the other three. He'd never seen these pegasi before. He looked around, but Brackentail and Stripestorm were nowhere.

"You can't escape us," said the white steed.

Star's feathers stood on end, and he was breathing

hard, prancing. "What do you want with me?"

Two stallions, a gray and a buckskin, clamped their jaws at the base of Star's wings. Another, a pinto, spoke, but not to Star. "We're ready, Frostfire," he said to the white stallion.

The stallion kicked off, angling his violet-tipped blue feathers, hovering over Star's head. "Let's go before those two colts we scared off tell Thunderwing we're here."

"No!" Star screamed. Searing pain ripped through his shoulders as the stallions lifted him by the roots of his wings and carried him into the sky. Below him the trees shrank, and Feather Lake contracted into a mere blue swirl. He dangled between the two sweating stallions, their heavily muscled wings pumping in synchronized rhythm as they headed east—toward Mountain Herd's territory. Star's scattered thoughts gathered into one heart-pounding realization. They were taking him to Rockwing!

Star had to get away before they reached the Vein, for if he crossed that into Rockwing's territory, it was doubtful he would make it out again alive. He thrashed and managed to yank one wing out of the gray's mouth. The sudden shift caused the buckskin still holding him to cartwheel into a nosedive. The two of them spiraled toward the dry foothills, Star's free wing whipping uselessly in the wind. The speed of the drop, the thrill of the heights, and the fear of the landing coursed through his veins like liquid lightning. Was this what it felt like to fly? Star wondered.

Star turned his head and saw the white stallion, Frostfire, follow them. The stallion curved his wings, banking sharply, and plunged toward the falling pair. He caught up to them and snatched Star's loose wing in his teeth, stopping his fall. Frostfire and the gray stallion worked together to stabilize their captive and resume their flying altitude.

"What's wrong with you?" Frostfire shouted over the whistle of the wind.

Star pinned his ears and glanced back toward Sun Herd's territory, shrinking in the distance. The sky behind him was empty. Where was Thunderwing? Brackentail and Stripestorm should have arrived in Dawn Meadow by now and sounded the alarm. Star knew that as overstallion, Thunderwing could assemble his flying army in minutes.

The stallions held him so tight he could feel each of their individual teeth. The foothills were behind him now, and ahead was the Vein, the neutral seam that ran between each territory of the five herds. Star had never traveled outside his own Sun Herd's territory.

He struggled, more afraid of Rockwing than of falling to his death; but the stallions bit into his wings harder, and droplets of blood oozed between his feathers. Star shut his mouth and focused on steadying his breathing as he sailed through the pale and chilly afternoon sky. The Blue Mountains rose up in front, framing Valley Field, the home of Sun Herd's closest enemy, Mountain Herd, and its over-stallion, Rockwing.

The steeds flew him up into the mountains and through a dark cloud. The mist blinded him, and the unreasonable fear that they would bump into something gripped him. He sucked in the moist air, choking on it, and his legs galloped for purchase; but he succeeded only in scattering the clouds. The stallions snorted with amusement and dropped toward the forest, their hooves skimming the top branches. Star's gut lurched from the rapid descent, and his damp hide and feathers caused him to shiver. Below he saw three deer hopping through the aspens, avoiding the wide, black shadows of his captors' wings.

After what seemed like a long while, they finally crested a ridge and entered Rockwing's territory. As they swooped over an alpine lake and a meadow thronging with Mountain Herd steeds, Star looked down to see the herd grazing or preening their feathers. A gold dun mare tilted her head skyward as their shadows crossed the sun. She noticed Star and neighed, "It's the black foal of Anok!"

Before the first echo of her cry had faded, the meadow erupted into chaos. Foals stampeded, mares bared their teeth for battle, and warriors took flight, their eyes glowing with a violent mixture of awe and terror. Frostfire and the stallions holding Star landed at the northern edge of the grassy valley. When Star's hooves touched the soil, he was let go.

Star's sore wings collapsed at his sides. Frightened, he turned in a slow circle. Thousands of pegasi faced him, their expressions fierce and their feathers vibrating. The Mountain Herd steeds were short, with wide faces and thick legs like tree trunks.

Star swallowed as fear washed over him. He wished he had not gone into the woods to practice flying alone. At the same time he thought how strange it was that this fierce herd was afraid of him.

The sound of flapping wings made Star turn his head as a brilliant silver Appaloosa with dark blue and gray feathers landed a winglength away. His thick neck was arched and proud as he trotted toward the black foal. "They call you Star?" he asked.

THE GUARDIAN HERD

SERIES

HARPER
An Imprint of HarperCollins Publishers

www.harpercollinschildrens.com